The God Cookie

"A quirky character with a goofy grin—that was me while reading every charming word of *The God Cookie*. With a truly fresh voice and more-than-witty, I'd say genius, dialogue, Geoffrey Wood combines incompetent employees, a bus stop full of eclectic characters, one lonely young woman, a seeking heart, and a fortune cookie, and somehow convinces me that God can speak into my world if only I will listen. Kudos to Geoffrey Wood. Long may you write."

—TRACEY BATEMAN, author of *The Drama Queens series*

"Geoffrey Wood combines his trademark prose—fresh and funny—with outrageous characters, a clever premise, and moments of beauty. I'll never look at a fortune cookie the same way again."

—MATTHEW PAUL TURNER, author of *Churched* and *The Christian Culture Survival Guide*

"Geoffrey Wood is one smart cookie. You'll be one, too, if you read this book."

—TODD HAFER, author of *Bad Idea* and *From Bad to Worse*

the
god cookie

the
god cookie

a novel

geoffrey wood

WATERBROOK
PRESS

THE GOD COOKIE
PUBLISHED BY WATERBROOK PRESS
12265 Oracle Boulevard, Suite 200
Colorado Springs, Colorado 80921

ISBN 978-1-4000-7344-3

Published in association with the literary agency of Alive Communications Inc.,
7680 Goddard Street, Suite 200, Colorado Springs, CO 80920, www
.alivecommunications.com.

Published in the United States by WaterBrook Multnomah, an imprint of The
Doubleday Publishing Group, a division of Random House Inc., New York.

WATERBROOK and its deer colophon are registered trademarks of Random House Inc.

Library of Congress Cataloging-in-Publication Data
Wood, Geoffrey, 1969–
        The God cookie / Geoffrey Wood.—1st ed.
        p. cm.
    ISBN 978-1-4000-7344-3
        1. Fortune cookies—Fiction. I. Title.
        PS3623.O6256G63 2009
        813'.6—dc22

                                        2008039500

Printed in the United States of America
2009—First Edition

10 9 8 7 6 5 4 3 2 1

Trust God and do the next thing...

—OSWALD CHAMBERS

Monday

Perhaps none of this would have happened had they not been arguing about golf balls.

They called each other, as men will, by their surnames—Parrish, Mason, and Duncan. Mason's last name, technically, was McDougherty, but he'd moved from Mason, Texas, when he was in eighth grade, so they'd called him "McDougherty from Mason" until everyone grew tired of that, and the city, not the surname, stuck. It *was* better than Doughy, after all.

The three worked at the coffee shop, Parrish's coffee shop—Fritter John's. Parrish's first name was John, they sold fritters, good ones, and everyone agreed that Fritter John's sounded to some degree like Friar John's, and he was a character in *Robin Hood* (or so they thought), and *Robin Hood* was a book they all could get behind.

At the strip mall across the street from the coffee shop there was an Italian grocery, Tony's, which had a few tables and a deli, and there was also a Chinese restaurant—Mr. Wu's Imperial Buffet. It was to that buffet one Monday afternoon the three men were headed for a late lunch. They'd eaten stromboli four days running, and

Mondays were Moo Goo Gai Pan Mondays. Mr. Wu made a mean moo goo.

On their way out the door, after they flipped the Out to Lunch sign and locked up, Parrish gave the sidewalk in front of his store a quick sweep, then leaned the broom against the table nearest the door so he'd remember to take it back inside after lunch. Picking up the broom, Mason used it as a baseball bat, swatting at a crumpled paper cup Duncan had dug out of the trash—a cup Parrish had just swept up. His pitch missed twice and, ragingly hungry, Duncan forfeited the game in favor of getting to the food. Mason, switching the broom into an imaginary golf club, gave the wadded cup a final swat into the parking lot, only to have Parrish fetch it and return it to the trash.

That's how the argument began. Nothing serious; their arguments rarely were, though each fought for his own—or any assumed—position with a solemn ferocity. The three had known each other forever, and arguing came as naturally as drinking espresso, both activities performed with convivial and cavalier abandon.

Nonetheless, Mason's poor (in Parrish's sage opinion) golf swing spurred a debate on form and finger placement. This took them across the parking lot. By the time they'd reached the opposite curb, they'd begun postulating the effects of a proper golf swing on, say, a racquetball. Naturally, squash balls came up. By the time they'd reached Mr. Wu's, the topic changed to the *differences* between squash and racquetball. And by the time they were filling plates at the buffet, having realized none of them knew the first thing about squash, they reinvigorated the "A Golf Club's Effect on Equipment from Other Sports" debate with the introduction of tennis balls. Here, all agreed, tennis balls would be no good. Finally, seated and eating, their conversation moved to a higher plane—they began arguing about the nature of golf balls themselves. More accurately, they argued about the little dents on the surface of golf balls.

"Purely cosmetic."

This was Duncan's position, the one he argued between forkfuls of rice and beefy soy bits, which he scooped into his mouth at an alarming pace. He was nearly finished with his second trip to the buffet while Mason and Parrish were still polishing off round one. In his defense, it was well past three o'clock. They often ate lunch this late in order to serve coffee to customers on *their* lunch breaks, but Duncan, though twenty-six years old, was still one of those tall, lean, unfillable sorts of men whose metabolism ticked and gnawed on par with a growing teenage horse.

"You eating that egg roll?" Duncan reached for Mason's plate, only to receive a swat to the back of his hand by Mason's fork.

"Give me a chance, Dunc."

"Well, hurry up."

"It's an all-normal-people-can-eat buffet," Mason reminded him. "You can go get six more egg rolls if you want."

Duncan gave a forlorn glance at the buffet, as if it were a ship far, far out at sea.

Mason's job, or so he took it upon himself, was to spend a large portion of the day reminding Duncan of the obvious. They were all roughly of an age, had gone to high school and college together, but Mason was the shortest of the three. Always had been. Not too short, not bad short, not dwarfishly short, just short*er* than his two friends. Perhaps this explained his constant need to be on offense, to have a fork at the ready to swat with, to continually pummel the most oblivious of the three with the obvious. Perhaps he was simply more down-to-earth because he was the closest one to it.

"Cosmetic?" Mason announced his displeasure loudly and in an upward direction, as if he were trapped down a well and calling for help. By this late in the afternoon, Mr. Wu's lunch crowd—though considerable, being a well-known and well-liked buffet—had mostly dissipated, so Mason could be loud. He could argue expansively with only a minimal return of odd stares. "Please!"

Parrish joined in. "Would you like to disagree or shall I?"

"Come on, it's obvious!" Mason pleaded.

The other two waited. They knew he wanted them to wait, that Mason liked a pause and wanted someone to beg him for his answer. Parrish and Duncan wouldn't indulge him so far as that—they wouldn't ask or guess—but they could appreciate the drama of a good pause. Besides, they were eating, and the food was tasty, and Mr. Wu had already begun to break down the buffet bar. He'd carried several big silver trays back to the kitchen, leaving empty, steaming holes amongst the food choices—holes that would no longer be refilled, not this late. They'd seen the last of the kung pao and chicken chow mein for today's visit, they knew, and that both saddened and invigorated their eating.

With great exaggeration, Mason cleared his throat. "Aerodynamics."

"No way." Duncan objected so immediately, a flurry of white rice fell from his mouth back into the plate over which he hovered.

"Yes, aerodynamics. The dents decrease wind resistance, like the fins on the back of a Camaro."

"They're not fins." Parrish gulped his Coke. "It's called a spoiler."

"I call them fins."

"You call them wrong."

"I like fins better."

"Forget it." Parrish waved a hand. "Instead, tell me how dents decrease wind resistance."

"They *in*crease spin, cutting the air more effectively, thereby *de*creasing resistance." Mason said it quickly, all in one breath. Sometimes enough words said extremely quickly was an easy win, or at least a serious advance.

"No, they don't," Parrish objected.

"Those fins don't," Duncan added through a mouth muffled with food.

"The fins *do*," Parrish clarified. "The dents don't."

Duncan shook his head and chomped the end off Parrish's egg roll. "Those fins don't. I know they don't."

"Yes, they do." Parrish elbowed Mason. "Tell him."

"He's right." Mason waved his fork. "The fins decrease all kinds of wind resistance. You put a Camaro with fins next to a Camaro with no fins, and you'll see which one's faster."

Duncan finished Parrish's egg roll. "I have done just that."

"When?"

Duncan swallowed. "Back in high school. Remember Walter Spivins, who had that maroon Camaro? Well, he was trying to decide if he wanted to go back and get the fins, so we raced his maroon one against Bill Finley's, out behind the gym after the state game."

"Bill Finley moved to Ohio the year before we went to state." Parrish looked around his plate, then under it, looking for his egg roll.

Duncan disagreed. "No, you're thinking of Bill—what's his name—the guy with the hats."

"That was Finley," said Parrish, taking Mason's egg roll, which he assumed was his, somehow either stolen or misplaced. "Finley always had two baseball caps hanging from the mirror of his Camaro, and Spivins's was fire-engine red, not maroon."

Duncan waved a hand, dismissing the details. "Whichever. The car with the fins lost, so I know fins are cosmetic, not functional. Just like those dents on golf balls."

"What kind of cosmetic effect do dents have?" Parrish challenged.

Duncan didn't answer. He just stared at the other two. Then, in a very addled way, said, "What?"

To this, neither Parrish nor Mason responded. They waited. Duncan could be addled, they knew. But Duncan also knew they knew, and he'd often hide behind an addled *what*, hoping the others would forget what they'd asked and move on. Sometimes he'd *what* just to give himself time to make up an answer he would then posit as absolute truth. This *what* was pure stall.

Finally, Mason restated, "How are dents cosmetic?"

Duncan stopped chewing—for him, a bold and singular move. "What?"

Parrish pursued. "Are those little dents aesthetically pleasing to you?"

"No." Duncan sounded wounded, hurt. "But…you know how when you swat a golf ball a billion times with a nine wood, you scuff it all up?"

"So?"

"So, you scuff and dent it up! If the golf ball were perfectly smooth and white, you'd see! Every little scratch!"

"So?"

"So they pre-dent golf balls so you don't feel bad after you ding them up. Purely cosmetic. Same reason you spackle a wall so it won't show scuffs."

Parrish put up a hand to stay Mason's attack and took this one himself. "So, according to this line of thinking, we should have scuffed and dented Finley's Camaro just in case he had a wreck or, say, drove down a particularly gravelly road?"

"Actually," said Mason, "Dunc did dent up Finley's Camaro pretty bad."

"I did not."

"You tried to haul that volleyball pole and two ice chests on top of it, remember?"

Duncan stared defiantly for a long moment, first at Mason, then Parrish, trying hard to bluff. Then he surrendered. "Okay, but if that pole hadn't caught that tree…"

"Nearly tore the fin off." Mason wiped his mouth with his napkin and pushed his plate to one side.

"I thought we were talking about golf ball dents?" asked Duncan.

"Gentlemen…" Parrish tapped the side of his glass with a spoon. "You're both wrong." He reached a hand across the table, twirled the round condiment rack that stood in its center, and carefully picked out his visual aid. "Look at this saltshaker." He held it aloft.

For a moment, three grown men stared at a saltshaker.

"What about it?"

Parrish rotated it with the tips of his fingers, catching the light as if it were a gem. "Look at the sides. Five, six-sided. It's not smooth; it's got sides. It's an octagon."

"That's eight," Duncan corrected.

"What is?"

"Octagon is eight. Octa—octa—octa. Like October, like octopus."

"Why are we talking about octopuses?" asked Mason.

"Octopi," said Duncan.

"Whatever!" Parrish shook the shaker dangerously in front of their eyes. "This shaker, we agree, it's got sides, right?"

They thought about it, but no one could find a way to argue that it didn't.

Duncan took the bait. "So?"

"Well…" Parrish let the shaker slip into his fist, grasped it as if he'd just solved the mystery. "Why?"

Like the characters at the end of an Agatha Christie novel, Duncan and Mason blinked stupidly at the events unfolding around them.

Sheepishly, Duncan tried, "Uh…aerodynamics?"

"No!" Parrish plonked the shaker down decisively on the table. "Grippability."

No one knew what that meant. No one knew if that was a word.

Mason picked up the saltshaker, stared at it. "Are you saying that the dents on golf balls are purposefully provided for added grippability?"

"Exactly."

"Whose grippability?"

"Not who…what."

Mason set the shaker down, completely lost. Duncan shrugged.

"Club grippability," insisted Parrish. "Grippability for the clubs."

"Are you serious?"

"Yes. The dents promote club grippability." From his seated position, Parrish mimed a demonstration. "So you can get in there and really grip the ball when you're teeing off."

"I'm getting teed off," said Mason.

Duncan agreed.

Mason pushed his plate aside and propped his elbows on the table. "You know, I've seen smooth, round saltshakers. Held them, gripped them…"

"No doubt," Parrish interrupted. "And when you've got chicken grease all over your hands, which shaker are you more likely to shoot across the table?"

Duncan shook a finger. "He's got a point."

"No, he doesn't."

"Even drinking glasses." Parrish picked his up off the table. "They have sides and bumps and curves and whatnot."

Duncan shook his head. "That's purely aesthetic. Cosmetic."

"No, it's not. It's for non-slippability—or, in layman's terms, grippability."

"But…," Mason said, still trying to understand, "how do dents on a golf ball allow a three wood being swung at full speed to grip it?"

"Have you ever tried to drive a golf ball without dents?"

"There are no golf balls without dents," Mason exclaimed.

"Yes, there are. I've seen one," Duncan offered casually. "Hey, hand me that saltshaker."

"No, you haven't." Parrish passed the shaker across the table.

"I have so. I used to have one."

"Where is it?"

"I used to have three. They come three to a box. I got a box of factory-defect golf balls that were completely smooth and dentless. Kept them for years."

"Did you ever try to drive one?" asked Parrish.

"No, I was afraid I'd lose it."

"What happened to them?"

"I lost them."

Much earlier that morning while eating powdered doughnuts for breakfast and discussing lunch plans, Duncan and Mason had planned to skip out and leave Parrish with the check. This was not unusual—neither the doughnuts nor the check skipping. Parrish was their employer; he owned a shop, they owned nothing; he made more money than they did, and as boss, it was his fault they didn't make more than they did. On average, they skipped out on him once or twice a week.

Duncan, far from following the nuances of Parrish's grippability argument and thoroughly out of food, had already begun thinking of leaving. He wanted to be ready to bolt whenever Parrish gave them the opportunity, so he thought through all the things he didn't want to forget when he and Mason scuttled out the front door and ran back to the coffee shop. He shoved his gloves and scarf into his coat pockets. He'd kept his coat on. He'd tied his shoes. He'd folded the section of newspaper he'd brought but had not read and placed it near his hand. Now, he slipped the saltshaker in his coat pocket.

But Parrish saw him. "What did you just do?"

"What?"

"You put that saltshaker in your pocket."

"So?"

Parrish paused, hoping Mason would jump in and help, but he only stared at Duncan in his coat, hoping Parrish wouldn't realize today was a skip-out day. Parrish had only caught them in the act of skipping twice, but when he did, they had to pay. Rules were rules.

Parrish tapped his finger on the table where the shaker had been. "Are you going to put that back?"

"Eventually."

"That's stealing."

"No, it's not. I'm borrowing it." Duncan believed this sincerely and couldn't understand why Parrish was troubled. "I have boiled eggs in my lunch."

"We're eating lunch." Parrish waved his hand at their empty plates.

"Yeah, but later I'll get hungry again. I need salt to eat a boiled egg."

Parrish looked at Mason, who merely shrugged.

"Put the shaker back!" Parrish said.

"We need a saltshaker at the store." Using his pinky, Duncan dislodged a piece of rice from a back tooth, then chewed it. "Besides, we eat here every day. I'll bring it back."

"Who are you?" said Parrish, the manager, the shop owner, a fellow orderer of pricey condiments. "You can't just take their saltshaker."

"I just did. I borrowed one of their many—"

"Well, yes, you can physically take it, but the point is you shouldn't."

Duncan looked to Mason for help, but Mason gave him a harsh stare. Duncan looked at Parrish, blinked as Parrish stared at him. "I'm leaving the pepper."

Parrish fell back in his chair and shook his head. "Tell him he's wrong, please."

Mason joined in. "You're definitely wrong. You're breaking the set. It would be better, both for covering your criminal tracks and for table condiment equilibrium, if you took both."

Mason handed Duncan the pepper.

"No!" Parrish stopped them. "You shouldn't take either. We know these people. You can't just swipe—"

"Fine. Here, here, here's the saltshaker. Take it if you're going to throw a fit." Duncan dug the shaker out of his pocket and spilled salt across everything as he put it back on the table.

But Parrish was genuinely concerned. "It's not a fit, but how do you not think that's stealing?"

Duncan looked at the napkin holder with a blank, helpless stare. Parrish swatted Mason's arm to elicit his help.

Mason leaned judiciously on the table, folded his fingers tightly together. "When were you going to bring the shaker back?"

Duncan answered listlessly. He was hot in his coat. "Today... tomorrow."

"How much salt were you going to use?"

"Two boiled eggs worth."

"And Mr. Duncan, did you, in fact, salt the food you just ate?"

Duncan tapped the saltshaker like a microphone, to see if it was on, then leaned over and spoke into it. "No, Your Honor, I did not."

"What difference does that make?" Parrish interrupted.

"He's entitled to some salt. If he didn't use salt during his meal, one could make the case that—"

"I don't want to be seen with either of you two."

"Order! Order! I'm not done!" Mason leaned forward, pulled the pepper close, and spoke into it. "And so, Mister"—he consulted his napkin—"Duncan, is it?"

"That is correct, Your Honor."

"Were you, in fact, Mr. Duncan, going to tell them when you brought the shaker back?"

"When I brought it back, I'd probably have said something."

"Like what?"

"Like...thanks for letting me borrow the saltshaker."

"Even though they didn't let you," Parrish argued.

Duncan covered his mike with his hand. "First of all, they wouldn't miss it. Second, whoever I talked to would probably think the other person had said I could borrow it and be fine. Third, it wouldn't be anywhere near the federal deal you're making out of it, and also, they have a thousand saltshakers. You can walk right over there to that stand where the iced tea's melting and find a little salt-shaker army of them. They wouldn't care if I borrowed one for the evening."

Parrish took the saltshaker and put it back on the twirly-rack. "You have no conscience."

"I have a conscience."

"Where is it?"

"Apparently, it's the smartly dressed cricket chirping out the back of your throat."

"Seriously, how do justify that?"

"I'm not justifying anything. I was borrowing. If it were wrong, my conscience would tell me so."

"It would?"

Mason interrupted. "His conscience has these little dents all over it for grippability…"

Parrish ignored this. "How would your conscience tell you?"

"Look," Duncan took the saltshaker out of the rack. "Say I borrowed this shaker to eat my eggs later. Later, eating said eggs, I'd happily salt away, no pang. Conscience silent." He demonstrated, shaking salt onto his empty plate, then looking up contentedly. "But, say, three days from now, if I found this saltshaker in my car, then I'd be like, 'Oh no, I've got to get that back to Mr. Wu's.'"

"I'm not sure that's a conscience."

"That's my conscience."

Parrish turned to Mason. "Tell him that's not a conscience."

Mason thought deeply for a moment. "I don't believe in 'the conscience.'" He used his fingers to make quote signs in the air.

There was a pause, then Duncan waved his hand for attention. "What'd he say?"

"I said I don't believe in 'the conscience.'" Again, Mason made finger quotes.

Parrish ran his fingers through his hair. "Oh, dear God."

"Exactly."

"What?" said Duncan.

"I believe there is no conscience per se. What is commonly referred to as 'the conscience' is really just a vestige of God's original voice in creation."

Everyone took a moment for that to linger.

"Wow," said Parrish. "Really?"

Mason nodded. "Yep."

"So, when Duncan finds the saltshaker in his car this Thursday, that's God originally telling him to bring it back?"

"Basically…yes."

"But the fact that Duncan has no problem stealing the salt-shaker in the first place…"

"Well, Dunc's apparently choosy about when he listens to God."

Duncan held his hand up high. "Wait a minute. What are we talking about?"

Parrish explained, "He's saying that what you and I call 'the conscience' is actually God talking a really long time ago, and that you have selective hearing."

Duncan looked at Mason. "That's what you said?"

"That's not what I said, but it's true."

"Really?" Duncan was suddenly fascinated. "Did God tell you something and I missed it?"

"Look." Mason pointed at Duncan. "Now he's got a conscience."

"I thought you didn't believe in them?" said Parrish.

"I don't."

"That makes no sense." Parrish shook his head. "I believe I have a conscience and that God talks to me, but I don't think they're the same thing."

Though Parrish missed the relevance and sipped his Coke, things grew deeply silent and serious at the table.

"So…" Mason straightened his silverware cautiously. "You believe God talks to you?"

"You know what I mean."

Mason folded his napkin back to its original square. "No," he said very calmly. "Categorically, I do not."

"Don't you guys ever…?"

Duncan picked up his section of newspaper and crammed it in his coat pocket. Mason raised his eyebrows, rather permanently.

Growing up, all three of them had been combed and dressed and carted to the same church. They'd all nodded with sleep in the same Sunday school rooms and found various occasions for skipping a service to walk down to the corner convenience store and drink sodas and eat chips and throw rocks at cats. Now in their twenties, all three had retained a more or less certain belief in God, the Christian one, though to be honest they rarely discussed it, not in any practical terms.

When thoroughly caffeinated, they could banter back and forth in a pseudophilosophical discussion about good and evil and how God juggled all that. But none of them had ever imagined being a missionary or a preacher or even a thoroughly good person, much less broached the notion that they heard God speaking to them. Now Parrish had claimed just that. And he meant it. It'd been on his mind of late, and yes, at times, he did think those passing hints and inklings in his mind might well have been divinely prompted.

Quietly, Duncan asked, "You're not hearing voices telling you to rob a bank or anything, are you?"

Parrish groaned. "Never mind."

"'Cause if you are," Duncan continued, "I apparently have no conscience, so maybe we could work something out."

"Don't you ever have a conversation in your head where one of the voices isn't you?" Parrish tried to explain. "Where one of the voices is in fact better than you, and…"

Mason burst with an interruption. "So you're not saying, like, ego versus superego minus id and all that, and you're not referring to some happy-happy self-talk sponsored by the collective unconscious. You're talking about the actual God actually talking to actual you? Like…like…your own personal revelation?"

"I don't mean that."

"What do you mean?" demanded Mason.

Parrish sighed.

Duncan laid a very serious hand on Parrish's arm. "Should we start calling you 'saint'?"

"We could rename the store," Mason announced. "Saint John's."

"We'd have to open on Sundays," said Duncan.

"People would think it was a church."

"And I looked up and beheld a latte…"

"Okay." Parrish scooted back his chair. "I have to go to the washroom."

"No, wait," said Mason, stifling a laugh. "We're sorry. Stay."

"Really." Duncan grabbed Parrish's chair. "We may not be here when you get back. Finish what you were saying."

Parrish hung his head for a moment, put his elbows on his knees, and pressed his fingers across his eyes. Then he raised his face, choosing to answer honestly. "I wasn't saying anything. I was just saying that there might be something *more* than conscience and *less* than inspired revelation, that's all. I mean, it's all over the Old Testament, God talking to people. How does that work today? Does it? Not the general 'don't do this' and 'do do that,' but to you—specifically. Is God speaking right now but we're just not listening?"

Here fell the longest, most serious pause.

Mason strummed his fingers on the table. "I still say they're aerodynamic."

Parrish crossed his arms. "Why do I talk to either of you?"

"No one else will." Duncan licked his thumb, dabbed up egg roll crumbs, then ate them. "Wait…" He looked up from his plate. "Who's that kid?"

Both Mason and Parrish looked around.

"In the Bible," continued Duncan. "Not the restaurant."

"Could you give us anything more?" asked Mason.

"That kid…" Duncan tried to snap his fingers, but they were too greasy. "His mother can't have a kid, but she wants a kid, so she talks to God about it and says, 'God, you give me a kid and I'll give him right back to you, I swear.' So God gives her a kid, so she does her part, she ponies the kid up to the old priest and ships him off to the temple. And so the kid, just a little kid, right, he grows up in the temple, and one night he hears a voice saying, 'Hey, you, kid!'"

"I believe that was Samuel."

"Right. 'Hey, you, Samuel!' So Sammy jumps up and runs to the old priest and the old priest says, 'Nope, didn't call you, go back to bed, kid.' So he does and it happens again, same song, second verse, and then a third verse, so finally it clicks with this priest—what with living in a freaking temple—this priest figures it's God. So he says, 'That's God. So next time you hear that voice, kid, don't wake me up.' So the kid does. He goes back to bed, and he hears that voice again, so this time to God, he says, 'I'm in.' "

Duncan looked to Mason, who looked to Parrish, who looked back at Duncan.

"That's in the Bible, right?" Duncan asked.

"Sort of," said Parrish.

"Good, I couldn't remember what book."

"Strangely," said Mason, "they put it in Samuel."

"Well, there you are."

Parrish and Mason waited. Sometimes, if they waited, Duncan would blurt out more information, useful information, actually finish a thing and provide them with the missing pieces that helped make a whole picture. This time Duncan just sat and scratched his ear.

"Hey, Dunc," Mason spoke gently, "that was beautiful, really it was, but Parrish and I haven't quite found the grippability…"

"The kid!" Duncan leaned in and repeatedly patted his hand on the table like he was calling for a dog to jump up on it. "Whatever else, you have to admit the kid was all in, right?"

Parrish grabbed his wrist to stop the patting. "Is this a poker metaphor?"

"Analogy," said Duncan. "Poker analogy."

"If we made you some little analogy note cards," said Mason, "would you hold them up when you recklessly swerve from paradigm to paradigm?"

"I'm going to the washroom." Parrish stood and dropped his napkin on the table.

"Look, Parrish, you're bent about whether or not God speaks and all that gray area between conscience and revelation, and all I'm saying is the kid had no problem hearing God 'cause his chips were all in."

"What does that mean, Dunc?" asked Mason.

"He was just a kid," said Parrish. "What chips did he really have?"

"Kid or not, his chips were all in, 'cause he had nothing else. What's that verse, 'Unless all ye become just a kid...'? Or his mother, same with her. When she slid all her chips on the table, she had no problem hearing God. So, practically speaking, I think it's a matter of what you're willing to wager. You know what they say."

For someone who had been planning to skip out on the lunch tab since that morning, it was ironic that he would finish his theological opinion with the words:

"You pay to play."

The washroom at Mr. Wu's was an enigma to Parrish and his friends. It was inordinately spacious, like bathrooms at a football stadium— a washroom as long as a pool hall. Four sinks lined one side below a huge, dingy mirror lit by long fluorescent bulbs, uncovered and hung on the wall along the top of the mirror. The ceiling had fluorescent bulbs of its own. Very bright, this washroom. The wall opposite the sinks was lined with shallow shelves, as if this had previously been a stockroom. Currently, the shelves were empty. Parrish knew health codes would never allow food storage here, and no customer wants to see huge cans of chickpeas and bags of rice stored in the same room as the toilets. And toilets there were—five stalls. Parrish had eaten in Chinese restaurants smaller than the washroom at Mr. Wu's. Had Mr. Wu brought tables into the men's washroom during his busiest times, he could have seated twenty-four more customers.

Though an inexplicably large room and an old, dingy one, the washroom was never dirty. A trace of bleach always lingered in the air, and the chrome on the faucets shone brightly. It even had homey touches—the hand soap, not in clanky metal dispensers but in store-bought bottles next to the sinks, came in floral and fruity fragrances that changed periodically. Apricot gave way to summer pear, which then turned to lavender.

Being tiled as well as spacious, the echo in the washroom was tremendous. Footsteps became ominous with amplified clacks and scuffs; the sound of running water from the sinks resounded like a miniature waterfall; a flush was nearly deafening, a roar and whoosh not unlike a fast train in a damp mountain tunnel. Parrish could always tell newcomers to Mr. Wu's buffet, if he happened to be in the washroom with them at the same time—they physically ducked and flinched and grabbed hold of a sink basin when an unsuspected flush occurred.

This was a reverberant washroom.

So reverberant, in fact, that as Parrish stood at the third sink from the door soaping his hands with a peachy lather, his mumble to himself did not remain to himself.

"Pay to play — to play — to play…"

His words echoed off the mirror and bounced from wall to wall. Hearing his own voice, he glanced around instinctively to verify he was alone. He shook his head, then looked again in the mirror, tilting his face left then right. He was growing a beard, or at least he'd not shaved in so long that he had substantial enough stubble to say so. As a beard, it didn't look great, uneven and spotty. "Scruffy face" were the next words he mumbled. The echoed f's fluttered about him like a trapped bird. He chuckled to himself.

"Is that what you want, God?"

He listened for his question to stop echoing, then waited, tilting his eyes slightly upward so as to address it to God there in the washroom at Mr. Wu's. If God were to answer, at least here he would be sure to hear it.

He heard only the sound of running water.

Parrish rinsed his hands, turned off the spigot with his elbow, then turned to the paper towel dispenser. He stooped, squinting through the dark plastic casing, but could see no trace of paper towels inside. Gingerly, using the tips of his finger and thumb, he cranked the handle, hoping to roll out some last shred.

Nothing.

He walked to the other end of the sinks, to the second dispenser, only to find the towel situation the same. Shaking his hands, he turned to see if any supplies were stocked on the rows of shelves, stuck back in some corner.

No luck.

He looked helplessly at himself in the mirror.

Certainly the emptiness of towel dispensers could be explained otherwise, but what if, Parrish suddenly thought, what if the dispensers giving-no-towels were like God giving-no-answer? What if he'd never risked anything, never put anything on the table but always expected God to play? Hadn't he treated God, often as not, more like a magic dispenser than a fellow player at a game of cards? Neither were particularly respectful metaphors of the Almighty, but at least one of them imagined God as a person.

"Okay, God." Parrish wiped his hands on the back of his pants. "I'm all in."

Coming out of the washroom, Parrish shook his damp hands, looked around for a cloth, a stack of napkins, a stray busser's rag.

"They stuffed you."

Parrish looked up. "What?"

"Your friends." Out the kitchen's service window, Mr. Wu pointed his spatula over Parrish's shoulder. "They leave before the check again."

Parrish turned. Vacant chairs surrounded the table where the three of them had eaten. In fact, in the whole restaurant, Parrish remained the only customer.

"They do that. And it's 'stiffed.'"

"Ah, yes. Stuffed you again."

Parrish nodded politely to Mr. Wu. Or he'd always supposed this was Mr. Wu. Though he'd eaten there a thousand times, he'd never properly introduced himself. But this man was clearly the owner and the lady with him in the kitchen was clearly his wife. They were the only two staff in the place and they did everything—cooked, cleaned, seated the tables, served customers, answered the phone— and the place was called Mr. Wu's Imperial Buffet.

"You're out of paper towels, Mr. Wu," Parrish said, pointing a thumb toward the washroom.

"Oh, sorry."

Mr. Wu turned and spoke to his wife in lengthy Chinese. She replied sharply without so much as a glance up from the onions and carrots she was chopping. The man dinged the edge of the spatula against the counter and stared at her, but she merely wiped her forehead with the back of her hand and continued her chopping. He shrugged and took off his apron.

Parrish watched as Mr. Wu passed by—a short man, his stride quick and dogged with feet slightly out-turned, his eyes down, fingers rattling through a ring of keys he'd taken from his pocket. Mr. Wu hurried to the door in the hallway near the washroom and unlocked it. The closet revealed shelves full of bound bundles of paper towels, rolls of toilet paper, boxes with garbage bags protruding from a slit, and boxes marked "soy sauce."

"How we on toilet paper?"

Parrish gave him a thumbs-up.

Mr. Wu chose a bundle of paper towels, then shut the door and locked it. Instead of proceeding immediately to the washroom, he ripped at the brown band around the towels and pulled out a small handful, then walked over and handed them to Parrish.

"My name not Wu, it Charles."

"Oh." Parrish took the towels. "Sorry about that. Who's Wu, then?"

"Wu just name for restaurant, like Ronald McDonald. Not real."

"Oh." Parrish dried his hands again before he shook Charles's hand. "I'm John, I run the—"

"Yes, yes." Charles set the paper towels on a table. "You make the coffee shop across the street. I see the cars each morning. You got Internet?"

"Yeah, had a thing hooked up last year."

"How's business?"

"We do fine. Good location."

"Yes, yes, location everything. Her name Min San."

Charles's wife had, very politely, taken off her apron and come out of the kitchen to stand beside Charles to speak with Parrish. She bowed slightly when Parrish offered her his hand.

"Very nice to meet you, Min San. You and your husband do a great job."

Both Charles and Min San frowned and shook their heads.

"No. Min San my sister." Charles stood there holding the wrapped parcel of paper towels. Min San looked desperately between faces to see that things were being explained. "And even if she not, she would not be wife."

"No wife." Min San gave Parrish a gesture like "safe" in baseball. "Got it."

That explained, Min San's face returned to its usual pleasantness and bright smile. She and her brother remained, facing their only customer as if they were glad to have someone to talk with besides each other.

"How long you been there?" Charles raised his chin, gestured out the glass toward Parrish's shop, then he crossed his arms and took a wide, businesslike stance.

"This is my fourth year."

Charles eyebrows jumped up then down, and he turned to translate to his sister. The translation volleyed back and forth between them, Min San asking questions and pointing at Parrish, toward his store, then a gesture that took in their own restaurant. Parrish didn't know what they were saying, but he could tell Min San understood more of his language than he did of hers.

"What did she say?" he asked.

"She say the fourth year a very good number."

Parrish nodded politely. He'd never really thought about numbers in quite that personal a way, certainly not regarding his business.

"This only our second." Charles punctuated this with two strong, quick fingers, then readjusted his stance.

Parrish knew that. He'd watched as the Mr. Wu's sign had been put up, as long trucks parked across the parking lot so furniture and kitchen supplies could be moved in, the grand opening announced with a huge red banner. Everyone at the coffee shop had been excited by the prospect of a new lunch option, something besides burgers or stromboli. He and the boys ate here—one of them if not all of them—at least three times a week. The food, though it would never make the newspaper's "Best of" section, proved consistently decent-to-good, and the buffet was ridiculously cheap—$6.99 all-you-can-eat, including a soda with free refills and one trip to the soft-serve ice cream machine. And, of course, a fortune cookie. All that, with tax, for less than a ten-spot—a godsend, they all agreed. Oh, and a fudge dispenser and sprinkles for the ice cream.

"Your business doing well?" Parrish asked.

"Oh, very good, good." Charles said this, looked to Min San, then shook his hand in the air. "Sometimes less good, but mostly good. Lunch very good here."

"Yes, the three of us like it." Parrish gestured toward his empty table.

They stood together in an awkward silence.

It seemed that both brother and sister didn't know what to say to that, about these people, his friends, who so often skipped out, leaving him to pay. Parrish knew they only ever saw the three men in context of the buffet, so in that light, the other two looked purely gluttonous and mercenary. Charles didn't speak—it would be ungracious to talk badly about a man's friends, Parrish imagined. Min San looked down at the floor, looping a strand of her jet black hair off her forehead and behind her ear.

"We should have you two over for coffee sometime...on me," Parrish said.

Charles nodded appreciatively, but Min San perked up immediately. "Do you have the peppermint lattes?"

Parrish laughed, because he hated peppermint lattes. He hated peppermint. He hated when people ruined good espresso with lots of milk, let alone flavored syrups, and he knew Min San must go to his nearby corporate competitors, the ones who put up huge candy-striped banners at Christmas and made their employees wear bright red elf shirts under their green aprons.

"Absolutely. Come on by, both of you. Please."

Charles nodded and shook Parrish's hand again. Min San turned happily and began to clear the plates from the nearby tables, her face almost childishly anticipating how soon she'd have her next peppermint beverage. Charles stepped over to Parrish's table and picked up the one plate Duncan hadn't cleaned spotless.

"You want to-go box?"

"Sure."

Charles hurried behind the counter where the register and the bowl of mints sat, stooped over and brought out a couple of the white foldable boxes, then began to box up what little Duncan had left on Parrish's plate.

"I can do that," said Parrish, but before he could take the boxes, Charles had already scraped both full and expertly folded the tops snug.

Parrish sat down to finish his Coke. Min San brought a bus tub over to a nearby table, set it down, and spoke discreetly to her brother. Charles stacked the two boxes he'd filled into a white paper bag, then helped his sister fill the tub with plates and silverware from the nearby tables, all while they quietly discussed something in Chinese. Min San stopped cleaning, pointed one strong finger into the palm of the other hand, and gave a final flourish of Chinese words. Charles shrugged and went back to the kitchen with the bus tub.

Left alone, Min San turned and stood next to Parrish's table, staring at him.

"You want to go get that latte now?" he asked.

She shook her head. Charles returned and stood next to her, said something to her in Chinese, and gave a gesture like he was scooting a child to jump in a pool.

Finally, Min San worked up the courage. "Excuse me, John?"

"What's up?"

She opened her hands gracefully, gestured to the empty chairs. "This happen too often, John. You maybe should find friends who do not steal from you."

Parrish laughed, but neither Min San nor Charles shared his levity. "I'll fire them this afternoon," he said.

Min San gave her brother a horrified look, pulled his sleeve harshly, then said another string of sharp things in her native tongue. Charles held up his hands and argued back. Her eyes filled up with tears and she fled to the kitchen, Charles quickly following.

Parrish had no idea what to make of this. He sat for a few minutes, sipping his Coke. He could hear them, barely, as they talked in the kitchen. He thought he heard crying. He reviewed his every word to see if he'd said something stupid. That was usually when Parrish caused crying.

Then he noticed the saltshaker was gone. He groaned and rubbed his temples. He hated them. Maybe that shaker was her favorite.

"Sorry," said Charles, returning. He held the little black tray with the check.

"Did I upset your sister?"

"No, no. She's…" Charles made a rising, wiggly gesture in the air with his hand.

"Min San want me to ask you"—Charles struggled with the impropriety of the situation—"to ask you not to fire them because of what she say."

Parrish laughed again. "I won't. I was joking. Tell her I'm joking. I've known those two forever."

Charles looked at him in stern disbelief.

"Really. If I fired them, they'd just come back."

Charles bowed. "Min San wanted me to tell you. She say she would not wish so much cause to happen from her few words." Very seriously, Charles delivered this message from his sister, then disappeared into the kitchen.

As Parrish sat, a strange sensation came over him, brief but significant—a fearful twinge. Prior to that moment, the washroom wager had held very little importance in Parrish's mind. He'd been sincere, as sincere as one will be talking to God with wet hands at the washroom sink of a Chinese restaurant. But suddenly, the full measure of what he'd done weighed down on him. Min San, so scrupulous, her serious and heartfelt concern over her own words, her sudden eagerness to correct what might have been a frivolous tap that set things in motion, cause and irreparable effect, words spoken and beyond reclaim—what if God had taken him seriously?

Momentary paranoia, nothing more. Parrish dismissed it. He

reached over to the tray with the check and the two fortune cookies. After all that soy sauce, a bite of something sweet would be perfect. He picked up one, put it in his coat pocket, then grabbed the other and tore it from its plastic.

Parrish cracked the cookie to pieces in his fist, then dumped and dusted them onto the little black tray. He pulled the lunch check out from beneath the shards, turned his head sideways to read it, then took several bills out of his wallet and stacked them beside his plate. Picking out one of the bigger pieces of cookie, he placed it on his tongue, crunching and chewing the sugary fragment as he unfurled the tiny paper scroll.

Did something divine happen during the short walk between the washroom and the table or was every step for years and years of his life bringing him to just this moment? Mightn't he just as easily have opened a trite, meaningless, random fortune, or at the propitious moment did the writing inside this cookie twist and burn with a new and miraculous message? From a timeless perspective, aren't both always true?

His jaw stopped midchew.

In simple black type, his slip of fortune read: TAKE THE CORNER.

"God told you to stand in the corner?" Mason asked skeptically.

"Geez, Parrish." Duncan looked at him soulfully. "What'd you do?"

The three sat around a small table at the coffee shop, the fortune in the center next to the second, unopened cookie.

Duncan pulled his sleeve over his hand and pushed the slip of paper away from him, so his fingers wouldn't touch it. "Why'd you open that, Parrish?"

"That's what you do with fortune cookies."

Mason swatted Duncan's hand, picked up the fortune and examined it. "And why, again, do we think this message is from God?"

In detail, Parrish explained the washroom wager, the strange sensation, the conversation with Min San.

"She's not his wife?" asked Mason, suddenly interested.

"Min San owns the joint," Duncan explained, matter-of-fact. "Charles just works there. Charles is getting his real estate license."

"How do you know this?" Mason flipped the fortune over, saw there was nothing on the back, then tossed it on the table.

"I talk to people, I don't just eat there. Min San is an amateur butterfly collector and she drives a black Dodge Hemi."

"When does he talk to people?" Mason held the unwrapped cookie up to his ear and shook it. "I never see him talk to people."

"He probably steals their mail. Where's the saltshaker?" Parrish demanded.

Duncan fished the shaker out of his coat and placed it on the table. "Since I paid for the buffet, can I go back and get another Coke?"

"You didn't pay." Parrish put the shaker in his coat pocket for safety.

"They won't care if I get another Coke, right?"

"He steals their salt," said Mason, "but now he's nervous there's an alarm on the soda machine."

Duncan gave them both a hard look. "I bet you thought his name was Wu."

"Can we get back to my fortune, please?" Parrish asked.

Mason called things to order. "Okay. Let the record show that I reserve the right to cross-examine at a later time regarding the divine origin of the message. But saying we go with this, what do you think 'Take the corner' means?"

"That's what I'm asking you guys."

"Okay, I'll play." Mason twirled a stir stick from finger to finger. "It's means…a turning point, big news waiting around the next corner, a pivotal turn in your previously mundane existence."

"Thanks."

Duncan tried, "Maybe it's like God calling the shot."

"What?"

"Pool, a pool game, shooting pool. You know, billiards? Fortune cookie off the coffee guy, corner pocket."

"Even if you're right, Dunc, what would that mean?"

"I don't know. I don't play pool."

Parrish sighed.

"Okay, wait," said Duncan. "It's a racing analogy."

"Metaphor," corrected Mason.

"Whatever. Like cornering, like you're taking a fast corner in your life. Brake going in, speed coming out, really lean into it—"

"It could be military metaphor," Mason interrupted.

"Analogy," corrected Duncan.

"Comparison!" Mason brandished the stir stick at Duncan. "Like soldiers taking a strategic hill. 'Come on lads, take that corner!'"

Parrish picked up the fortune and desperately read it again on the chance there was some clue he'd missed.

Duncan's face grew very serious and he spoke, as if prophesying. "Parrish will soon be offered a promotion. A high-salaried position in a local law firm with a company car and box seats at the stadium, and his own office. And when they offer, he's supposed to take the corner office."

"God's telling him to take the corner office?" Mason asked.

"We're guessing. That's a guess."

"That's a stupid guess."

"It's as good as yours."

"Why would God tell him that?"

"So he wouldn't be too greedy, think too highly of himself. Just take the smaller corner office, be satisfied with what's given as opposed to scraping for too much."

"Wow, suddenly you're Gandhi on crack. What if the corner office is the best office?"

"It's my guess, so it isn't. At least my guess has a moral attached. I think if God's giving out directives in cookies, then there's going to be a moral element attached, not some military, macho, attack-the-hill scenario."

"Taking the hill could require courage. That's a moral element."

"Only if there's a tank or a sniper guarding the hill."

"Gentlemen." Parrish laid his hands flat on the table. "Whether or not you take this seriously, I do. Could we please just try to imagine what God was getting at instead of arguing?"

Mason harrumphed. "Well, you'd think God could do a little better than just a phrase all by itself like that."

"Isn't that a sentence?" Duncan asked.

"Yes," confirmed Parrish. "It's a sentence. An imperative one."

"Ooh!" Duncan became scared all over again. "God would definitely be imperative."

"All I'm saying is, as sentences from God go," Mason clarified, "it's a very short, not very informative sentence."

"He didn't have scads of room," said Duncan. "It's a tiny piece of paper."

"God couldn't write on the back? Use a smaller font?"

"But if three words is all we get," Parrish redirected, "what do we do with it?"

"Let's not do this 'we' stuff." Duncan put his hands safely away in his coat pockets.

"It's probably a typo, Parrish." Mason leaned his chair back so the front legs were off the floor. "Don't get huffy, I'm just suggesting. I once had a fortune cookie that said: GOOD THINGS COME IN MALL PACKAGES, but I didn't think the Almighty was sending me shopping."

"I once got a dud," Duncan offered.

"A dud?" Mason asked.

"Yeah. Ate my chow mein, cracked open my cookie, no fortune."

"All cookie, no fortune?"

"Exactly."

"Did you speak to management?"

"No. I ate half the cookie, then left feeling mildly adrift and hopeless."

Mason sighed. "You need to see a doctor or get cable or something."

Parrish interrupted them. "It's not a typo. Look, it's perfectly centered, there's no spaces, no letters missing, three words in perfectly black ink: TAKE THE CORNER."

"It's a cookie!" To punctuate, Mason dropped all four legs of his chair to the floor. "If you don't like this fortune I'll get you another one."

"This is the one I was supposed to open."

"Because God brought you this cookie?"

"I thought Min San brought him the cookie?"

"Guys, can we focus?" Parrish begged.

"Well…" Duncan took a mug off the nearest shelf to play with. "Could it be a translation problem?"

The other two stared at him.

"Like…from the original Chinese?" Duncan tried not to look over at the soda machine.

"How do you dress yourself and get to work each day?" asked Mason.

Duncan blinked. "What?"

"No one's translating fortunes for cookies!" Mason barked. "Fortune cookies aren't even Chinese! They're American."

"No way."

"The Chinese don't have fortune cookies, Dunc."

"Don't do this to me. Parrish? I know they do!"

"No, they don't, we can go right now—"

Duncan pivoted violently in his chair. "So who came up with fortune cookies, then?"

"Californians, I believe," said Mason.

Duncan buried his face in his hands.

"Hold on." Parrish searched his pocket for the plastic wrapper, uncrumpled it. "Look, the wrapper says 'Made in New Jersey.'"

Mason grunted. "You can't trust anything out of New Jersey."

Duncan showed his eyes. "Isn't that the Godforsaken State?"

"Garden State."

"Oh, right."

"Anyway," said Parrish, placing the wrapper on the table as evidence, "it's not a translation problem unless the factory typesetter in New Jersey is originally Dutch or something."

Duncan leaned over the table so that his cheek almost touched the wood. "Wait, now you're saying they don't even make the cookies here—at the restaurant?"

"They use fake shrimp, Dunc. Why would you think they'd have homemade cookies?" Mason said, then turned to Parrish. "Let alone divine ones!"

Duncan seemed to be in physical pain. "How do you fake shrimp?"

Parrish and Mason stood up, taking a moment to allow Duncan to catch up, to figure things out his way, to let him grieve. Parrish walked over to the coffee machine and fetched Duncan a cup of coffee and one for himself. He sat down and sipped silently.

Mason took a brownie out of the pastry case and brought it back with him. He sat down, chewing, and watched Parrish's eyes. Finally, with a mouthful of brownie, he said. "Parrish, get a grip. God doesn't use fortune cookies."

"Who says?" asked Parrish.

"God didn't give Moses ten fortune cookies in a to-go box. God didn't lead the Israelites through the wilderness with a neon all-you-can-eat sign. And God doesn't speak to people in bathrooms, public or otherwise."

"Technically," Duncan said, "the circumstances shouldn't matter in situations regarding divine intervention."

Both Parrish and Mason looked at him.

"Loaves and fishes, man." Duncan placed his coffee on the table in front of him and leaned his face over it. "You're working with low principal, which makes it all the more miraculous."

"That's redundant," said Mason.

"Fake shrimp." Duncan wagged his straw at both of them slyly, like he'd figured out the joke they'd played on him. "That's redundant."

Mason shook that off. "No, Dunc. 'All the more miraculous.' That's redundant. It's either miraculous and therefore securely in the grander, the 'more' category, or it's not, and it's earthly and explicable."

"You can have miracles more miraculous than others," Duncan insisted.

"So you know some miracle hierarchy? You could make a chart with class-A and class-D miracles?"

"Yep."

"Can you give me an instance of the semi-miraculous?"

"The two of you having jobs," said Parrish, "that's semi-miraculous to me every day."

"It was his idea to stiff you." Duncan pointed at Mason. "But seriously, there's that time that disciple—I don't know, not one of the lead guys. A supporting disciple, Nathan or Jeremy—"

"Jeremy was not a disciple."

"Whatever. Anyway, he gets sent ahead on Palm Sunday—although it wasn't Palm Sunday, not yet, 'cause the whole palm frond thing hadn't happened—but that Sunday, I think Luke tells this, ol' Nate is told to go toward town, stop the first stranger he meets, and say some code thingy like, 'The raven is ready.' And this guy will just give him—"

Mason gripped the table. "The raven…is ready?"

"For once, just listen, would ya? He stops a total stranger and the stranger gives him this horse."

"It was a donkey," Mason corrected.

"Maybe it was a pony," said Duncan.

"There is not one pony in the whole Bible."

"There are several ponies in the Bible."

Mason took out his wallet. "Here's a twenty. Go buy a concordance, look up 'pony'—"

"Listen, it might not have been translated 'pony,' but a pony is a small horse. That's how you get donkeys. You breed normal-size horses with little ponies—"

"That's a mule! You breed horses and donkeys, that's how you get a mule."

"Would you guys shut up?" Parrish yelled.

Mason licked the brownie off his fingers. Duncan slurped at his mug without lifting it from the table.

After a safe pause, Duncan spoke quickly. "Guy stops a guy on the road, says something cryptic, other guy gives him a small horse-like creature for free."

"Your point?" asked Parrish.

"That's semi-miraculous."

"Define that," said Mason.

"An occurrence of the extremely coincidental without being necessarily supernatural."

"So?"

"Well, the pony event is only a somewhat miraculous event, whereas something like raising the dead—"

"Guys!" pleaded Parrish.

"My point is: If you're dead, you're dead, but a guy could already have a horse waiting."

Mason and Parrish waited.

"If God intervenes through a circumstance, say, a cookie, the quality of the cookie doesn't matter. The more impossible the cookie, the more clearly divine the intervention."

"So if God gave you this fortune, Dunc," Parrish asked, "what would you do?"

"Oh no, no, no! That's your cookie, pal."

Mason tried to help. "He's only asking what if—"

"No dice. He's already eaten his fate."

Mason held up his hands. "What, so now it's a fate cookie?"

"That's a trouble cookie, that's what that is. He should never have opened that cookie. Probably much safer not to have gone and done that. Who says the corner won't come and take him?"

Parrish pointed accusingly at Duncan. "You're the one who said all that stuff about Samuel. 'You pay to play.'"

"I never told you to do it!" Duncan shook his head vehemently. "That's crazy! I had no idea you'd march into the washroom and mouth off to God. Last thing you need is to dare God to get involved. Have you never read anything? What happens in books to mortals who get mouthy with deity types? Insolence, that's how it looks from the deified point of view. Even the more benevolent versions are often benevolent in the most irregular of ways. It's benevolent for somebody else, maybe, but usually pretty hard wear and tear on the messenger. Brother, you're just begging to be burned at the stake or crammed in an old log and sawn in two. There's a whale somewhere right now whose fish brain just got your name and file downloaded. You need to put that cookie back together, pronto. Look, here's the wrapper."

"Everyone needs to calm down!" Mason pounded the table for attention. "Okay, you got a weird cookie. So what? I don't mean to swat your ego here, buddy, but this smacks a little narcissistic for me. God is not trying to communicate to you through a cookie. It doesn't work that way. God's not all Jack-and-the-magic-beans and tooth-beneath-the-pillow voodoo. You don't just close your eyes, flap open your Bible, and slam a steak knife into a verse. It's that sort of thinking that leads to witch trials and Senate probes."

Both Parrish and Duncan stared as if they'd been scolded for horseplay at the swimming pool.

"That's all I'm saying about this." Mason leaned back, folded his hands.

Parrish turned to Duncan. "Should I open the other cookie?"

"Ah! I'm done." Mason stood, pushed his chair in with a shove. "Do what you want."

Duncan shook his head. "I wouldn't."

"You never know," Mason mocked ominously, "maybe there's a prepositional phrase in there."

"Oh, crap. You think it's a two-parter?" asked Duncan.

"Who knows, Dunc? Maybe the other cookie is really the first cookie. Maybe it says: UNDER NO CIRCUMSTANCES..."

Parrish's eyebrows rose as he considered that possibility. "I almost opened that one first."

"God's out to get you, Parrish." Mason whistled eerily. "Maybe it says: THIS COOKIE WILL SELF-DESTRUCT IN FIVE, FOUR, THREE..."

Duncan put his fingers in his ears, closed his eyes. Mason swatted him.

"No more cookies. I mean it." Duncan stood, following Mason's lead. "You've got enough trouble, Parrish."

"Thank you for your help," said Parrish, looking up at them. "You've both been bastions of enlightenment, and I appreciate your thoughtful candor."

"You're welcome," said Duncan.

"He's making fun of us, Dunc. Don't be nice to him."

"No, he's not." Duncan turned to Parrish doubtfully. "Are you?"

Parrish nodded.

"Well, figure it out yourself then." Duncan picked up his coffee and gave one last noisy slurp. "God didn't give us the cookie."

"Go away," Parrish said quietly.

"Yes sir!" Duncan saluted, then marched behind the counter to brew more coffee.

Mason turned back to Parrish. "You coming back to work?"

"I need a walk," Parrish answered, staring at the fortune where it lay on the table.

Mason dropped his head, sighed. "Then I'll leave you alone with your cookie."

As Parrish stepped out the front of his shop, he zipped his brown corduroy coat up to his neck and hunched his shoulders. The wind was a brisk February one, so cold it made him blink. He wrapped his long scarf twice around his neck and buried his stubbly chin in its protection. He started walking, nowhere at first, just straight across the parking lot. Then he considered going back to Mr. Wu's, to do what, he was uncertain. Maybe Charles would also tell him there was nothing to the fortunes inside cookies, maybe that would help him let it go. Maybe Duncan was right, Parrish thought, maybe he'd give this fortune back, switch out for another, maybe there was such a thing as a fortune cookie trade-in.

Parrish walked at a clip across the parking lot, a weaving route in and out of parked cars with his hands buried in his pockets. Parrish looked at his wristwatch—nearly five o'clock. Duncan hadn't rolled in until ten, so he'd stay until close, and though Mason was already off, he'd probably stay to make more messes. But Susan would be in soon. He had recently hired her, someone who actually knew how to clean, who liked to clean, actually saw its benefits. The store would be fine without him.

At the curb, he stopped in the patch of grass, waiting for a break in traffic so he could cross. A long city bus pulled down the street right in front of him, so slowly and close he could've reached out and run his fingers along its dirty side. The bus's brakes puffed and released as it halted at the corner. The hydraulic doors exhaled several passengers flipping their scarves and managing gloves and stocking caps as they stepped down the ramp stairs. They exited quickly, without a word to each other, dispersing in every direction. Parrish recognized one of his regulars, or he recognized the Green Bay Packers toboggan, which the man wore in cold weather or hot, rain or shine. He never would've guessed that particular triple-shot-extra-foamy-cappuccino drinker for a bus rider, but that just showed how little he knew.

Parrish glanced down the street in the opposite direction, toward an intersection with a light where this side street connected with a major one. The after-work traffic pulsed in full swing, and the light shone green for the traffic coming toward him. He could have bolted, but he'd have had to take his hands out of his pockets, so he waited.

In his coat pockets, Parrish dug and curled his fingers downward. He didn't like gloves, didn't like the way he couldn't pick up things when he wore them, but he'd have taken a pair then. In one pocket, his hand found the unopened fortune cookie, in the other, his fingers flipped at the piece of paper till they recognized its shape.

He took another glance toward the busy intersection, then back toward the bus stop.

He stared. Nothing special drew his gaze, just an average bus stop on a typical street corner. There was nothing remarkable about the corner—it was simply the nearest one. He tried to empty his eyes of the thought behind them.

It was already past time for his postlunch espresso. He should go back to the shop. He suddenly felt an urgent need to finish all his supply orders before he went home. Besides, it was too cold to stand outside. A chill wriggled up his spine.

He listed all the things he'd rather do.

Then he walked to the corner.

The bus stop was the kind with a single small sign posting the route number and two companion benches situated one next to the other, both facing the street. Attached to the sign with a heavy chain was a round public trash can of thick, metal mesh. The trash bin was mostly full, and Parrish wondered who, if anyone, ever emptied this can. He'd never seen someone do so, but then again, he'd never given it any attention. The benches were typical—thick, dirty wooden slats with dark green, chipping paint, the ends of the slats bolted to a concrete frame that made up the sides, back, and armrests of the benches. Perfectly ordinary.

As Parrish arrived, the bus's engine roared as the hulky vehicle slowly pulled itself away from the curb, puffing clouds of black diesel exhaust as it picked up speed. Three people remained after the bus's departure—two women, both seated on the benches, one reading, one knitting, and a man leaning on the route sign, lighting a cigarette.

"Blind," the man said, the lit cigarette bouncing in his lips.

Parrish glanced at the smoker. "Sorry?"

"That driver." Cigarette-man cocked his head the direction the bus had gone. "He's legally blind. You can wave your hands all day, jump up and down, but he won't see you."

Parrish nodded in appreciation for the inside information.

"You have to slap the side of the bus or beat on the door half the time to stop him," the smoker continued. "He shouldn't be driving. He can't see."

"Thanks," Parrish said, then avoided further conversation, having no wish to explain why he was at a bus stop with no intention of catching a bus. But as he stood there, turning in a circle, it was clear he didn't know what he was doing. Both women gave him an investigative glance. The girl on the bench closest to him stared longer, less approvingly, then returned to the book she was reading.

"You mind if I sit?" he asked her.

She did not acknowledge him. With a gloved hand she adjusted her glasses, then turned a page in her novel.

Parrish sat anyway, and though he sat as far to one end of her bench as he could, this earned him a second disapproving stare. She was a young woman, not much younger than himself, Parrish guessed. She wore a gray, puffy, knitted-wool toboggan and wool gloves and was bundled in a long gray Burberry coat, which covered her almost completely. He could see only a hint of the mint green scrubs she wore as pants—a doctor, a nurse, maybe a dental assistant. She divided the space fairly between them, gathering her backpack and day planner closer to her end.

On the other bench, the older woman knitted. Maybe his mother's age, she was also bundled in a long wool coat, navy blue, but she wore no hat and her gloves lay neatly on the bench beside her so her fingers were free to do their work. Several plastic shopping bags of yarn surrounded her. Parrish glanced back and forth. The two women sat at opposite ends of separate benches, as far apart as possible.

When the man finished his cigarette, he grimaced as he removed the cigarette butt from his lips, threw it to the ground in front of

him, then put his hand back in his warm pocket. This discarded cigarette nub, and the smoke that trailed it, received a glance from the
book reader and a breathy huff that steamed from her mouth into
the cold air, then trailed over her head.

The man grinned at Parrish, shrugged, then rolled his eyes.
"Forty minutes," he then announced. "Maybe forty-five. Buses run
pretty much on time, at least."

"Appreciate that," said Parrish.

"Where you headed?"

Parrish paused. "Nowhere, really. But thanks."

The man nodded, but frowned as he considered that answer.
The aloof young woman apparently had exquisite hearing. She
immediately turned and gave Parrish a hard stare. Even the knitter
raised her eyebrows while she looped a stitch.

"So…" Cigarette-man adjusted his shoulders, uncrossed his legs,
shifted into a tougher-looking lean on the signpost. "You just hanging out at bus stops today?"

There it was, Parrish thought. In less than five minutes, he'd
completely failed at avoiding it, and now he either had to come out
with the impossible answer or a credible lie. Very funny, God. And
because this whole bit seemed God's, Parrish felt distinctly disin-
clined to lie, but neither did he want to tell the truth. And what was
the truth? God via cookie had sent him here? Did he even believe
that? Even if he did, he couldn't say out loud. He looked up at the
white, puffy clouds that promised snow.

But cigarette-man proved insistent. "I said, 'You just hanging
out at bus stops today?'" His tone turned aggressive.

Parrish smiled. "Today, yep."

Both women registered the tension in the cold air. The reader's eyes scanned the book more quickly, and the knitter's fingers increased their knitting.

Cigarette-man gave Parrish another chance. "Why you hanging out at bus stops today?"

Parrish nodded agreeably to himself, accepting the situation. God wanted him to get beat up. What was it, Monday? The coffee shop would be slow on a Monday night, so one of the boys could slip away to drive him to the emergency clinic. No problem. It was cold, so the first punch would sting, but maybe the guy would want to get his fists back in his pockets as soon as possible. Good fortune, all around. Heck, he was sitting next to someone in a health care profession.

Having gone this far, Parrish decided to go the next step. He looked up at the man and very kindly asked: "Actually, I was wondering if you needed anything?"

The man cocked his chin and stared defiantly. "You selling something?"

"Nope."

"What're you selling?"

"Nothing."

"Whatever you're selling, I don't need any."

"Nope. Not selling. Just thought if you needed something, maybe I could try to help."

The man pushed off from the post and took his hands out of his pockets. Sure enough, fists. His eyes searched across the parking lot, then up and down the street, as if checking to make sure no cops were around.

Parrish looked down at his boots. He didn't have to offer his face to be punched, did he? The turn-the-other-cheek thing only applied to second punches. His left boot had come untied, but as he reached to tie it, he saw cigarette-man's black shoes step forward and square off in front of him.

"Well, guy, I need a million dollars."

Parrish shook his head, nearly laughing. He dropped the laces, and leaned back on the bench. "I haven't got a million dollars."

"I thought you wanted to help me."

"Sure, but—"

"You ain't got a million dollars? What good are you, then?"

"If you need some cash, I can give you—"

"I don't need your money, kid! What do you think I am?"

"Maybe I was supposed to help someone else. Sorry I bugged you."

Parrish felt the hair bristle on the back of his neck. If he stood, he knew the man would shove him and they'd fight. But if he looked away again, that was just asking the guy to keep on coming. He took his hands out of his pockets and put them in his lap very carefully. Nothing aggressive, but at least he could block a punch. Parrish sighed and looked directly up at him, as unafraid as possible.

The man stood with a wide stance. His face surged with anticipation, like he wanted one thing more to justify his desire to pound the stranger seated before him.

"I don't believe he meant any offense."

Both men turned as the knitter said this. She didn't plead, nothing fretful, just casually mentioned it, looking at the men with kindness in her eyes, then returned to her knitting. At the same time, a car horn honked.

The man looked over to the parking lot, raised his chin, and waved. "That's my ride." He delivered this with a finger pointed sharply at Parrish, like a warning—he was leaving unless someone wanted him to stay. Anybody? He took shallow, quick breaths, cracking his knuckles on one hand, then the next. Then he reached around to his back pocket. Parrish flinched slightly, but the man only took out his wallet, withdrew a dollar, and threw it in Parrish's lap.

"Here. Buy yourself some sense." He walked off to meet the car awaiting him.

Parrish took a deep breath, staring down at the dollar. He glanced over at the knitter. "Thanks."

She gave him a kind smile, let her motherly eyes linger on him for a moment, reassuringly, then returned to her knitting, completely unperturbed.

"How much sense you think I can get for a dollar?" Parrish asked her.

The knitter shrugged.

Parrish heard the young woman next to him mumble, "Not enough." When he turned, she was reading diligently.

Parrish decided to go. That was more than enough God stuff for the day. He would walk back to the safety of his coffee shop, have a round of espressos with the boys, make great fun of fortune cookies and angry dollar-throwing men, and thank God he didn't have to ride the bus on a daily basis. But both from habit and adrenaline, he nervously checked the bench to see if he was about to leave anything—a glove, a scarf, his pride. He glanced down, saw his untied boot, and when he leaned down to tie it, there, way up underneath the bench, as if the wind had blown it up against the concrete leg nearest him, he saw a folded piece of stationery paper.

He picked it up. It was blank on the outside, but he could see writing on the inside, so he opened it. It was a letter, of sorts. Very short, but with no sender's name, no name for whom it was being written to, no names at all. He read it quickly—a sad letter. With it open in his lap, he leaned back on the bench.

"Did you drop this?" Parrish asked the knitter.

She looked up, glanced down at the letter in his hand, then smiled and shook her head.

He turned to ask the girl the same, only to find her already staring harshly at him, her book closed in her lap, her face indignant and appalled.

"Did you just read that?" she asked.

Parrish looked down at the note, then back at her. "Yeah," he admitted.

The girl blinked disapprovingly. "You read it. Just like that?"

"Pretty much."

They stared at each other. The girl gave a disgusted huff.

"I've known how to read for a while now," Parrish said.

"Is that yours?"

"No." Parrish held it out, perfectly willing for her to take it. "I just found it."

The girl tilted her head and her eyes went unbelievably small as she squinted at him over the rim of her glasses. She wasn't unpretty, Parrish thought, until she did that with her face.

"Under the bench," he added, as if this might help.

Though she didn't say the words, her eyebrows bunched eloquently, and he received the insult—you jerk—without any translation problems. Then she shook her head, sighed, and sank her attention back into her book.

Parrish stared at her, stunned, but she took no notice, having dismissed him entirely. He glanced at the knitter, hoping for a commiserative shrug. The knitter only smiled and pulled more yarn free from the plastic bag sitting on the bench next to her. She showed Parrish her work, spreading it out and holding it up properly so he could see what it eventually would become—a dark blue sweater.

Parrish folded the note closed. He almost put it in his pocket, but if he put it in his pocket and stood to leave, she might tackle him, accuse him of stealing. He considered throwing it back under the bench, only to imagine her muttering about litter and civic duty. Who was this woman, anyway? His intention, although peculiar, had been benevolent, and he wasn't often benevolent, so he didn't like missing credit for it when he was.

"So…," he said, "you don't think I should've read a note I found on the sidewalk?"

She shut her book. "No," she answered assuredly.

"What do you care?"

"It belongs to someone else. Maybe it's personal."

"Is it yours?"

"No. But you didn't bother to ask, did you?"

"I asked her." Parrish pointed to the knitter. The reader looked over at the knitter.

"He did," the knitter verified.

The girl huffed again. "Still."

Parrish cleared his throat. "Ma'am, is this your note?"

The girl was not amused.

"Seriously, if it's yours, take it. I didn't mean to invade your—"

"It's not my note. That's not my point. My point is that it's not your note, so you shouldn't just open it up and read it."

"What am I supposed to do with it?"

"You could try to give it back to its proper owner or throw it away."

"You say that like it's a rule or something."

"It is a rule."

"Whose rule?"

"Everybody's but yours, apparently." The girl waved a hand with an air of finality.

Parrish looked around for everybody, for anybody, but saw only the three of them. He wished Duncan or Mason could hear this. They'd have had a field day with some girl on a bus bench declaring arbitrary rules for humanity. Exasperated, he dropped the note on the bench between them.

The girl glared at him.

"What?" he said.

She shook her head slowly, incredulously, then gave up, pulled her backpack closer to her, unzipped it, and began to wedge the book she'd been reading down into it.

Parrish picked up the letter, unfolded it again.

The girl gasped. "What are you doing now?"

"I'm going to reread it."

This time she used the words. "You're a jerk!"

Parrish had had enough. "Look, lady. First, I've already read it, so what does it matter if I read it again? Second, you just told me to find who it belongs to and give it back to them, right?"

The girl stared at him, refusing to blink, her nostrils flared.

"Well, how do I do that unless I read it?"

"You don't have to *read* read it. You scan for an address or name or something, that's all."

"It doesn't have any, look!" Parrish held the letter out to show her, right in front of her nose. He held the letter up for a long moment, long enough to watch her eyes as they moved along the few lines, to notice how they softened as she took in the letter's sadness, then he whipped the letter away so suddenly that her eyes met his.

"Ha! You were reading it!"

The girl immediately turned her head away, as if shamed. "No!"

"Yes, you were."

"I was looking to see if there were any names—"

"No, you weren't scanning. That was reading."

"No, I wasn't."

"Excuse me." The knitter interrupted. "If the letter isn't yours, maybe you shouldn't keep reading it."

"Thank you!" said the girl, blushing with anger. "Either find who it belongs to or throw it away."

"That probably would be the polite thing," the knitter suggested.

"Unbelievable," Parrish mumbled to himself. "One unbelievable day."

The older lady looked up at the sky and nodded as if she agreed with him but thought it a good thing. The girl sat clutching her backpack as if protecting it, as if keeping the bag between her and the letter would somehow distance her from the fact that she'd read it too.

"I think I was supposed to read it," Parrish said softly.

Both knitter and reader looked at one another.

"Excuse me?" said the knitter.

"I was sent here," said Parrish. "To find it. I think I was supposed to."

The girl's eyes went incredibly wide. "Someone sent you here to pick that up?"

"I think so, yeah." Parrish looked to see if the girl thought he was crazy. She did.

"Who sent you?" she asked.

"Can we discuss that later?"

"You just said—"

"Look, it's personal, okay?"

"Kind of like someone else's letter? That kind of personal?"

"Exactly." Parrish bobbed his knees up and down to warm his legs. "I wasn't trying to be a jerk, okay?"

The girl said nothing.

"You work at that coffee shop," asked the knitter, "across the street, right?"

"Yes ma'am. That's my shop."

The girl gave one quick glance across the street to verify there was a coffee shop.

"That's it, then. I thought I recognized you," said the knitter happily. "I thought at first maybe I saw you on the news or something, but you're not a criminal at all. You're that coffee guy."

"Right," said Parrish.

"My Arthur, he loves your shop," continued the knitter. "Well, he did. My name's Rose." The knitter put her yarn aside and offered Parrish her hand. "Rose Miranda."

"John." Parrish said. "Nice to meet you, Mrs. Miranda."

"Please, call me Rose."

They shook hands.

Not a part of the bus stop introductions, the girl awkwardly occupied herself with the zipper on her backpack. Sitting between the two, Parrish felt introductory. "This is Rose," he offered.

The girl brightened and leaned to see Rose's face. "I'm Audra."

"Nice to meet you. Audra, this is John."

Audra's eyes moved hesitantly to Parrish's face and she forced a smile toward him. Parrish acknowledged her effort, tipping back his chin and giving a slight nod.

An awkward silence followed the awkward introductions. Parrish turned to Rose. "You talk like he doesn't come in anymore."

"Arthur? No." Rose sighed. "No, he doesn't." She continued her knitting.

Parrish looked at Audra and for the first time, they shared a glance that wasn't hostile. They shared the same concern—the way Rose spoke, they couldn't tell if Arthur was no longer in Parrish's coffee shop because he was no longer among the living. Parrish gave Audra a pleading glance.

She released her bag and shrugged with a helpless gesture of her hands.

He glanced at Rose, then back at Audra and mouthed, "What do I say?"

In reply, Audra mouthed, "You don't."

So Parrish turned and asked, "Did we give him a bum latte?"

Audra pressed the fingers of both her hands into her forehead.

"No," Rose continued happily. "Arthur doesn't drink coffee anymore. Not yours in particular, but coffee in general. Doctor's orders. Oh, but when he did, he'd have coffee all day. And he'd always come home with one of your paper cups. He said you guys know how not to ruin a good Costa Rican."

"I'm proud of our Costa Ricans," he said to Rose, then gave Audra a quick wink.

"That's what Arthur guessed. He could guess a pot of coffee from the aroma. From across a room. Costa Rican, Kenyan, blah, blah. Anyhow, I went once or twice with him, and that's where I've seen you. Glad you're not a criminal."

"Always felt glad about that myself."

"I mean I guess you're not," Rose laughed. "A criminal, I mean. You could be a criminal with a day job, but that'll usually show up in the end, won't it? I mean, money missing from the tills, late for work, that sort of thing."

"I have a couple of criminals working for me now. Neither is punctual."

This comment induced another awkward pause from the threesome.

Audra leaned forward to address Rose. "Excuse me."

"Yes, dear?"

"Would you give us your opinion on something?"

"For what it's worth, sure."

"Your coffee guy, he just found a note on the ground, folded up—"

"Yes, I heard."

Parrish interrupted. "What is it with you?"

"No, wait." Audra made a patting gesture in the air. "Calm down. We disagree, so let's get another opinion."

"I'm sorry she's bothering you, Mrs. Miranda," said Parrish.

"Don't apologize for me," Audra said defiantly.

"Please, call me Rose."

Audra continued unabashed. "Should he have read someone else's note?"

"It was lying on the sidewalk!" Parrish said.

Rose paused as if she were choosing her words carefully. "It might be best to return it to its owner, if that's possible."

"That's what I was saying," said Audra smugly.

"But it doesn't say whose it is," Parrish argued. "So technically, even though it's personal, I don't know who that person is, so I haven't invaded their privacy."

Rose considered this. "That's an idea, yes."

"Whether they know it or not, it's a question of prying into someone's affairs," insisted Audra.

"Well, if they didn't want us prying," Parrish said, "maybe they should've taken better care of the note."

"You found it, so you have the right to pry?"

"Maybe I can help."

Audra shook her head as if she'd suddenly awoken. "And who are you to go out prying and helping?"

Parrish said nothing. It was ridiculous, he admitted that to himself. He didn't look remotely like a helper. Besides, there was no way to find out whose it was.

"Does the person in the letter need help?" Rose stopped her knitting, concerned.

Parrish handed her the letter.

Audra clapped her forehead with her hand, her shoulders fell limp.

"Oh, let it go!' said Parrish. "I've read it, you've read it. She might as well read it!"

"I don't have my reading glasses," said Rose, handing it back to Parrish. "What does it say?"

Parrish took the letter, cleared his throat, then paused to see if Audra would object.

She threw her arms up in a gesture of surrender.

Parrish read aloud:

I watch you every day.

What gets you up in the morning? How do you go on? The way you're treated, what's happening to you… I don't know what to do anymore. Home, what should be a home, how did that become nothing but this trap?

I don't think I can go on. Too much bad for too many days, nothing but the awful feelings all the time. Then I wonder how you must feel. It scares me what I might do. I want to quit, quit all of it, quit everything, quit today. Only one thing stops me. What would it do to you if I disappeared? I can't stay much longer. Who will love you when I'm gone?

"Well, I don't like the sound of that." Mrs. Miranda clucked her tongue.

Parrish folded the letter and tucked it away in the breast pocket of his coat. Audra sniffed, pulled her collar tighter against the wind. Her left ear was uncovered outside her toboggan, so it shone bright red with cold, as rosy as her cheeks. She pulled the edge of her hat over the exposed ear and sniffled again. When she glanced at Parrish, he looked away.

"And there's no name, no address?" asked Rose.

Parrish shook his head.

"Pity," she said, mostly to herself.

No more conversation passed between the three. None of them wanted to dismiss the sadness of the letter with small talk. Audra returned quietly to her book, occasionally jotting reminders in a thick, black day planner. Rose continued her sweater, but now and again she looked up and considered, then hummed a sigh. Parrish began imagining his next espresso.

A short man in a long wool overcoat strolled down the sidewalk, leading a St. Bernard on a leash. Actually, the dog strolled, tongue-wagging, his paws plodding heavily and the leash strained taut, not quite dragging the man, but enough to make him follow at a brisk, staggering clip.

As they passed the bench, Parrish spoke up. "Excuse me."

The man turned, yanked at the leash numerous times. The dog did not acknowledge the tugs, apparently never knew anything about them.

"Bellamy! Whoa!" the man commanded to no effect, then turned himself, lowered the leash so he could step over it and prevent a tangle. Bellamy found Parrish, trotted back to him, and brashly nosed at Parrish's hand.

"Bellamy, sit!" called the man, assuming a stern tone. The dog sat, more tired than obedient. He panted and stared at Parrish as only a big, friendly dog can, flopping a damp paw onto his knee.

"Bellamy, down!"

"He's all right," said Parrish.

Audra smiled and leaned over to scratch behind one of the dog's substantial ears. This delighted Bellamy, and his paw renewed its insistence on Parrish's leg.

"Sorry to interrupt your walk," said Parrish, "but did you, by any chance, drop a letter near this bench?"

The man stood still for a moment but said nothing.

"We found a letter under this bench." His gesture included Audra, who immediately withdrew her hand from the dog's ear and went back to reading.

The short man huffed. "You stopped me to ask me that?"

"When we read it…" Parrish glanced at Audra, thought better of it. "When I read it, it sounded important, like whoever lost it might need it back."

The man looked at Audra to see if she owned any responsibility for this. She never looked up, not even when she brushed a muddy patch off her coat from Bellamy's pawing. She rubbed it clean with the palm of her hand and continued reading.

"I didn't drop anything," he said, annoyed, then pulled the leash hard. "Bellamy, come!"

The dog stood reluctantly, panting rhythmically in steamy puffs until his droopy eyes looked down and he took a licking interest in Parrish's boots. Working in a coffee shop, Parrish's boots often sported vanilla syrup, chocolate powder, crumbs of all kinds.

"Sorry," said Parrish.

The man turned his back to him. "Mrs. Miranda, good to see you."

"Oh." She looked up and answered politely. "Yes, good to see you too."

"Bellamy! Walk!" The short man yelled these one-word commands like he was performing a magic trick, a poorly practiced one. After a series of tugs on the leash, the man finally straddled the large dog and pulled him by the ears simply to turn his attention back to the sidewalk. The dog didn't seem to mind this treatment, rather responded as if it were usual, even affectionate, and licked his owner's hands. Once turned, the dog started his trot down the walk again.

Parrish watched as they made their way down the sidewalk until they disappeared. Only then did he notice Audra staring at him.

"What?" he asked.

"Don't tell people I'm a part of…whatever it is you're doing," she said.

Parrish buried his hands in his coat pockets, shifted himself higher so that he sat on the backrest of the bench, his feet on the slats of the seat, and hung his head to observe his freshly licked boots.

At this, Mrs. Miranda checked her watch, stopped knitting, examined her progress, tugged at a few loose sprigs, then gathered her things into the plastic bag. She took a brisk breath, placed both hands flat on her knees. "Nice to meet you both," she offered.

Parrish nodded and Audra smiled.

Mrs. Miranda stood, looping the plastic bags over her arm, and walked down the street, away from the busy intersection and toward the rows of houses and apartments.

Several more times, Parrish tried. People who hopped off the next bus, people who happened past, he begged their pardon, then asked if they had at some point, perhaps yesterday, dropped a letter. He held it out enthusiastically, tried to give it away, to prod it into hands that might identify it. He gave each stranger a discerning squint, hoping to spy some hidden reserve of sadness. Each time it was the same. Not only did no one show the slightest recognition of the letter, those who actually understood his request frowned suspiciously as if they recognized the telltale signs of madness — his.

It grew darker. Dusk rose upward, and the gray of the concrete seemed to thicken, loosen, then float free. The gray seeped, emanating until it hung above the bus stop and the parking lot, muting everything imperceptibly through shades of haze. It moved across the cloudy white sky, which purpled briefly before all went a darker gray, and the wind blew colder. The streetlamps high above the bus benches buzzed and blinked awake.

He watched Audra slip a ticket stub in her book to mark the place and gather her things. She stood, pulling on a pair of heavy wool gloves. Keeping her fingers outstretched, she made room inside the gloves by wiggling them.

"So?" she asked. "How'd it go?"

Parrish stood up tall on the bench seat, then hopped down to the sidewalk.

"Genuinely, I'm interested." Audra shouldered her bag. "You said you were sent here. To find that." She pointed, then cocked her hip. "You seemed so certain an hour ago. So?"

"I feel painfully foolish," he answered, shoving the letter in his coat pocket, away from sight. "Thanks for asking."

"I'm not making fun, I'm—"

"Yes, you are."

"Some. Yeah."

She arched her back opposite the bend of her slouched posture, put a hand atop her hat so she wouldn't lose it, then collapsed her stretch with a yawn. "You have to admit it's interesting for an afternoon at the bus stop."

"Glad I could entertain."

"You started this conversation. Don't get huffy that I'm willing to finish it. Fair?"

"Fair enough."

They both stood shivering a bit in the wind.

"You going to tell me who sent you?"

"No, I don't think I am," he said testily. "Fair?"

"Okay. But what are you going to tell this mystery person about—can I call it your 'mission' without you getting bent out of shape?"

"Sure."

"So?"

Parrish looked at this girl, this stranger. He could understand, even excuse, her amusement, though it was at his expense. When she used a heavily gloved finger to push the glasses up on her nose, then wrinkled her nose because of the cold and sniffed, she seemed almost decent.

"I hadn't really thought about it," he admitted. "Maybe I was wrong."

"Wait," she said. "Now you're not sure you were told to come here?"

"The more I explain this, I assure you, the less sensible it's going to sound."

Her eyes narrowed suspiciously.

"Can we drop it?" he asked.

Dropping it seemed an allowable solution in Audra's world. She reached over and swatted a few St. Bernard hairs off the arms of his coat. "I don't want you to feel foolish. I was just curious."

"Kills cats, I hear."

"Dog person," she said. "Wouldn't own a cat."

"Probably a good thing. For the cat."

She smiled widely at him, her first real smile since he'd met her, and her forehead smoothed brightly. "What happens next?" she asked, pointing at the letter in his pocket.

"Next?" Parrish gave a distant glance toward his coffee shop.

Later he would wonder exactly why he said what he did. At that exact moment, had he relied on his feelings—what with the cold, the failed attempts, the near beating, and the overall hassle of the past hour—he felt thoroughly done with the cookie fortune mission. He had no "next." But for some reason, when he looked back at the girl's smile, those inquisitive eyes blinking behind the brown-framed glasses, he decided.

"I guess I'll be foolish again tomorrow."

Audra shifted the weight of her backpack more securely on her shoulder, sniffled, and put her free arm across her chest and looped her fingers on the pack's strap so that both her hands held it tightly.

"Keep warm," Parrish offered.

"You too."

He watched as she walked away, head down, taking the sidewalk the same direction Mrs. Miranda had gone, toward the neighborhood of houses and apartments where porch lights and windows awoke against the gray evening like candles suddenly uncovered.

Parrish walked back toward his coffee shop, taking his time.

Perhaps it was the cold, perhaps he was less than properly caffeinated, perhaps it would be fair to say that he had a bad habit of indulging and fanning a cranky spark. Regardless, as he walked, he stoked his smoldering mood—he mumbled to himself, reviewed his ongoing list of general complaints, replayed specifically the troubles he'd just suffered.

"Buy yourself some sense."

He repeated the cigarette-man's threat audibly, loudly, with a mocking voice. He stared at his own reflection in the windshield of a Honda, then responded sarcastically to his own face with a courage he hadn't found when the smoker stood over him.

"Maybe I can borrow some of yours?" he complained.

He walked on, his hands cold, so he kept them in his pockets, scratching his stubbly cheek against the shoulder of his coat as he walked. He needed to shave. He hadn't in a few days for no particular reason other than he had no boss—other than himself—to tell him to do so, and what there was of a beard was at just the length to itch considerably. He didn't like itching. But he didn't like shaving, either, so he did the sensible thing—he kicked a rock.

It bounced across the asphalt toward a parked Buick. He watched helplessly, immediately regretting his rash choice, his bad aim, his stupid rock-kicking foot. He bobbed and leaned in hopes of controlling the course of the projectile, and, for once, it worked. At the last moment, the wayward rock skipped beneath the parked car.

"Take the corner."

He said this out loud as well, but with less taunting, more a grumble. What was that about? He looked for another rock to kick. And what was the point of owning your own shop if you still had to shave all the time? He was not at all comfortable with this new gig, this all-in wager. Duncan's idea, no less.

With his hands in his back pockets and slouched forward, he trudged across the lot, navigating around meandering cars that searched, slow and senile, for the best spots to park. He wondered what the procedure was for calling God off. Could he put God back where God had been earlier that day and, in all honesty, where Parrish had kept God every other day before this one? In all honesty, Parrish had to admit that he was cranky with God.

Outside his shop, he straightened the tables and threw away a few empty cups and stray lids. It was dark by now, and the small patio area was lit, but not brightly. Most of the light outside came from inside, shining through the glass door. He stopped and stared through the glass before going in, a cranky manager secretly observing his staff.

Susan was working. Parrish watched as she swept, dusted, refilled things, and swept and dusted and refilled things at the same time. She happily gathered plates and wiped down tables, and not just the tabletops. She took the rag and wiped down the legs and bases of each one, bent down and pinched crumbs off the floor with one hand, dropped them into a pile in the other, then walked over to the trash and dusted her palms. Then—and for Parrish it felt almost like watching the end of a movie where the guy and girl stroll hand in hand toward a hopeful future—he watched as Susan went to the sink and actually washed her hands—with soap—before helping the next customer. And she dried them on a paper towel instead of her apron. He loved Susan, really.

He did the math in his head. If he fired the other two, could he then pay her enough to work, say, sixty-five hours a week? She went part-time to college, and he knew she'd taken this job to save up for a car. He had a car. Not a good one, but if he slept in the back of the shop beside the coffee roaster, slept on the huge burlap bags of green coffee beans, he could give Susan his car and a raise.

Parrish leaned his shoulder against the glass door and stared at Duncan and Mason. He knew they wouldn't be working, and he enjoyed catching them. It was their game, his management style, their employee-employer dysfunction, and it had its finer points. Catching them would not get them to work, not that simply. They were amoral when it came to employee guilt. The goal in catching them was to score so that the following day, having a point against them, they tried all the harder not to be caught again. Parrish would then increase the number of times he walked randomly through the shop, forcing them to feign labor more often.

He could count on their laziness. It was a rock, a tide, an arithmetical certainty. With any effort on his part, eventually, he would catch them again. That would be two points to their zero. (They never scored on him, because [a] he worked, and [b] if he ever messed around, they gladly joined in, causing a split decision.) Competitively, they'd be determined not to go down three to zip. They'd prepare things they could grab and pretend to be doing whenever he came through — lean with a broom nearby, take an overloaded garbage bag out of the garbage can and tie it off so they could pick it up when he appeared. (And this was almost like taking out the trash.) This continued until, finally, being lazy required so much effort, so much work, Parrish achieved what he called The Creeping Realization. He loved The Creeping Realization. Like half-and-half added to a black cup of coffee, it slowly, swirlingly permeated their minds that the normal work might actually be easier than the work involved in avoiding work.

Parrish slipped inside the shop, careful with the door so the bells wouldn't jangle. Duncan, he knew, was still on the clock, but

Mason's shift had ended at five—if he had remembered to clock out, that is. They were busy. They were stunningly industrious about all things non-work-related. Mason was busy speaking to a couple, two regular customers, asking if they could move to another table. Once they had, he stood in their vacated chairs so he could reach the top shelf of the retail wall. The display—a pound of coffee, a mug, and a gift basket—he shoved recklessly to a back corner of the shelf, placed a metal steaming pitcher in its middle, then very carefully turned the pitcher and moved it backward and forward from the wall.

Meanwhile, Duncan worked busily at wadding paper pastry bags three at a time into tight paper balls, which he then wrapped with excessive amounts of duct tape, forming shiny, silver, sticky round balls. He pressed and formed each tape ball in his hands until it was perfectly round, as perfectly round as he could make such a thing. Roughly a dozen he'd made so far, and seemingly eager to make a dozen more, Duncan found himself out of duct tape, the new roll—which Parrish had bought two days ago—completely gone.

"You can't leave that crap up there, it'll mess up my backboard shots," Duncan said, observing the shelf.

"You're fine," Mason replied without turning around.

"No, it's not. Take that stuff down."

"Don't have anyplace to put it. Anyway, you can't use a backboard. That's against the rules."

"What rules?"

"Tape-ball rules. It's about arc, using good arc. If you know what you're doing you don't need a backboard."

"Why can't there be a backboard?"

"Because there isn't one in tape ball, that's why. How many did you make?"

Duncan counted. "Thirteen. Is there more tape?"

"I told Parrish to buy some the other day," answered Mason. "Did he only buy one roll?"

"I only found one. Check that cabinet by those whatsama-thingys."

Mason ignored the request. From past history, Parrish knew that Duncan was in charge of making the tape balls. Mason just set up the goal, the basket. He jumped down from the chair, backed up into the middle of the store, eyeing the steaming pitcher, then stood in the chair again to make adjustments.

"Is that centered?" he called to Duncan.

Parrish stepped up behind him. "A little to the left."

"You think?" Mason never looked down. "The handle, should it be turned to the very back, or just to one side, like this?"

Parrish put both hands on the back of the chair, then with one hard shove, tilted the chair backward as far as he could. The steaming pitcher clanged as it fell from the shelf, and Mason had to grab the wall and put a foot on the table to keep from sprawling.

"What the— oh, hey, Parrish."

Hearing this, Duncan looked up from his tape balls. "Parrish, is there another roll of duct tape somewhere?"

"I think you've made enough," Parrish replied with quiet restraint.

"No, we got thirteen, you can't have an odd number."

"I think thirteen's enough."

"Two teams, no way. Unless Susan wants to play. Susan, you want to play?"

Susan distanced herself from what was about to happen by sticking her head into the pastry case, adjusting the trays, and removing a cake in order to serve a slice to a customer.

With a shaky degree of caution, Mason climbed down off the retail shelves until he was on all fours in the middle of the little bistro table. He looked like a frightened dog at the veterinarian's office. "Hey, Dunc, I think thirteen's enough."

"No!" Duncan whined as if he'd been waiting all day for this game of tape ball. Then, suddenly, he looked up, very puzzled. "Is thirteen divisible by three?" He addressed this question eventually to Susan, but she kept busy slicing cake for her customers. "Look, we'll just throw one ball away. Twelve is good. Twelve's divisible by everything. There's a reason twelve makes a dozen. Besides, this one's kind of oblong anyway." Duncan stepped back, pretended to dribble, then reared back with a jump shot that sent the tape ball toward the garbage can beside the brewers, missing terribly. "See? Oblong."

Parrish watched Duncan calmly, then turned to stare at Mason.

"Hey, man, we just finished up with straightening the back room, like you told us, so we thought we'd take a quick break, for five minutes and—"

"Are you on the clock?"

Mason glanced toward Duncan, then over at Susan, then smiled at the customers seated at their new table, then looked blankly back at Parrish. "Which clock?"

"Get off my table and punch out."

"Come on, I always forget to clock out."

"Get off that table!" said Parrish.

"Back room looks great, though," said Mason.

"Hey, Susan?"

"Yes, Mr. Parrish?"

"Did you clean the back room?"

She paused. "They did help me a little with the—"

"Thank you for cleaning the back room, Susan."

"You're welcome, Mr. Parrish."

Mason climbed off the table. "She's always stealing the credit for stuff we—"

"You, shut up," said Parrish, pointing a finger in Mason's face. "Hey, Susan, can you drive a manual?"

"Manual?" she asked.

"A manual. A manual car. A car with a stick shift."

"A stick shift? No, I…"

"Never mind," Parrish said. "And you two, clean this mess up."

"Take one shot first," Mason said, scooping up the steaming pitcher and jumping to put it back on the high shelf. "Dunc, throw Parrish a tape ball."

"Heads up!"

Parrish turned to tell him not to throw, but Duncan was far too excited and, this time, more accurate. Parrish stood still as the tape ball bounced off his cheek, then rolled under the pastry case.

"Hey, Mason?" Duncan blinked when he saw the numb stare on Parrish's face. "Parrish doesn't want the tape ball."

"I think you're right, Dunc."

Parrish hopped once to grab the steaming pitcher off the shelf, then handed it to Mason. "Have you clocked out yet?"

"On my way."

"Clock out, then put that display back. And put it back right."

"I'm just going to clock out," said Mason, "then I've got to get on that display."

"Sounds great. Hey, Susan?"

"Yes, Mr. Parrish?"

"Would you make sure he does it right, please? And you can call me John or Parrish, if you want."

"Yes, Mr. Parrish."

In the back room, Parrish threw his coat and scarf on the back of his chair, then sat at the computer for the rest of the evening, typing in his shipment orders for the week. After a while, Susan brought him a latte—a fine one, very foamy and in a porcelain cup, three shots of espresso poured through so the foam was marked with the tasty brown crema of the shots. She delivered his drink to him at the back desk, the cup on its proper saucer, a tiny round cookie on the saucer's edge.

Parrish leaned back in his rolling chair and rubbed his neck. "Thank you, Susan."

"Oh, you're welcome." She picked his scarf up off the floor where it had fallen and hung it over his coat.

"Hey, Susan, care if I ask you a series of crazy questions?"

She put her hands in her back pockets. "Okay."

"Why do you work so hard?"

Susan laughed. "I don't. Not really."

"Yeah, you do. And not just comparatively. Why?"

"Thanks. Uh…the way I was raised, I guess." She leaned against the rack to think of a better answer, but couldn't. "Why do you ask?"

"Is Duncan working?"

She looked down at her arm and scratched it. "He's trying to…I think."

"Great," said Parrish. "Do you believe in God?"

"Me?" She blushed as if he were joking with her. But he waited quite seriously, so she answered. "Not much. Why do you ask?"

"If you don't believe in God, would it be silly to ask if you believed God still did things?"

"What things?"

"*Thing* things," he said. "Anything, something. Here and now things."

Susan considered her answer. "Well, if you do believe in a God, that sort of makes it more likely that you'd believe God might, right?"

Parrish shrugged, took a sip.

"Do you?" Susan asked.

"What?"

She narrowed her eyes. "Believe in God?"

Parrish returned his cup to its saucer. He stared into the computer screen. "Always have, yeah." His answer seemed to surprise him.

"I sometimes wonder," she added, "if believing changes anything."

"Good point," Parrish said, then wiped the foam from his lip with his sleeve.

Susan bounced her knee, shifted her weight, then bit her lip. "I read the other day where they found coral-encrusted bones and chariot wheels at the bottom of the Red Sea."

"No way?"

"They did."

"That's crazy," said Parrish.

Susan hummed thoughtfully.

Parrish took another sip of his latte. "Thank you for this."

"Sure." Susan pushed her weight off the rack and went back to the front to help a customer.

The evening passed without further incident.

Parrish piddled around the back room well after closing time. Occasionally, Susan or Duncan came through the back, looking for the broom, bringing dirty cups and dishes to wash in the sink. He could hear Mason's voice echoing from the front, reading the interesting bits of the newspaper out loud to anyone who would listen. Though off the clock, Mason hung around. This was not unusual, not for any of the boys. Whether on the clock or not, all three could usually be found in the coffee shop or thereabouts. They had long since realized that's why they worked in a coffee shop—they would go to one regardless, so it was better to get paid for it.

Parrish sat down to his computer again to finish typing his cof-

fee order. He heard Susan say good night to the boys, then call out
to him.

"Good night, Sue!" he called back.

Then Mason and Duncan traipsed into the back room, dropping a few last plates loudly into the deep metal sinks, then propping
themselves comfortably about—Mason on a huge burlap bag of
beans and Duncan on the desk where Parrish worked.

"Where'd you go when you left Wu's?" Duncan asked.

"Had an errand."

"What errand?"

"Have you clocked out?"

"Oh yeah, I meant to tell you." With great concentration, Duncan bit at a hangnail on his thumb. "I forgot to clock in."

"That'll save me a bundle, thanks."

The three sat in silence while Parrish typed. Mason perused the
sports page, and Duncan, his eyes somewhat crossed, finally snipped
the troublesome nail with his front teeth, then shook his thumb, surprised by his own self-inflicted pain.

"You know, Parrish," Mason said, attempting an apology, "if
you'd been here, we never would have started the tape-ball game."

"Yes, you would've."

"No," he argued, "you would've started mumbling and hidden
the duct tape."

"And why, do you think, I would do that?"

Mason shrugged. "You've always been a mumbler."

Parrish stopped typing, shoved Duncan's foot off the seat of
his chair, then turned to Mason. "Did you know that the cost for

one person to eat the buffet at Wu's is cheaper than a roll of duct tape?"

"I did not know that," Mason answered with mawkish wonder, tired of Parrish's mood. "Hey, Duncan, don't eat the duct tape. Mr. Wu's is cheaper."

Hearing his name, Duncan looked up from his fingernails. "Oh yeah, where'd you go after you left Wu's?"

Mason stood and swatted Duncan's shoulder with the newspaper.

"What?" Duncan protested angrily.

"Let's go. Leave him to his duct tape."

"We're out of duct tape," said Duncan.

"He knows."

Parrish sighed. "I went and hung out at the bus stop for a while."

"Why?" asked Duncan.

"Just did."

Mason gave Parrish an odd stare. "The bus stop…at the corner?"

"That's the one."

"Why?" Duncan repeated this rapid-fire like a toddler, which earned him a second swat from Mason. "Why do you keep hitting me? I don't get it. Why'd he hang out at the bus stop?"

"Let's go, Dunc. I'll explain it in the car." Mason picked him up off the desk and pushed him through the doorway.

"Is this a trick?" Duncan said from the hallway. "What's in your car?"

"Get your coat. Let's go."

There were the sounds of a slight skirmish in the hallway, then a flutter of whispers. Parrish heard Duncan's boots as they tromped out through the darkened coffee shop. After a moment or two, Mason stuck his head into the back room and slapped a hand over the light switch, flipping it on and off several times until his friend looked his way.

"You okay, Parrish?" Mason asked.

"See you tomorrow."

"Have it your way," Mason said, then disappeared.

Parrish stopped typing, listened as Mason joined Duncan at the front door, heard his keys, the bells jangle as the door opened and closed, then the click of the bolt as they locked Parrish alone in the shop. He waited. Sometimes they did that only to creep back to the office and scare the daylights out of him. Sometimes they hid behind the counter in the dark and jumped him. Parrish continued to listen but heard nothing except the hum of the heater and the fall of new ice in the ice machine. He walked to the front, peeked out the glass door until he saw both their cars' headlights illuminate, then drive away.

He found the pot of coffee they'd left for him on the burner, so he poured a cup on top of the remnants of his latte, then walked back to his desk. Setting the cup down, he leaned far back in his chair, put his hands behind his head and his feet up. He sat that way for a while, then swiveled his body, reaching his hand into the pocket of the coat he'd hung on the back of the chair. He took out the letter and unfolded it. His eyes skimmed to the final sentence:

Who will love you when I'm gone?

Tuesday

The next day was warmer, sunnier, and the wind softened to a less than frigid breeze. Not that a February day in the city ever completely lost its wintry demeanor—the trees still stood bare and thin, the concrete walks still gray and drab and dry. Fronts had been threatening snow for days. For a week the sky had been nothing but a puffy, seamless sheet of white, and this Tuesday had begun the same. But as the day progressed, the grayness receded like a mist, the sky's white became more illumined from behind, then occasionally a patch of blue would open. Then another here and there, until blue touched blue and they became background for streaks and wisps of cloud. Sunlight, rays of it, gave a brightness like spring, a direct and golden-yellow brightness unlike the trapped, refracted glow of a winter's day, and to that homogeneous cityscape that lay so inert and wide and flat, just a few spring rays of sunshine gave a sudden depth and dimension to everything. Individual things came alive, as if each stood brightly before you, each with its own story.

Parrish shared the day's disposition. A short but good night's sleep restored him with a fresh supply of morning optimism and the stormy proceedings of the previous afternoon receded so far that he could not even recall yesterday's mishaps enough to take serious notice of them. It had been a Monday, after all. He chalked all wrong up to that fault, cheered himself with the thought that Monday was over for the week.

This morning, he'd arrived at the shop at five in order to open at six. He set up the coffee machines, made his to-do lists, untied the stacks of newspapers, and flipped the sign to Open. Only a few customers graced him with their presence that early, and their needs met, he'd had his four shots of espresso, a blueberry fritter, and all seemed buoyantly right with his world.

He preferred opening alone on slow mornings. He could blare the music loudly, his favorites, with no squabbling as to what to play. He could set up everything the way he liked it done. Long ago, he'd realized how much more he got done alone in those two hours when he let Duncan sleep in until seven, and a bustling, productive start always made the whole day run more smoothly.

He had espresso waiting for his friend when he came dragging in, eyes half-closed and foggier than usual, even for Duncan. They ran the commuter rush speedily and efficiently. As the rush settled down, he consulted his lists and attacked his tasks with a caffeinated vigor. He ordered in stromboli from Tony's for lunch and sprang for the tab without a word of complaint when Duncan couldn't find his wallet.

He worked the rest of his shift, then well beyond it, well into the afternoon until Susan joined them. He was a manager, after all. His shift ended when all that needed doing was done, and that never happened. But he enjoyed the day, especially savoring the sense of accomplishment when he looked at his long, mundane to-do list with lines drawn through nearly every task. The only item left at the bottom of the pad: Bus stop.

Slightly past five that afternoon, he grabbed his corduroy coat off his chair in the back room, tore the list off the pad, and crumpled it, dropping it in the wastebasket under his desk. He leaned over the mouse pad and logged out of the computer screen, then walked to the front and headed out for his last to-do, his God one.

"You gone?" Duncan asked, leaning sadly against the espresso machine.

"Got an errand." Parrish kept walking so Duncan wouldn't trap him in a conversation.

"You coming back?"

"Chances are high, yes." Parrish pushed his arms into his coat and pulled his scarf out of his pocket, but when he opened the front door and felt the temperature, he shoved the scarf away again.

"Need a coffee before you go?" Duncan called out.

"Mason'll be here soon, Dunc. You'll make it." He waved through the glass as the door shut.

Approaching the bus stop, Parrish saw Mrs. Miranda and Audra seated exactly as they had been the day before, one knitting, one reading. The bus had just come and gone—he could still smell the diesel fumes—and so had the passengers who'd exited the bus. All that remained were the two ladies on their benches. He took a casual lean against the route sign.

"Afternoon, Rose."

"Good afternoon, John," she replied. She pulled her plastic bags of yarn closer, clearing a place, welcoming him to sit.

Parrish put up a hand to politely refuse.

Audra looked up from her book. She blinked at him behind her glasses, tried to smile, which didn't work, so then she tried not to show that she'd tried. Parrish gave her a friendly wave. Her eyes returned to her book.

Parrish looked at her as she read. She wore her same wool coat, a long gray Burberry with a thick belt and six oversized buttons in two parallel rows on the front, wide, high lapels, and a collar with another large button so it could be popped up and buttoned all the way up to the chin. It was a good city coat, though it didn't look new. The fashion and cut of it seemed hand-me-down, maybe once expensive but now worn and comfortable like an old favorite. Though it was sunny, she wore all but the collar buttoned, and Parrish could see her slim, bare neck. Her gloves and scarf lay in a heap on the bench between her backpack and the armrest nearest her, leaving the rest of the bench free, open. Her gray knit toboggan lay beside her gloves, so Parrish got the full effect of her hair—lots of hair, long and curly and brown, very frizzy but in the good way, occupying a style somewhere between permed and unattended. He wondered how all her hair fit up in that hat. Again, he noticed her scrubs, hanging loose and baggy from below her knees, where the Burberry stopped, down to her running shoes. This time the scrubs were powder blue, the only thing she wore that wasn't gray.

"Doctor?" Parrish asked.

Rose glanced at Parrish then over to Audra, who finally looked at her, then up at Parrish.

"Scrubs." Parrish pointed.

"Oh!" Audra gave her own clothes the glance of someone who dresses functionally, who rarely took inventory of how she looked. "Nursing student," she answered factually.

"First year?"

"Fourth."

"Ah." Parrish looked down at his boots, pointed the toes together. Whatever compliment he might have paid her, he'd just erased. So he said, "The fourth year's a very good number."

Audra scratched her cheek and stared at him blankly, then dismissed his strange comment. She flipped a new page, stretched out her legs and crossed them at the ankles, slouching back into the bench.

Rose glanced at the two, then resumed her knitting with a sly smile.

Parrish gave up on conversation, went to work. He scanned both directions down the sidewalk and glanced across the parking lot, but no one came. He saw a couple of people at a distance—a homeless guy, that tall man in the nice suit who ordered lattes, a lady with two young children—but none of them came near his corner. So he watched and waited.

Half an hour passed. No one came. Parrish adjusted his stance and bent his knees, the route sign on his back becoming less and less comfortable.

Rose's fingers knitted with only minimal assistance from her eyes. She noticed him fidget. "Does your shop serve breakfast?"

"Fritters."

Audra shot her eyes at him over the rim of both book and glasses.

"Rectangular doughnuts without the holes," he explained. No one here needed to be told what a fritter was, but it was an odd word said all by itself like that, and Parrish was in the habit of immediately explaining to customers with an economy of words.

Audra said nothing.

"Either of you want anything?" he asked. "Coffee?"

Audra looked to see if Rose might accept, but Rose declined, so Audra shook her head too. Parrish smiled at the way her voluminous hair continued shaking "no" for a moment longer than the rest of her.

The elderly gentleman with the cane hesitated at the opposite curb, watching traffic. A younger person would have bolted, would have already seen three chances to do so, but at his age he waited until absolutely no car threatened. None turning at the intersection or pulling out from the parking lot. This took time. Finally, the street completely deserted, he began to cross the road slowly, his stoppered cane placed securely down, then each foot catching up with it. Once in the street he began to hurry, which meant he no longer looked up. Head down and eyes focused solely on the shuffle of cane and feet, he blindly trusted that no car would turn and suddenly strike him. When he reached the opposite curb, he stretched out a hand, wrinkled and spotted with age, and grabbed the bus route sign to help his step up.

Parrish hadn't seen him, leaning as he was with his back on the sign. He felt him first, the man's hand grabbing at the signpost then clasping Parrish's shoulder as he brought both feet up to curb level. Parrish turned, instinctively grabbing the man's elbow and supporting it. Once the old man had firmly found the sidewalk, he patted Parrish's arm.

"Thank you, young man."

He wore black suit pants and a black vest, both unpressed, and his once-white dress shirt had yellowed, especially at the collar. His collar had no buttons, only holes for a tie clip, an accessory given up with the advance of trembling in his hands, and lay open to the chill. He wore a black trench coat, very wrinkled and missing a button near the middle, a stitch marking the empty place like a winked eye. His hair, what little there was of it, wafted thinly and stuck upward from the breeze.

The old man stopped in the middle of the threesome, breathing fast and shallowly, and with a shaking hand he pressed his hair flat, or so he thought. Then he rummaged in his coat pockets, both inside and out, withdrew a white handkerchief, silk and expensive, though it too had seen better days, and dabbed his lip while he looked at the sign, the benches, the strip mall nearby, all in an effort to place his location. His eyes were not dim with age. He saw this corner clearly but in years long gone, so that what he did see bewildered. He remembered several other versions of this corner he had seen come and go, so getting home required travel both through space and time.

He raised a wavering finger and pointed in the direction of the houses and apartment buildings. "That is Hawthorne, isn't it?"

"No sir," Parrish said. "This is Belvedeere. Hawthorne runs the other way, right over there, see?"

"Of course!" The elderly man shook his head, dismissing the confusion, the mirage. He patted Parrish's arm again, then pointed his finger back and forth. "I've walked down this street a thousand times, young man, would you believe that? For the past fifty years. Hah! Fifty years and that..." He pointed his cane, raised it as high as his arm could lift it, then fixed his eyes as if he were aiming a rifle. "That is still Hawthorne."

He rummaged his coat pockets just as thoroughly to put his handkerchief away. Then he began to walk slowly toward the street Parrish had pointed out to him. Audra pulled her legs beneath the bench so they wouldn't be an impediment to his path.

"You going to make it, or can I help you home?" Parrish offered.

The elderly man had to stop completely and turn to see Parrish. He shook his head. "No, thank you. It's not far now. Hawthorne's the place, but I thank you for speaking."

Then the man just stood. He said nothing, his face tilted slightly downward, but they could see his quick, shallow breaths.

"Excuse me," said Parrish.

The man raised his face. "Yes?"

"If you passed by here yesterday, did you by any chance drop this?" Parrish took the folded letter out of his pocket and held it up.

It took several seconds for the recognition—what had been said, whether he had walked here yesterday or not, and dropped what, what Parish held in his hand, a folded letter—but when the recognition came, the elderly man began trembling. He rummaged his coat again, dug at his pockets and pulled them inside out. His eyes glanced up at Parrish desperately, then down at his hands, his mouth open but speechless except for a few panicked sounds.

"My letter!" he said with a gasp.

Audra straightened and put her book on the bench. Parrish took a step forward and put out a steadying hand, so agitated was the old man's response. Rose set her knitting aside.

Once certain that he'd checked every pocket of his frumpled coat, the man finally reached out, his fingers gently gesturing for the letter to be put in his hands. When Parrish did, the elderly man clutched it against the buttons of his vest, slowed his breathing, and closed his eyes. When he opened them again, they were damp.

"Oh, thank you." He reached a trembling hand toward Parrish, to take and hold his. "Thank you, young man. You have no idea what it would mean to lose this." He put the letter safely in his coat pocket so his other hand was now free to take Parrish's shoulder. "Thank you."

Audra gave Rose a shocked glance. Rose clapped her hands together in surprise.

"Glad we found you," Parrish said. "We found the letter yesterday."

"Yesterday's letter?" The elderly man asked as if to verify. "Oh, my, yes. Thank you all."

"We were trying to figure out whose it was," Parrish confessed. "I hope you don't mind, but we read it."

Audra cleared her throat.

Parrish corrected. "I read it, and we…" Parrish looked to the ladies for help. Rose picked up a knitting needle and poked it in the air as if prodding Parrish onward. "Are you…okay?" Parrish asked awkwardly. "Do you want to talk?"

The man's face beamed. Again, his eyes glistened damply. He took out his handkerchief and wiped them before he answered. "Yes, that would be…yes." He looked at Parrish's face as if he'd just recognized an old friend that he'd long since assumed, like the neighborhood around him, had faded and gone. "I could make us a spot of coffee? I live on Hawthorne. We could talk."

Parrish looked triumphantly at Audra who, at first, could only manage the most stunned of looks. Then hurriedly, she shoved her hat and gloves and book in her bag, zipped it and slung it over her shoulder, then jumped up and came to Parrish's side.

"What?" she asked innocently.

The elderly man took her hand too, patting it as happily and easily. "This way," he said, then slipped the cane off his wrist and turned to lead their way.

Audra began to follow, but Parrish gave her bag a slight tug.

With a flourish of her frizzy hair, she turned. "Oh, I'm going with you."

It was cold in Mr. Crawford's house, somehow colder than it was outside. When he offered to take Parrish and Audra's topcoats, the two politely refused and kept them. Taking off his own coat and hanging it on the rack, Mr. Crawford escorted his guests into a parlor of sorts, made his way to two lamps, and turned them both brightly on.

"I'll fix us some coffee," he announced with hostly pleasure, then shuffled off to the kitchen.

It was a large house, and the parlor appeared unused. Stacks of boxes were piled neatly in one corner, along with a few bound stacks of old newspapers. The thick drapes were drawn closed, and from the dust that flew when Parrish shook one, they had been drawn for some time. Audra paced around the room, looking at all the photos and paintings—on the end tables, the walls, the mantel above the fireplace.

Parrish walked over to the fireplace. "Think it works?"

"I'm sure it isn't gas, if that's what you mean," she said.

"No, I'm wondering if I put wood in this and burned it if the whole house would catch fire." He knelt down and looked up the chimney, then yanked at the flue, which moved neither in nor out.

Audra watched with fascination. "What are you doing?"

"I don't think this has been opened in forever."

"He can't haul logs at his age," she whispered. "Are you going to build him a fire?"

"I might build me a fire," said Parrish, examining the tongs and the shovel that leaned in a brass stand beside the fireplace.

"What were you going to use for wood?"

"I thought I'd break the furniture into pieces."

Mr. Crawford returned with a plate of cookies. "I wouldn't trust that chimney, young man."

Parrish stood, dusting off his hands. "If you get that cleaned out, I bet you could have a nice roaring fire in here. Audra volunteered to go get us wood."

"Thank you, dear," Mr. Crawford said to her, taking Parrish seriously. "I don't believe I've used that fireplace since my Cecelia passed."

"Is this her?" Audra asked, picking up a framed photograph.

Mr. Crawford blinked, trying to see which picture she held. Audra brought it to him, holding it out in front of her. He recognized it on her way and began to smile before it ever reached him. He tilted the frame gently in her hand so they could both look at it at once.

"Yes." He smiled warmly, a smile that settled deeply through him, and for a moment he seemed to forget his guests and the letter and the pot of coffee, even the plate of cookies in his own hand, and simply stood, touching his fingers to the figure in the photo.

Audra held the picture, but she watched his face. "She has cheerful eyes."

"Yes, she did," the man agreed, smiling at Audra gratefully. His hand released the frame to her, and she walked it over to Parrish.

"That was our fifteenth anniversary," said Mr. Crawford, wagging a declarative finger in the air. "We flew to Cape Cod for a long weekend. Or was that our sixteenth?"

Neither Parrish nor Audra spoke; they simply waited politely for more.

"We were married forty-eight years," said Mr. Crawford. "Cecelia passed away seven years ago come this May." He spoke to no one in particular, offering this information to the parlor in general, as if speaking aloud helped him sort the times and dates. Finally his eyes returned from where they'd gone. "Do either of you take cream?" Slowly, he set the plate of cookies on the glass coffee table in front of the sofa.

"No, thank you," said Audra. She returned the frame to its place.

"Young man?"

"No cream for me."

"Do you care if I peek at the rooms?" Audra asked, selecting a cookie.

"Please, make yourselves at home."

When Mr. Crawford shuffled away again to the kitchen, Parrish grabbed the elbow of Audra's coat. "How do I bring up what the letter said?"

Nibbling a cookie, she shrugged. "That's your problem. I told you not to read it."

"You wanted to come along. Now help me."

"I came to observe. I have no idea how you'll do that." She pulled her sleeve free and walked down the hall.

"Where are you going?" Parrish whispered.

"Snooping."

Parrish watched her leave the room, heard her footsteps on the wood floor down the hall. He stood in the cold parlor alone for only a moment before he followed.

She'd announced that she'd be snooping and that's precisely what she did. Parrish trailed behind, snooping on her snooping, watching her open doors, step into each room and wander through curiously—

the sewing room, a dusty book-lined study, two guest bedrooms. In what must have been Mr. Crawford's bedroom, there were a few signs of life—a comb and some mail on the dresser, the bathroom light left on, probably forgotten, and the sheets and bedspread on the bed, though not properly made up, had been pulled up to the headboard in a casual effort. Parrish watched as she tucked in the bottom corners and smoothed the bedspread flat. She smiled at Parrish as she squeezed past him in the hall and went to the bottom of a large staircase. Though it was inviting, she didn't venture upstairs, but only took a moment to run her fingers along the smooth banister. The hall behind the stairs revealed another door to the kitchen, which she gently opened. She peeked in. Parrish caught only a glimpse of Mr. Crawford's back before Audra put a finger to her lips, and quietly shut the door.

"Satisfied?" Parrish asked as they returned to the parlor.

"Almost," she said, then began to investigate the embroidery on the sofa cushions, gently tracing the threads with a finger. Parrish laughed at how closely she brought her face to them.

"One day," he said, "you'll need to get over this shy problem."

Without looking up, she frowned sarcastically. "Oh...," she said, then spun and straightened to face him, the soles of her sneakers squeaking on the hardwood. "Did you see the coffee maker in the kitchen?"

"No...," Parrish said hesitantly. "Why?"

Audra put her hands behind her back and swayed. "Well, he's using coffee out of a can that looks roughly pre–World War I and dumping it in a rusty percolator."

Parrish paled and collapsed in a large armchair.

Audra leaned or knelt at every photo, straightened a doily or two, and ran her finger once across the dusty mantel. "Doesn't this make you sad?"

"It's dusty," Parrish said. "Cut the guy a break."

But Audra shook her head as if he hadn't understood her meaning. "No, look around. The sofa pillows need fluffing, the lampshades aren't straight, the whole house wants a broom and a mop. The curtains need to be taken outside and shaken out, then aired on a line. Clearly, nobody's cleaned properly in a very long time, but everything is so arranged and placed. Just so. A woman's eye." Audra sighed.

"And this is sad?" Parrish asked.

Audra put a hand on her hip and shook her hair at him. "It's sweet and sad, yes. He's lived here for nearly seven years without changing the way his wife arranged things. He lives like a caretaker, a curator of her house, more than the owner. Keeps his own things to a minimum—the coatrack or that strangely shaped ashtray on the hall table for his keys and pocket change. And the dish rack beside the kitchen sink held only one cup, only one plate to dry. That's adorably sad."

When she turned again to see his response, Parrish said, "Sure, okay."

Mr. Crawford reappeared. This time he held a large silver tray with a matching silver dish heaped with sugar cubes who knew how old. He set this beside the plate of cookies.

"May I help pour?" Audra asked.

"No, my dear, I can still manage. Now where are those good cups?" He turned to a large china cabinet, opened it, and began touching the cups and saucers stacked inside. He found the ones he wanted—white porcelain with a dark burgundy leaf design—and took out three sets slowly, piece by piece. These he brought and set on the silver tray on the coffee table.

As he did, they heard the oven timer beep.

"Coffee's ready," the old man announced.

The timer beeped loudly and continuously for the time it took him to find his way back to turn it off. They heard various clanks and the tap turned on then off. Finally, Mr. Crawford returned, set the coffee carafe in the middle of all, then slowly slid an armchair closer, gesturing for them to take the sofa.

Everyone took a seat.

Both Audra and Parrish sat stiffly, nervously on the edge of the sofa as Mr. Crawford served them. The carafe he'd transferred the coffee into looked heavy and worrisome, not to mention full of scalding coffee. The old man's arms shook slightly as he tipped the spout over their cups, pressing one finger on the ill-fitting lid to keep it from falling off. They breathed more easily once he'd set the carafe firmly back on the tray.

"Are you two happy in those coats?" Mr. Crawford asked.

"We're fine," Parrish answered.

Audra, apparently not the kind of girl who liked being answered for, reached over and gave the side of Parrish's leg a terrific pinch.

Parrish winced, he squirmed, he wriggled dangerously, but managed not to cry out. He glared at her.

"I guess it is cold in here, isn't it?" Mr. Crawford said, then looked around the room as if he were seeing it for the first time in a very long while. "Gloomy?"

"The coffee will warm us up," Audra suggested brightly. She picked up a cup and saucer, handed it to Mr. Crawford, then did the same for Parrish, smiling as if no pinching had occurred.

Still jumpy from the pinch, Parrish took the cup and saucer. The coffee table stood just far enough away to make it a shaky stretch to pick up his cup and put it back every time he wanted a sip, so he balanced the cup and saucer awkwardly on his knee. When he did so, he realized his knees were bouncing. (He did not want to ask this man about his sad letter.) He could not stop his knee from bouncing, let alone balance breakable things on a bouncing knee, so he cheated—he looked to see how Audra solved the problem. She balanced her cup and saucer daintily on her knee, but she never took a sip. She was also cheating. Not once did she raise the cup to her lips. Then he remembered what she'd told him about the percolator and the old can. He lifted the cup to his nose, took a whiff of the sour brew, then quickly deposited cup and saucer back on the table.

"How is it?" Mr. Crawford asked.

"Great!" They looked at each other, both saying the same thing at once.

"I'm glad," Mr. Crawford said, enjoying another sip.

Parrish cleared his throat so loudly that Audra blinked protectively and shielded her cup. Parrish leaned forward, laced his fingers seriously. "Mr. Crawford, may we ask you about the letter we found?"

Audra reached to pinch him again, but he caught her hand this time and pressed it into the sofa.

"Oh my, yes, I wanted to tell you about that!" Mr. Crawford put down his cup, laid his napkin on the arm of the chair, then slowly stood again, as if he were going somewhere. "It must be yesterday's or the day before. Excuse me a moment."

Mr. Crawford left the parlor.

Parrish turned to Audra with a sharp look. "So why are we pinching people?"

"Yes," she said. "Why are *we*?"

Both stared silently at the other.

Slowly, Mr. Crawford returned. From his bedroom, he'd fetched a framed letter and brought it to them. "My Cecelia was a bit of a poet," he said. He handed the framed letter to Parrish. As he looked at it, Audra peered over his shoulder until he passed it to her.

It began with "My dearest." It was written in a woman's hand, though the cursive was shaky and words jumped the lines now and again. An old hand. It was dated May 9 seven years earlier.

Mr. Crawford sat in his armchair. "When Cecelia became ill— she developed cancer and was in and out of hospitals and treatment centers—but toward the end, she had to stay in the hospital. That's when she wrote this."

"She wrote to you?" Audra asked, voice melting with compassion. "Were you called away?"

"No, no." Mr. Crawford laughed lightly, as if it were absurd to think he would have left his wife's side. "Cecelia liked letters. Writing them, receiving them. In the hospital she wrote as long as her strength would allow—letters to family and friends. I offered to write for her, to have her dictate, but she said that wouldn't be the same. I remember she asked me, 'Would it be the same for you if it weren't written in my hand?'"

Mr. Crawford shook his head tenderly as if he were answering his wife once again.

"I spent every day with her, every night on the little couch-bed they provided. She lingered on, suffering terribly for weeks toward the very end. With the breathing tubes, she could no longer speak, not with any ease. But she wrote, always wrote, always asked for more paper, more envelopes. So I'd fetch her more."

Mr. Crawford stopped, sipped at his cup of coffee, squinched his face as if he'd forgotten how hot it was, then continued his story.

"And one day, she finished a letter and sealed it in an envelope. She set it on the food tray beside her bed. I remember I'd put on my gray scarf and that very coat." He pointed to the hall where his coat hung. "I asked how she was. She nodded. Fine. I told her I was going down to the newsstand for a paper, did she want a magazine? She shook her head no. Would she be all right while I stepped away? Her hands trembled."

Mr. Crawford looked down at his own.

"She pulled her hand from beneath the sheet and placed it on the envelope. 'Do you want me to mail that?' I asked. See, I didn't know. And she smiled at me. Then very clearly, as she'd done a thousand times before, she shooed me with her hand and sent me away."

With the tongs, Mr. Crawford plopped another sugar cube into his steaming cup.

"I was gone so few minutes. I know she meant it to happen the way it did, because it was such a short time. I only rode the elevators to the lobby, bought a *Wall Street Journal* and a cup of coffee, stood for a moment to sip it, then went back. When the elevators opened on her floor, I saw the crowd of nurses at the door to her room. I dropped my coffee. I remember worrying someone might slip and fall, but I left the puddle, hurried toward that crowd, and looked inside her room. A nurse was checking her pulse, but the machines told us what we all already knew. And her hand was on this, still lay on this letter."

Mr. Crawford took the framed letter back from Audra and set it gently in his lap.

"That last letter was to me. I didn't understand until I saw the envelope had my name on it. I couldn't understand at first why she would send me away. Oh, we'd long since said all we needed, settled up with the fact that she was indeed dying, and dying first. That's how she wanted to go—to write what she most wished to say, then slip away. I had it framed."

Parrish and Audra sat in silence.

Mr. Crawford's eyes trailed down to his cup and saucer, shaking slightly in his hand above his lap. The tiny sound of porcelain rattle was the only noise in the room besides the hum and click of the waning light bulb beneath the lampshade.

He sipped again, then replaced cup to saucer, saucer to table. "You two make a handsome couple."

Audra's knee jumped, spilling a little coffee into her saucer. Parrish cracked every knuckle on both hands.

Mr. Crawford struggled out of his chair again before either of them could correct his mistake. For an awkward moment, he stood deciding how best to do something, then shuffled into the hall, where he opened a closet. He cracked the door just wide enough to slip his thin frame into the closet, bend down, and retrieve something. Returning to his chair, he brought back a shoe box, which he set on the table next to the tray. On the box's side, in black marker, was written: January–February–March 2009. Mr. Crawford lifted away the lid, put it underneath, and fitted the box into it. Inside were stacks of envelopes bound in rubber bands and a few envelopes that were loose, leaning next to the bundle.

"I've kept up the correspondence, so to speak." He took out a few of the envelopes and handed them over. "These are from February."

Audra took one, as did Parrish. The writing on the front was in a shaky hand, a recent date sat in the top right corner of the envelope, and both were addressed the same—To My Beloved. Neither Parrish nor Audra knew what to say. Audra ran her fingers along the edge of the envelope she held, as if to verify its existence. Parrish leaned his neatly back into the box with the others from the month.

Mr. Crawford reached a slow hand to the sugar tongs, daintily picked up a cube by its edges, and dropped it in his cup. "It used to have a real bench…"

Parrish looked up at him. "Sorry?"

"A real bench. Not that concrete jutting up. At that corner, a real bench with legs and a back, smooth wood and curling wrought iron, like in a park. Or the kind they used to have in parks, I should say.

There was a birdbath too. No, it was a sundial! Yes, they kept geraniums or some such planted around it. Used to be a nice corner before they widened and paved that road, began the buses up and down. And that lot across from the bus stop, that wasn't there at all. It used to be one large field. The old fellow who owned that, he was mean and wouldn't sell an inch of it even when the city offered him outrageous money. He had to die before they could get a hold of that. His son sold it. At least, I believe it was his son."

Parrish glanced at Audra. She listened to Mr. Crawford, her face enraptured.

"So you've lived here all that time?" she asked, reaching eagerly for another cookie and placing it on her napkin.

"Yes, we did." Mr. Crawford surveyed the parlor with a contented gaze. "We bought it outright and never thought of moving, even when the neighborhood began to change." He positioned his cup and saucer a tad more squarely on the table.

Audra's attention drifted back to the shoe box. She placed her cup and saucer on the table, then slowly picked up the stack of envelopes bound with a thick rubber band.

"May I?" she asked her host.

"Certainly."

She fingered through the stack, tilting her head to admire the dates on the envelopes, which were in order by month and day, going all the way back to New Year's Day of that year. She thumbed the edges of the envelopes, flipping through them quickly so that the words *To My Beloved* wiggled and moved as if they were being magically rewritten. She shook her head with disbelief and gave Mr.

Crawford an unreserved look of appreciation. "I could be wrong, but I think you are amazing, sir."

"Daniel," he said.

"Daniel it is," she said, gazing at him, her smile widening in a warm and steady progression across the features of her face until her shoulders relaxed completely and she sat beaming at him.

Parrish pointed. "So this is only one box of…"

Mr. Crawford rose to his feet without hearing the end of the question. He gestured for them to follow, then led them to the closet in the hall. This time, with a flourish, he pulled the knob with both hands while backing away so that the closet was fully revealed to them. There were no coats, no clothes hanging on the one rod below the hat shelf. Only shoe boxes, dozens of them, from the hat shelf high to the closet's ceiling, stacked on the floor all the way up to the rod, and above and around and behind it. The closet was crammed nearly to capacity with shoe boxes, each marked with heavy black marker. In the shortest stack near the front of the closet, where Mr. Crawford must have bent and taken away the box he'd brought them, the next box was marked: October–November–December 2008.

Again, Audra reached out to verify with both hands, like a child in a toy store. She dusted the dates on the sides of the boxes, cracking a lid here and there barely to peek inside, careful not to disturb the overall order. She ran her hand along the wall of shoe boxes, her fingers thumping down a long row of them.

"I write to her every day." Mr. Crawford held the door for them proudly, pleased to have someone see his work. "Seven years come this May."

He watched proudly as Audra finished her investigation, allowing her to linger. When Audra finally realized the two men stood watching her, she blushed and stepped shyly back, and he shut the door.

They returned to the parlor.

"So that is why, young man, I am very grateful to you. If I had lost even one letter, after so many... Well, it would be a loss to me." Mr. Crawford rested his palm on the side of the carafe to see if it was still hot. "More coffee?"

Both refused politely.

Parrish glanced at their cups. Neither of them had drunk what they already had. He watched Audra nibble a cookie, sitting perfectly content on the sofa beside him. Maybe she hadn't put the pieces together, but the letter he'd read yesterday was far from a love letter. The sadness of that letter was, if anything, a cry for help, and he didn't know how to help, especially when Mr. Crawford served coffee and cookies and showed off the boxes as if they were an achievement. Certainly, he was lonely here in this big house, his lifetime companion gone, but Parrish didn't want to bring it up. Then again, why else was he there?

Parrish leaned forward, put his elbows on his knees. "Mr. Crawford, the letter I returned to you, may I see it again?"

"Certainly." Mr. Crawford reached into the pocket of his suit vest and withdrew the letter, then handed it to Parrish.

"What I wanted to ask you—"

As Parrish spoke, Audra slipped her hand into the crook of his arm. It looked affectionate, as if they were the couple Mr. Crawford had taken them to be, after all. But then she gave Parrish's arm a subtle but startling tug before he could unfold the letter. He turned to her, annoyed, but she tugged again, pulling him slightly toward her. She whispered in his ear, then released his arm and looked to see if he'd understood.

"Oh." Parrish looked again at Mr. Crawford. "You took that out of your vest, didn't you?"

Mr. Crawford hooked a finger in his vest pocket, then nodded. "Yes."

"The letter I found," asked Parrish, "the one I gave you…didn't you put that in your overcoat?"

"Front left pocket," Audra added.

Mr. Crawford blinked, and his head wavered, confused. He extended his hand and took back the letter he'd just given away. He unfolded it, his eyes scanning up and down the page—he recognized it as his own. Then he stood slowly, walked to the hall, and fished through the pocket of his coat hanging on the coatrack. Finally, his hand deep in the pocket Audra had identified, his motion stopped. He slowly withdrew a second letter and stared down at the two in his hands.

"How did I…"

"Our mistake," Audra interrupted. "You were worried you'd dropped a letter to your wife, that's understandable. One of those is ours."

"Ours?" Parrish turned to her. Audra squeezed his knee, then patted it as if they'd been together for years.

"I'm very sorry." Mr. Crawford's wrinkled face blushed with embarrassment. "I dragged you here and talked your ears off—"

"No, it's fine," said Audra. She reached for the old man's hand until he stepped over, took hers, and she sat him back down. "We've enjoyed talking with you."

"I wasn't who you were looking for," he said, then straightened the rumples from his vest by tugging hard on it. "I do apologize."

Audra kicked Parrish's foot.

"Right," he said. "Our mistake. My mistake. Don't worry about this letter." Parrish took it and put it quickly away in his coat. "Tell us more about what that corner used to look like."

They heard story after story.

In great detail Mr. Crawford explained the neighborhood and its various manifestations over the years, the transformations that turned the corner from a grassy spot with a sundial into a bus stop with a trash can, told the true and unimaginable explanations for why certain roads ran the way they now did, recalled some of the walks he and his wife had taken through the changing neighborhood, their favorite paths, step by step.

When the grandfather clock in the hall chimed eight o'clock, Parrish turned to Audra, who nodded in agreement. Simultaneously they stood, excused themselves, and wished Mr. Crawford a good night. They waited politely for him to pull himself once again out of his armchair. He showed his guests to the door, and standing beneath the porch light, Audra and Parrish gave Mr. Crawford their good-byes and thanked him for his hospitality.

"Anytime," Mr. Crawford repeated again and again. "You're welcome anytime."

The two walked down the path toward the sidewalk, then turned to wave. Only after they'd crossed the street did Mr. Crawford shut his front door and turn off the light.

It was dark by now. The sky had cleared earlier and was cloudless and speckled with stars. Parrish and Audra walked slowly, side by side, back the way they'd come. Neither spoke for some time, both needing the silence to process and shape the past two hours, and both willing to let the other do so. Their elderly host had assumed they were a couple, and strolling as they did now—on a brisk and starry night, both their heads drooped slightly, only occasionally glancing at the other—anyone peeking out a window might have assumed the same.

Parrish broke the silence. "Okay, that was unusual."

Audra stopped walking.

"What?" he said. "That was definitely non-usual, the whole event."

She raised her eyebrows and crossed her arms decidedly.

Parrish halted a few steps ahead to wait for her. "I like the guy, but come on. Didn't any of that strike you as bizarre?"

Audra stepped up to him and quickly pinched his arm through the folds of his coat.

"Stop!" Parrish winced. He thought he'd be ready for the next pinch, but she'd surprised him again. "Okay, we need to talk about that."

"That's the sweetest little man I've ever met," she argued. "Those letters! That was the sweetest thing."

"That's what I said." Parrish zipped his coat up to his chin. "Bizarre."

Audra huffed the exact huffing she huffed when they'd first met. "Do you think you'll ever be loved like that?"

Parrish blinked as he considered her question. "Haven't thought about it."

"Do men ever think about that?"

Parrish rubbed his arm where she'd pinched him. "If we do, I don't think we know we do."

Audra sighed.

The two stood on the sidewalk and stared at one another.

"Is it colder out here now," asked Parrish, huddling with a shiver, "or was it just freezing inside his house?"

"Both." Audra opened her backpack to find her scarf.

"I need a cup of coffee. A proper one," Parrish said. "You want coffee?"

Audra frowned, checked her watch as if she were needed elsewhere.

"If I say he was sweet, will you come?" he asked.

"He *was* sweet," Audra insisted with mock hurt.

Hunching himself down into his coat for warmth, Parrish grinned up at her ridiculously. "The most sweetest."

Audra tucked her scarf into the neck of her coat.

"Come on." Parrish laughed, then began walking. "I know this terrific little coffee shop."

Mason was concerned.

Earlier, he'd slipped into the coffee shop around fifteen to six.

Technically his shift had begun at five, so he had peered through the glass door, and not seeing Parrish, snuck in quietly. He'd quickly taken his coat and scarf off and thrown them in a cabinet, then grabbed an apron (which he never wore unless he was in trouble) and tied it on as he hurried behind the counter. Immediately, he pulled himself a shot of espresso in a tiny ceramic cup. If he didn't have a cup of coffee in his hand, it would be obvious that he hadn't been there long. With his espresso, he then took a leaning stance by the sink and tried to look nonchalant.

Duncan watched all this from where he was seated on the counter. After a few deep breaths, Mason looked at Duncan and jerked his head toward the back room.

"Parrish been back there awhile?"

"You're late."

"We know that. Has Parrish been looking for me?"

Duncan explained when Parrish had left, how he'd left, that he'd mumbled something about an errand, that he, Duncan, was very bored, and that Parrish would probably be back later.

Susan came out of the back with a rack of clean dishes and metal pitchers.

"Parrish not back there, Sue?"

"Nope." She wore her black hair pulled back, but the steam from the sanitizer had caused several strands to loosen and fall in her face. "I haven't seen him since he left, what, an hour ago?"

Hearing this, Mason pushed himself away from the sink, yanked off the stupid apron, downed his espresso, then ran over to the big glass windows at the front of the shop. He couldn't see well enough, so he borrowed a chair from a table where a customer sat alone, dragged it over to the windows, stood on it on his tiptoes, and looked out again. Not seeing Parrish at the bus stop, he climbed down.

"Where'd he say he was going?"

Duncan shrugged. "I don't think he said."

Wiping water off the plates, Susan said, "He told me earlier he was walking over to the bus stop."

"Again?" Mason stood back up on the chair and stared out the window.

Duncan played with the buttons on the register. "What are you doing?"

"His car's out there. His car's working, right?" Mason jumped down and stormed behind the counter.

"Why wouldn't his car be working?"

Mason walked over to Susan. "Did he say he was riding a bus somewhere or just going to the bus stop?"

Susan thought about it. "I didn't really pay that much attention." She handed Mason a small saucer, which he turned over in his hand, uncertain where those were kept. Susan grabbed it and put it beneath his cup.

Duncan yawned. "Why would he take the bus somewhere?"

"The question is, why would he hang out at the bus stop?"

Duncan thought about that hard. "Why is that the question instead of the one I came up with?"

Mason pulled himself a second espresso and returned to his original lean on the sink.

"You're acting strange," Duncan said. "Pull me one of those."

Mason didn't, instead throwing Duncan one of the ceramic cups. Duncan bobbled it twice before he caught it, while Susan winced, her shoulders up, waiting to hear ceramic shatter. Duncan jumped off the counter, then realized he'd jumped off on the wrong side, the customer side. Instead of walking around the counter, he sat on it again, then hoisted his feet high and pivoted. Trying to make his boots clear the register, he knocked a can of pencils, the tip jar, and a small basket of chocolates onto the floor. Duncan set his espresso cup on the counter and began picking up his mess. Susan helped him.

"Why are you worried about Parrish's car?" he asked.

Mason shook his head. "I'm not, Dunc. I'm concerned that he's gone to that corner two days in a row. I'm concerned that he's following directives from a fortune cookie, and I'm concerned that if he's committed for insanity, he'll lose this shop and we'll have to start paying for our coffee."

"Oh, right." Duncan looked around like a dog chasing its tail, finally locating his cup behind him on the counter. He hopped down and walked over to the espresso machine. "You really think he thinks the corner in the cookie is the corner at the corner?"

Mason said nothing, just brooded with the cup and saucer close to his lips and waited for Parrish's return.

Parrish held the door for Audra and showed her to a table. She swung her backpack off her arm and placed it on the floor, then took off her heavy wool coat and dropped it in a chair. Besides the loose blue scrubs that tied at her waist and the striped running shoes, she wore a bulky cotton sweatshirt, dark gray and cut wide at the neck. It drooped low off one smooth shoulder, exposing the white, ribbed tank top underneath. She took off her glasses, laid them gently on the table, then suddenly bent at the waist, tossing her considerable hair forward so that the curls dangled over and around her head. Using the hair band she wore on her wrist, she wrangled her hair, gathered and looped and cinched, so that when she stood upright again, it was pulled back. Not in what could properly be called a ponytail—it wouldn't do that, it couldn't—more just sending the wild dark brown hair in a backward direction as opposed to a hair free-for-all. She polished the lenses of her glasses, held them up to the light for inspection, then returned them to her blinking brown eyes.

"Parrish," yelled Mason. "Come here for a second."

"What's up?" Parrish asked as he walked over to where Mason and Duncan were standing behind the counter. Duncan looked normal, for Duncan, but Mason stared at Parrish, grinning like an addled cat.

"I get it now," said Mason, then he winked.

"Get what?" asked Parrish.

"Your sudden interest in bus stops," said Mason, pointing quickly over Parrish's shoulder. "Makes more sense once you see Ms. Bus Stop."

Duncan looked. "Hey, Ms. Bus Stop's pretty."

Mason winked again.

Parrish picked up a rag and swatted Mason across the chest, then gave the rag to Mason so he could swat Duncan.

But Parrish, too, had noticed. Previously, she'd been that mouthy girl with the backpack, slumped on a bus bench and swaddled beneath woolen layers of winter gear. Suddenly, here in his brightly lit shop stood a woman, and quite a nice-looking one at that. He threw his coat on the chair with hers.

"What do you want to drink?" Parrish asked Audra as he returned to their table.

Audra stretched her arms above her head and smiled. "Let's see what you got in this place."

Like customers, the pair walked over to the counter and stared up at the menu board.

Duncan and Mason both stood professionally at the register.

"Evening, Parrish," said Mason, looking only at Audra. "What can I get you two?"

"You want a scone, carrot cake?" Duncan asked her with even less subtlety. "There's fresher cake in the back."

The customer Susan had just served the fresh carrot cake, overhearing Duncan's remark about the cake, now poked doubtfully at his slice.

"Hey, Sue," said Parrish. He touched his index finger to his thumb then tilted that near his mouth—the international signal for "I need espresso."

Susan nodded.

"One espresso…on the house." Mason waved his hand benevolently at Parrish, then snapped his fingers at Susan.

Susan's eyes went dangerously wide.

"Duncan, make me an espresso," Parrish said quickly. "Susan, how about a break?"

"Thank you!" She pulled off her apron and stormed into the back.

"Don't snap your fingers at Susan," Parrish said to Mason. "She'll kill you."

Mason ignored him. "And what may I do for you…Miss… Miss…" He used his deep voice, the one he reserved for answering the phone.

Parrish frowned suspiciously. "Why are you working?"

"I was scheduled at five."

"Oh, yeah, I left at five. You're late. But I'm asking why you're *working?*"

Innocently, Mason shrugged.

Duncan, with an espresso cup rattling nervously on the saucer in his hands, walked slowly toward Parrish, both eyes fixated on the cup. "Take it, quick!"

Parrish did. "Who told him about saucers?"

Mason cleared his throat. "Our espresso is best served in a demitasse with a saucer."

"What's a demitasse?" asked Duncan.

Audra lowered her head, snickered, then glanced up at Parrish.

"Please, can we save the idiot act for tomorrow?" pleaded Parrish.

Audra placed a hand on his arm. "I'll just have a cup of tea. Do you have lemon?"

All of them took this news hard: she was a tea drinker. Mason and Duncan frowned grimly toward each other and tried not to meet Parrish's look. She'd been so pretty, but rules were rules. What happened next took approximately thirty seconds with a rapid-fire, pointed, and well-rehearsed delivery.

Mason took a deep breath and began. "Did she say tea?"

On cue, Duncan followed. "Tea, like some restaurant tea?"

"Where's that tea book?" Mason demanded. "Wait, I remember tea!"

"Is tea that beverage that tastes so bad you need to put fruit in it?" Duncan asked.

"It doesn't taste at all, really."

"You tasted it?"

"No, I saw someone else once. It's mostly hot, colored water."

"Like coffee?" asked Duncan.

"No!" Mason pounded the counter. "And don't let me hear you talk like that again! Coffee, as we know, is that epiphany occurring when exotic, arabica, highly caffeinated beans roasted to chestnut perfection are delicately ground, then expertly infused into— ecstatically merged with— triple-filtered artesian well water, creating a steaming libation of dense, rich, roasty, life-enhancing body not unlike drinking filet mignon or, say, liquid bacon. Tea, however, is more like dirty dishwater. Think dishwater insipidly stained into this thin, pitiful, orangy—"

"Orangy?"

"Often. This watery, orangy brown, like a glass of Dr Pepper with its ice all melted and held up to the sun. But it's served hot."

"No!" Duncan bit a knuckle. "Maybe that's just people drinking weak coffee?"

"No, it's much worse than weak coffee. Tea's meant to be that weak."

"Why?"

"I don't know! But it's made out of dried leaves. Go out back and scrape up some dead leaves. She's thirsty."

Nobody moved. Duncan didn't go out back, Mason didn't ring anything on the register. Both stood waiting for Audra's response. And, as Parrish knew from practiced experience, there was no possible customer response except changing the order to a coffee drink. Audra stared across the counter. Perhaps they meant to be funny, but their faces were as serious as stone. Speechless, she turned to Parrish.

"You done, boys?" Parrish asked.

Duncan and Mason swapped a satisfied look.

"Sorry, Audra," Parrish said. "They do this. You should have told me you were going to order tea, and I would have gotten it for you."

"I…I didn't know," she said.

"You should probably go back to the table. What kind do you want?"

"Green tea, please."

Mason threw up his hands, and Duncan bowed his head. Even Parrish gulped.

A few moments later, Parrish brought a mug of hot water steeping with two green tea bags over to their table, along with his cup and saucer of espresso.

"Thank you," said Audra.

"I should have warned you about those two," he said, taking a seat.

"Do customers ever come back here a second time?" she asked playfully.

"Tea-drinking customers?" Parrish raised his eyebrows. "No."

The two sat at a small bistro table situated up against the huge glass windows that entirely spanned the front of the shop. Their table was near the front door and its jangle of bells, but the customers were thinning and the table was set quietly off to one side.

Both had grown up here, and Audra attended university downtown, the same Parrish had attended. Parrish attempted to explain his medieval studies degree, which was always a crapshoot. There was no direct and clear line to be drawn from the study of medieval literature and the learning of dead languages to the running of a coffee shop. He liked Latin; he liked coffee. That was it.

Parrish lived alone, nearby, in an apartment that he rarely saw. He spent most days, all day, in his shop, and that suited him fine. He'd considered clearing out space in the back room for his clothes and television. It wasn't as if he hadn't slept on the huge burlap bags of green coffee beans on more than one occasion. They were not uncomfortable, and he'd calculated the financial boon were he to make it a permanent move. Couldn't he keep a towel and a bar of soap at the YMCA? Was this too much information?

Audra shook her head vehemently, commended such man-thinking, and encouraged him never to stop thinking that way. She herself had recently considered finding a better place, closer to school and the hospital, where she wouldn't have to commute by bus every weekday morning. She also lived in an apartment nearby. Living with people was trouble, she agreed. Nursing school, the fourth year, was mostly practicum, hands-on in a hospital. Every weekday, she worked harder than the actual nurses while paying for the privilege, then rode the bus home. On that bench, she read for an hour or so until the light ran out—for enjoyment, not school. She liked the cold, and besides, it was getting out of the house.

"How well do you know Mrs. Miranda?" Parrish asked.

"I don't, really." Audra dunked the tea bags up and down in her mug, then squeezed them out with the spoon. "I see her most days, but I never introduced myself."

"Why not?"

Audra shrugged and blew on her tea. "I never felt the need to strike up conversations with strangers at a bus stop."

Parrish remained silent.

"I don't think she rides the bus, though," she added thought-fully. "I've never seen her ride a bus. She knits."

"If both of you hang out at a bus stop, why were you giving me a hard time?"

Audra ignored the question. Instead, she busied herself with opening a packet of honey. She squeezed it thoroughly, stirred until it melted into her tea, then licked her thumb. "Are you ever going to tell me who sent you to find a letter at a bus stop?"

With his hands in his lap, Parrish lowered his face over his cup of espresso on the table, distracting himself by smelling the roasty aroma. He wasn't sure he wanted to answer her. This girl was mouthy, he thought, but he appreciated mouthy. He'd been shocked when she'd come along to talk to Mr. Crawford—that took moxie.

Moxie and mouthy. And he'd been glad she'd come along. Watching her now, as she sipped her steaming tea, her glasses fogged over and her cheeks dimpled, he thought he could definitely like this person.

But if he answered her question truthfully, he would secure an insane check mark beside his name. Now, here, at this table, he cared whether or not she thought he was crazy. But he was not dishonest. He was too honest, in fact, to even come up with a story other than the real one.

So he said, "Thanks for coming along today."

Audra smiled at him suspiciously. "Seriously?"

Parrish nodded.

"If you're serious, then you're welcome," she said. "Why did you say that?"

"This might be the last time you talk to me, so I figured I ought to thank you while I had the chance."

Then he took a deep breath and, as briefly as he could, explained the problem with golf balls, with Duncan's saltshaker, the semibiblical allusions to Samuel and Texas hold 'em, his washroom epiphany, and the subsequent conclusion concerning the cookie fortune— both as directive and divine.

Audra sipped her tea and tried not to show any clinical surprise. "Really?"

"Sounds a bit off. But there you are."

"Well, it's not knitting."

"Nope." Parrish took the fortune from his pocket and handed it to her. "Do you believe God would use a cookie?"

"Who said I believed in God?"

"Do you?"

Audra glanced at the slip of paper, front and back, then returned it to him. "May I play devil's advocate?"

Parrish sighed. "I've always wondered, when people say that, does the devil need an advocate?"

"Poor choice of phrase. May I speak frankly with you?"

"Sure."

"You say *that* fortune"—she pointed with her spoon, then licked it—"you say that was God, that God sent you to the bus stop. And today, you thought Mr. Crawford was the letter's owner, but we found out otherwise. Does that strike you as a wrench in God's plan?"

"Technically, all God told me was, 'Take the corner.' I went on the idea that maybe I'd be of assistance to someone. I thought this more appropriate than demanding everyone leave my corner. The letter came next, so I sort of assumed I was meant to find its owner."

"But you didn't find the owner. And please, I don't mean to be a jerk, but…you were wrong, right?"

Parrish nodded. "I was wrong in thinking the letter was Mr. Crawford's, correct. But then again, he did need someone to talk with."

"So?"

"So, that's what *he* needed." Parrish sipped his espresso. "We did that for him. In fact, you did that better than I did."

"Whoa!" Audra set her mug on the table with a loud thump, spilling a splash of tea. "You think God sent me along with you?"

"I'm figuring this out on the fly." Parrish dabbed up the spill with a napkin. "I think I'm supposed to look for the letter's owner, and if, along the way, God uses whatever God uses to do whatever God wants, couldn't that be part of the providential plan, so to speak, as opposed to a wrench in it?"

Audra stirred her tea silently for a minute before she resumed her argument. "But if God sent you to find the owner, shouldn't you have found the owner?"

"Maybe I will. But I think talking with an old guy—a sweet old guy—was precisely what God wanted to happen. I ran into Mr. Crawford while I was on cookie business. Maybe I'm supposed to be available to help whomever God puts along the way. And whether you believe *you* were sent or not, you helped too. Mr. Crawford adored you. He doted on everything you said like some long-lost daughter."

Audra eyes fell shyly. "Do you always think like this?"

"No, I never think like this. Or I never used to. I don't really know if I should now, but if you go with the assumption that God sent you to a bus stop, then you look at everything a little differently."

"You're aware that's not the most stunningly normal behavior?"

"Very aware, yes."

"Good."

"Good?"

"It'd be more worrisome if you didn't."

"Sorry to worry you."

"Don't worry. You don't."

Parrish fell back in his chair and gave a short burst of a laugh. He smiled at first, but when he shook his head, the smile became a smirk.

"What?" she asked.

"Are you always so tough?"

Audra blinked with genuine surprise. She pushed her glasses further up her nose. "I'm not so tough."

"I thought you were going to punch me when I met you."

This pleased her. She pulled both legs up into the chair and sat cross-legged, her back very straight, like a dancer. "What, you can deal out tough, but you can't take a little in return?"

"I take it quite fine," he said. "Let's say it's worrisome to me."

"Sorry to worry you. May I?" She nodded toward his espresso. "I've never tried it."

Parrish slid the tiny cup on its saucer across the table. Audra, propped on one elbow, held her face above it and sniffed. She gave Parrish a troubled look, then skimmed the end of her middle finger across the brown froth on top and popped it in her mouth. Instantly, both her eyes closed tight and she frowned, then stuck out her tongue.

Parrish pulled the saucer back his way. "Acquired taste."

She took a gulp of her tea to wash it away and wiped her lips with her napkin. "Yack!"

Parrish checked over his shoulder to make sure no one had seen her blatant coffee disrespect. "Don't go out of your way to like it."

"Why would anyone *want* to acquire a taste for that? To me, *that* is bizarre."

"You can dump sugar in it," he offered. "Make it sweeter."

Audra smiled playfully. "I thought you didn't like sweet."

"I don't, no." Parrish sipped his coffee. "And I didn't say Mr. Crawford wasn't sweet, just the way that all played out, that was unusual."

"Sure, if you think God made you follow him home."

"Exactly," Parrish agreed.

"I was kidding."

"I'm not, unfortunately. But isn't it weird how trying to give back the letter, we ended up getting all that?"

"Yes," she said assuredly. "It's weird."

Parrish spun his espresso cup on its saucer, pushing the tiny handle around in a circle with his finger, the way one might swirl a finger in a sink of water to test its heat. Then he decided. "Since we're speaking frankly and I've been fairly frank with you about some fairly odd beliefs," he began, "tell me, what do you believe?"

"I try not to," she replied quickly.

"Tell or believe?"

"Both."

"I don't believe that."

"What?"

"That you don't believe in anything."

Audra shrugged. "Believe what you want or don't."

"That, that right there," Parrish leaned forward, pointed a finger, and tapped it on the tabletop. "That's the tough girl bit I'm talking about."

"Shut up!" she said, pretending offense.

Parrish pursued. "You dish, but you won't lay down a card of your own."

"That's not true. I've told you all about myself."

"You told me the *safe* stuff."

"I don't *know* you."

"I'm not asking for dark family secrets," Parrish argued, "just whether or not you think my story's crazy because you don't believe in God at all, or because you believe in a God who would have nothing to do with a crazy person like me."

"I'll let you and God sort that out."

There was a long pause. Audra filled it by reaching up to her hair and recinching the wild tangles by the handful. No matter how expertly she chased and gathered it, some strand or two escaped and dangled across her face or beside her ear. With a huff, she finally took the band out completely and started from scratch, her head tipped downward and her back totally straight, tying it off like she would a sack. When done, she smiled at Parrish but said nothing, then turned and gazed blankly across his shop, sipping her tea.

Parrish slouched back in his chair, slid his hands on either side of his cup, and strummed his fingers on the table. He examined her profile, her hair, her sipping, her distance, her silence, then chose his words carefully. "You are not exceedingly honest."

With the mug at her lips, Audra coughed and put a hand to her chin. "Excuse me?"

"You said you wanted to speak frankly." He upturned his hands on the table. "You ain't honest."

"No. I'm just not blathering out my thoughts indiscriminately."

"Ouch!"

"Sorry!" She reached out a hand in mocking comfort. "Did I just dish? Was that harsh?"

"Harsh, oh no, not harsh." Parrish rested his hands atop his head. "Just scathingly self-protective."

"You're not being frank; you're an idiot."

"And you have avoided my question."

"What question?"

"God—you believe in God or not?"

Audra sighed heavily. Parrish wondered if she was annoyed just as much by her own refusal to answer as his refusal to stop asking, or because she hated the thought of backing down.

"I can't just say yes or no. My beliefs, if any…" Audra consulted the inside of her mug and her eyes grew humorless. "Let's just say they're in a holding pattern."

"Oh, that's clear."

"You wanted an honest answer, John. That's a precise and honest answer." Her voice, her eyes, pleaded slightly. "Fair?"

Parrish took in her eyes, and his voice softened. "Fair."

A short silence followed. Parrish let it remain. He'd already pushed too far. He sipped the last dregs of espresso out of his cup, overturned it, then set it gently on the saucer with a light clink.

The bells on the front door jangled as a young mother with a stroller backed inside, or tried to. The front wheel of the stroller caught itself on the doorjamb. Parrish jumped up and held the door for her, then bent down and freed the wheel. She thanked him politely, then, with a completely harried look, tried to manage her diaper bag and the stroller while she looked for a table. Parrish found one for her and told her to sit. He took her order, then brought it to her without a fuss. She thanked him and paid. He pulled a second chair nearer her, took her bag off the floor, and placed it in the chair so she wouldn't have to move again at all.

Audra watched him with a confused and curious look, like measuring the instinctive kindness against his obvious oddities.

When he returned to their table, she picked up her mug and held it a long while before she sipped. "Anything else I can clear up for you?"

"Why'd you become a nurse?" he asked without a beat.

"You never run out of questions, do you?"

Parrish flipped his fingers, pointing them absurdly in differing directions. "You asked me to ask."

"I did. But you talk like a date-match service."

"We make a handsome couple," he said, parroting Mr. Crawford's remark.

"I'm leaving now."

"Come on. The nurse question's the most normal thing I've said all day."

"Fine," she said, pushing her hands out in the air, clearing imaginary room for her answer. "Though my eyes are hazel, my favorite color's green, thus the tea. I enjoy swimming, but not in winter, and I've always wanted to help humanity through the healing arts."

Parrish nodded. "Wow."

"What did I win?"

"Well, Audra, you'll be leaving with my undying devotion and the toaster. Is that the real answer?"

"That's my real answer. I always wanted to be one, since I was a little girl. Nurses help people, that's all I could ever think I'd be useful doing."

"Why do you want to help people?"

"Why not?"

"*Buzz*. Oh, I'm sorry, the judges want the toaster back."

"People need help, John. Since I was a kid…I don't know. I imagined, if you could help people—*see* that, I mean. It's gratifying to see people fixed up. I mean, you can *see* stitches. They were bleeding, now they're not. A child in fever and pain, finally comforted, falls into a cool, peaceful sleep. I get to see that on a daily basis."

"So…and I don't mean to push too hard here…but perhaps you'd say you believed in that?"

"Most days. On good days."

"What about the bad ones?"

"Not everyone gets fixed, John."

He wondered what that meant but didn't ask. He was, slowly and very unsurely, realizing when to drop a thing with her. He was beginning to know her.

Audra's attention drifted to the other tables—a student hunched over his laptop, an older couple sharing a cookie broken in pieces on a napkin. She smiled at the young mother, tending her baby in the stroller, her table littered with baby gear.

After her moment, she returned. "Why'd you open a coffee shop?"

"I always wanted to help humanity through the caffeine arts."

"Smart."

"Seriously. To see a customer who can't even open their eyes at six in the morning, who can barely show up, mostly dressed, clutching a handful of correct change, in need of coffee. It's beautiful, really. No one speaks—just a hand overturned, coins rolling on the counter as they reach for the coffee already sitting in front of them. To watch that—someone sitting down and popping off a lid, hovering over the steam of a cup of perfectly brewed joe. They sip, and that tension between their eyes releases, their eyebrows come to life. You see the happy blinking after the first blush of caffeine rises to their cheeks and they can face the day, a productive, caffeinated human being."

"You're a pusher."

"Coffee enabler may be slightly below nurse on the benevolent occupation list, but let's not look at it in terms of addiction."

"I'm sure your customers, your victims-slash-junkies, think of you as a saint."

Parrish winced. "Let's not use that word."

"Junkie?"

"No, saint."

"Why not?" she asked.

"Heard it already this week."

Audra looked at him in confusion.

He didn't explain. Instead, he asked, "I don't know if it's harder just to be odd, or to be odd because God told you to."

"I'd think it'd be easier," she said. "You'd have someone to blame."

Parrish put his hands in his pockets and sat for a moment. He took out the cookie fortune, tilting his head to look at it again. Audra reached out a hand and he dropped the tiny slip on her palm. She propped her elbows on the table, held the paper between the thumb and finger of each hand, and leaned her face close, her eyes looking over her glasses as she flipped it front and back. She handed it back to him and he put it away.

"Do you really believe you'll find the owner?" she asked.

Parrish sighed, then shrugged. "I think I'm supposed to keep trying."

"What happens if you do?"

"I ask if I can help," he replied. "It's God's deal. I guess God'll fix that when I get there."

Another silence fell between them.

Parrish broke this one. "Does all this sound crazy to you?"

"Maybe not crazy," she said hopefully, kindly. "Equal parts weird and well-meaning. A dash of Messiah complex."

"Thanks."

"And all because of a cookie." She laughed. "The God cookie."

"I'm cutting you off." Parrish tried to take her mug, but she shielded it with her arms.

"The adventures of Parrish and the amazing God cookie."

"The green tea's gone straight to that frizzy head of yours."

"Excuse me!" She sat up straight, put a hand to her hair, and slid it back to check the band.

"You've got great hair, I'll say that."

"Is that a compliment?"

"Messiah complex?" he asked. "That was a nice thing to say?"

"This place got a dictionary?" Audra looked around the shelves. "I'm pretty sure *frizzy* is not a compliment."

"It is from where I sit."

Audra tilted her head, then lowered her face over her mug. Despite much effort not to, she smiled.

"Last question," he said.

"Promise?"

Parrish nodded.

Audra grabbed her mug with both hands, readying herself.

"When's the last time you believed?" he asked.

"What do you mean?"

"You said you're in a holding pattern. When's the *last* time you remember not being in the air flying circles?"

"You got any more hot water?" she said, looking over at the counter.

"Come on. All the green tea you can drink on the house, free, eternally. Last answer."

Audra sighed. The last question was clearly tricky. Decidedly, she pushed her mug to the center of the table and took the challenge. She shifted, put her feet up on the seat of the chair where her coat lay, wrapped her arms around her knees, and leaned her chin on them. Her expression drew inward as she considered his question. Then her jaw tightened. She'd found her answer. She aligned her feet together primly, pointed her toes, then straightened her neck to speak.

"When I was little, six or seven I think, I was in this play. Not a real play, a church thing—Christmas pageant. I was in this angel costume—don't laugh!—white with silver sequins, white leotard, ballet shoes, feathery wings made out of this paper frame with lots of feathers sewn on, a coat hanger halo, the whole bit. I had one line to say. I have no idea what it was, I can't remember. I didn't remember it that night either. But I do remember that I was on the stage alone. I stood right at the edge, curling my toes in the little slippers over the lip of the stage, and the audience was totally in the dark. I couldn't see them, because there was this massive spotlight on me, but I could hear the rustle of people in the audience. I put my hand up to shield my eyes, but I couldn't see past that bright light in my eyes. I knew I was supposed to speak, but I couldn't for the life of me remember my line. I just stood there, my heart racing, my knees shaking. I froze. I thought I'd ruined everything. But as I stood there squinting, I heard my parents whispering. They were four or five rows back, and I could see their heads silhouetted, just barely. I heard my father's voice, heard him whisper, 'Is it too early to applaud? Look, she's so beautiful.'"

In her mind, Audra seemed to stay on that stage, lingering there a moment longer. Then, as if someone harshly called her name, she withdrew. Her eyes quickly met Parrish's, to read them closely, to see if they hid ridicule. She looked around the shop, took her feet off the chair, crossed them beneath her again, and forced an awkward smile. Then she reached a hand and stubbornly, triumphantly, turned her mug until the handle pointed toward Parrish.

"I'll take that green tea now."

It grew late.

They finished another round of drinks, watched the other customers leave, and shared a couple of chocolate biscotti over one crumb-covered plate. As closing time approached, Susan began her final and most serious sweeping of the lobby, and Duncan and Mason argued, then cut a deck of cards to decide who would take out the trash. Duncan won with a nine of spades. They could have stayed past closing, of course—it was his shop after all—but Audra checked her watch and realized she hadn't eaten. Parrish apologized and offered to get her something. She wasn't hungry, but she had to go home. She pulled her legs from under her, stretched them awake, then stood and pulled on her heavy wool coat.

"Do you have far to go?" Parrish stood as he asked her this and pushed in his chair.

Audra gave him a look—something between suspicious, lonesome, and tired—he couldn't tell. "Not far," she said, spooling her scarf around one hand as she pulled it out of her coat pocket. "I'll make it from here."

Parrish held the door open for her as she walked out. "Have a good night, tough girl."

She smiled at him over her shoulder. "Thanks for my eternal tea."

Wednesday

The next afternoon, the boys were ready.

At five o'clock, bus stop time, both Duncan and Mason stood behind the counter, waiting for Parrish to come out of the back room. Mason had made them both fresh cups of espresso, double shots, and when Parrish walked out, they said nothing at first, just grinned like a couple of pleased and mischievous boys who'd put toothpaste in his shoes or a scorpion in his pillowcase.

Parrish eyed them suspiciously, a warning of a face, then deliberately looked away. At the espresso machine, he poured a pitcher full of milk from a jug, then steamed it to a swirling froth. He flipped two cups off the top of an upside-down stack, caught both in the other hand, then pumped chocolate in the larger and two pumps of vanilla in the shorter. He considered for a moment, then added a dash of almond flavor to the cup with chocolate. He high-poured the hot milk into the chocolate-almond cup, getting a good height above the cup so the gravity of the milk's fall mixed the syrups into the froth, pushing it to the top of the drink. Then, with a large, flat spoon, he held back the foam as he poured milk into the second drink, then scooped three dollops of thicker foam on top. That done, he tossed the spoon like a throwing knife into its designated water bin. He washed the pitcher quickly under the tap, then upturned it with a spin onto the drying mat. With a bartender flair, he spun the whipped cream canister in his palm, topped the larger drink with a fluffy, swirling peak, then twirled the canister back precisely in its place. He pinch-flipped lids one by one into his hand, capped both drinks, then fit them snugly into a carrying tray.

The boys merely watched, waited. Then Mason cleared his throat loudly, overly long. "Hey, Parrish? Who the drinks for?"

Parrish didn't look up from his business. "Leave me alone."

"You drinking hot chocolate now?" Duncan asked.

"With almond, no less?" added Mason.

"Do you want me to start ordering those boxed tea sets?" Duncan asked dryly.

"Cozies!" suggested Mason. "We could order tea cozies for every table!"

"We'll have to start prepping sliced lemon." Duncan shook his head.

"Which means going to the grocery, what, two, three times a week?" Mason calculated on his fingers.

"That'll cost gasoline and whatever fruit costs." Duncan wrung his hands worriedly.

"Plus the cozies," said Mason. "We're going to have to raise our prices."

Parrish drank a shot of espresso. "Leave me alone, both of you."

Duncan craned his neck, shifting his head back and forth to better examine his boss. "What's different about him today?"

"I don't know, but something has been different all day, hasn't it?" said Mason. "Hey, Parrish, did you *shave*?"

"That's it!" Duncan shouted. "He's groomed himself!"

"A whole new 'groom' mentality!"

Parrish picked up the tray of drinks and shoved past them. "When you guys are ready to clean out those grease traps, hop on it anytime, okay?"

"Hey, what time is it, Dunc?" Mason asked innocently.

"I don't know," he shrugged. "I just saw a bus. Maybe it's five."

"Hey, Parrish, it's five o'clock."

Parrish pushed his way backward out the front door, trying to get away, but not before Mason called out, "Don't forget your cookie!"

The bus huffed away from the curb as Parrish arrived. He delivered the hot chocolate to Mrs. Miranda, who put aside her knitting to take the cup with both hands, then thanked him. She mentioned that his beard looked nice and asked if he'd shaved, and he explained that her hot chocolate had a dash of almond. He hoped she liked that. She did. Then Parrish turned to Audra.

"I guessed you for a double-tall-two-pump-vanilla-percent-extra-foamy latte."

"I'm all that?"

"As far as froufrou goes, you're marginally sweet, yet sensible. A perfectly proportioned drink."

Audra raised an eyebrow, but smiled. She closed a finger in her book, took the cup, and brought it to her nose. "Smells good."

"I know you like tea, but try it," he said.

That done, he went to work—cookie work. He paced, watched for passersby, and checked to make sure the letter was still in his pocket, easily accessible for a quick-draw when the need arose. Parrish paced with determination. What he lacked in belief he made up in sheer stubborn nervousness. The few people who exited the bus had walked away and were nowhere to be seen. He stared in every direction and scanned the parking lot to see if anyone was heading his way.

Fifteen minutes passed, then another fifteen. All the while Parrish paced, and no one walked by. Waiting—for anything—had always proved the hardest thing for him to do. Waiting *wasn't* doing, it was the opposite of it, and his life had been built on overactivity, on caffeination. Explain the task, then leave it for him to manage as he saw best. He preferred doing. He mentioned that to God, reminded God as to his preferences.

Still no one came.

Another fifteen minutes passed, and Parrish began to doubt. He doubted the letter, the bus stop, the cookie had anything to do with God. Why would it? He'd simply imagined this situation. All that had happened could much more easily, much more sensibly, be attributed to random chance and imagination. What made him think God would do things the way *he'd* imagined they should happen? He tried to put doubt out of his mind, but doubt was like trying *not* to hear the neighbor's loud music—once you'd heard it, you couldn't then not hear it, no matter how loud you turned your own volume up.

Perhaps his doubt had something to do with the fact that he'd shared his story with the girl who, he knew, now watched to see how this would work out. If it didn't work out, he'd not only feel the normal amount of foolish, he'd have bonus foolish. He already cared what she thought of him, and that realization made him angry with himself, which only fed his self-doubt. He glanced at her nearly as often as she glanced at him.

Finally he confronted his doubt instead of trying to ignore it. He admitted that he wanted God to prove him right in front of Audra, so he could look good. He wanted that *more* than he wanted to help the hurting person who'd penned the letter, and that was surely wrong. So he tried to focus his motivation, to purify it, get it all in one basket. He tried to convince himself that he was doing the right thing with no ulterior motives. This was, of course, silly. Like holding a beachball underwater, trying *not* to think of the ulterior only made it more exterior, and a motive, now surfaced, could no longer be submerged merely by command. He doubted not only God but himself now.

Another fifteen minutes passed and Parrish stopped pacing, leaned limply against the signpost. God would never show him the letter's owner. He gave up.

The daylight had begun to wane—a grayness had lowered over the parking lot in shades, imperceptible as it happened, but noticed over spent time. It grew slightly colder, and the wind awoke and began to prowl.

Audra raised her book closer to her eyes, huddling her hands together as she held it. Rose checked her watch, then began to bundle her things in her plastic shopping bag.

"Time to make dinner," she said. "Thank you again, John, for the drink."

"Anytime."

"Audra." Rose moved closer to where she sat and spied the knitted toboggan she wore. "If you had to pick a color for another one of those, what color would you like?"

Audra laughed with a girlish smile—eyes closed and her chin thrust forward. "Oh, no, Rose. You don't have to do that."

"I'm going to, so you'd better pick the color you like."

"Oh, anything," she said. "You choose."

"John." Rose turned. "What color would *you* like to see Audra's hat?"

Parrish walked over to the bench, jumped up on it, and sat on the backrest beside Audra to get a better view of her hat.

"I don't know." He considered his choices. "She says her favorite color's green."

Audra twisted around and gave him a look.

"Green it is," announced Rose. "That narrows it down to about a million greens."

Parrish nudged Audra's arm with his knee. "Tell her which *green* you want."

"Who *are* you?" she said.

"Oh, let's not go back there." Rose wiggled her fingers in the air to erase that between them. "Just pick a green."

"I don't know!" Audra shut her book, pulled at the lapels of her coat. "Primary! Primary green!"

"Primary?" Rose frowned. "Is that a color?"

"Your basic green," explained Parrish. "Stoplight green."

"That's almost blue, really," said Rose thoughtfully.

"Green-light green, I should say. The green they put in books to teach a kid green. That's primary green."

"Well, I never knew."

"Please, stop staring at my head!" Audra held up her hands claustrophobically.

Rose hitched her bag over her arm. "I'll match the green in a children's book. You two have a pleasant evening."

"You too, Rose," said Parrish.

The two watched as Rose walked away.

Audra adjusted her coat, resituated her hat, pushed strands of her hair up in it, then stared blankly at Parrish.

"What?" he said finally.

She shook her head disapprovingly, then thumbed the pages of her book, letting them drift open in her lap. "How's your mission today?"

"You're watching it," he answered.

Audra took in their surroundings, gave a long look over each shoulder, checked her watch, looked for the next bus, then turned back to Parrish.

"May I ask a question?" she said.

"Why not?" he said gruffly.

"I thought you said *whoever* comes along, that's the person you're supposed to help?"

"Can I help *you*?" he asked.

"No."

"Do you *see* anyone else?"

"Yes," she said.

Surprised, Parrish looked up.

Audra grinned. "But you don't, do you?"

She didn't help him any more than that, just kept her eyes on him. He stared first at her, then slowly looked left, then right, all around. Like a game you play in the car on vacation, Parrish searched in every direction for the thing she could see but he couldn't. He asked her for a hint, but she only hummed and rolled her eyes side to side, then up and down. Parrish shoved his hands in his coat pockets, tired of games. Then he saw. Across the side street sat a small house with a grassy yard. Lying beneath the yard's only tree, Parrish saw a homeless man.

"Oh no…no," he mumbled. "No way. I know that guy."

Audra's eyes blinked innocently.

"No, *that* guy messes up my shop on a daily basis! He annoys my customers, leaves grocery sacks full of old pants in my bathrooms…"

Audra said nothing.

Distressed, Parrish turned his entire body away, banishing her entirely. He shook his head, pulled his coat collar up high around his neck, and hunched down into its warmth. He fumed a bit, acted thoroughly unappreciated, and though Audra said nothing else, he sang the word *no* over and over to himself while he bounced his knees. Suddenly, he turned sharply toward her. "You're kidding, right?"

"It's not *my* rule, Parrish. *You're* the one who made it up yesterday. I don't care what you do."

He tapped her on the shoulder. "Lady, you're not right."

"Maybe not, but maybe…how did you phrase it?" Audra

scowled, slumped, dropped her voice low, and buried her hands in her coat pockets—her best Parrish impression. "You're not *exceedingly* honest."

Parrish's mouth gaped open, partly because it was a terrible and unflattering impression, but mostly because he'd been caught, and he knew it. Not only by his own dumb rule, but by the fact that he hadn't even *noticed* the homeless guy. He'd dismissed a person's existence simply because he didn't *want* to talk to him. He considered pulling Audra's gray toboggan down over her face.

She refused to look away, even giggled.

After a silent moment, Parrish stood up on the bench. "Hey, guy!"

"Parrish!" Audra swatted his leg with her book. "Don't!"

"Hey, guy, I want to talk to you!"

"What do *you* want?" called out the homeless man. He recognized Parrish as well.

"I want to talk. Come over here."

"You come over *here.*"

Parrish dropped his head to his chest and sighed. Then he hopped down from the bench. "I'll come halfway. Meet me at the sidewalk."

"Look, I ain't in *your* stupid shop, I ain't in *your* stupid parking lot. If I walk over *there,* you'll call the cops on me or something. You got something to say, walk it over to *my* tree."

"That's not your tree, Jake."

"Ain't your tree either...Jake!"

"Okay." Audra held her hands in the air, hostage style. "I think I've started a fight. Maybe this isn't such a good—"

"You coming?" Parrish cut her off with a fierce glance.

Audra paused, giggled, then swallowed it. She gave Parrish a solemn salute. "Yes sir!"

The homeless man lay stretched out in the grass, just his head resting on the trunk, his neck at an angle that could not possibly be comfortable. He wore a dirty, tattered pair of corduroy pants and a filthy high school jacket, the kind with snaps and sleeves a different color from the rest. It had a football emblem over the heart, but with his neck crooked that way, his ratty beard was long enough to cover most of it. The skin of his face and his fingers was dirty or windburned or both, and though the hair on the sides of his head was long and scraggly and black, he had a dirty, windburned bald spot on top. The homeless guy put a dirty hand up to shield his eyes and get a better look at who stood over him.

"Okay, look, guy," Parrish began, "there's no way to explain this, but…is there some way I can help you out today?"

The homeless man said nothing.

"Look, I'm serious. Have you eaten today?"

The man looked at Audra. "What's he up to, lady?"

"He's attempting a good deed," Audra said softly. "I think."

"Oh!" The homeless man weakly banged a fist on his chest. "So I'm your good *deed* for the day, is that it?"

"Let's wait to see how this tumbles out," Parrish said. "Have you eaten?"

"Let me get this straight." The homeless man made a sawing gesture with his hand that was everything but straight. "Every other day, you throw me out of your coffee shop, you tell me to go away, you yell at me—"

"I don't *yell.*"

The homeless man turned his face to Audra and shook a finger at Parrish. "Right there! Did you hear him?"

When Parrish looked at her, Audra remained silent but gave him a pained shrug.

"You're *always* yelling." The homeless man mimicked Parrish. "Get out of my shop! Get out of my garbage! Get out of my chairs! Get out of my bathroom!"

Parrish put his hands behind his back and spoke very calmly. "Right. 'Cause I don't want you in my garbage, I don't want you sleeping in the chairs, I don't want you screwing up my bathrooms."

"I *trash* the bathrooms 'cause I know when I come out, you're going to *yell* at me."

"I know this!"

"Now you're coming over *here* to yell at me." He gestured widely to indicate his tree, his yard, his grass.

Parrish's voice became intensely quiet. "Audra, am I yelling?"

"Not now." She put a hand on his arm. "But I'm afraid you might have a stroke."

Parrish ignored her touch.

Audra clasped her hands together tightly and rubbed her palms worriedly.

Since the homeless man wouldn't sit up, Parrish squatted beside him. "Are you hungry?"

"Give me a couple of bucks and I'll go—"

"Nope, not cash." Parrish adjusted his stance, grounding his balance firmly. "You want food, I'll get you food, but what do I get?"

"What do *you* get?"

"If I buy you dinner today, how's that help you get off the streets?"

"It doesn't."

"So help me figure this out."

The homeless man waved his hands in the air limply. "For a guy doing a good deed, you sure are pushy. Did you shave?"

Parrish stood up, took a lap around the tree, then squatted on the other side of him. "Do you have a place to sleep?"

"I'm homeless, Jake."

"I got that. Have you been to the shelter?"

"Yeah, yeah, yeah." The man swiped the air with his hands and closed his eyes, paddling to get away from the shelter. "I slept there last night. They'll probably let me in again."

"Okay! Progress!" Parrish looked up at Audra with an expression between madness and glee. "But you can't sleep there forever. How do we get you a job?"

"I don't want a job."

"This is where the homeless thing kicks in, right?"

"Don't preach to me about my life."

"You're right, I won't. But how do I help you get a job?"

"At the shelter, they're trying to get me to put together a...a résumé, go to some interviews."

"How's that coming along?"

"Man, I was lying by this tree…"

"This is not going to be the kind of pocket-change experience you've grown accustomed to."

"Shoot, I see that."

"We need to start thinking about the bigger picture."

"Dude, I'm homeless. *We* ain't got no bigger picture."

"How do *we* help you get one?"

"Know what?" The homeless man opened his eyes wide. "I'm tired. Leave me alone."

Again Parrish looked up at Audra, either for help or permission to quit. His fingers yanked at the grass, pulling it out in clumps.

Audra knelt in the grass beside them both. She put a hand on Parrish's knee, shook her head gently, trying to release him from this particular mission.

The homeless man grumbled blearily, twisting his head back and forth. Audra looked more carefully at the man's cloudy eyes and tried to diagnose their unsteadiness. She took his wrist and felt his pulse. He let her take his wrist without seeming to notice.

"Parrish, I think we should call an ambulance or—"

"No!" The man swung one arm wildly. "No cops!"

Audra backed away, falling to one side and catching herself with one hand on the grass. Parrish put his hands out to shield her from being hit.

"It doesn't do any good to call an ambulance, let alone the police," he said. "They don't do anything. They can't."

"They'll lock me up again," the homeless man yelled, but less to them than to some imagined policeman in his mind.

"We're not calling the cops, okay?"

"Okay, Jake. Okey-dokey."

Parrish grimaced at the homeless guy, then said, "But you need to eat something."

"I don't want anything you *got*!" He spat the last word at them.

Parrish ran his fingers wildly through his hair, looked up to where Audra now stood. "This is the part I don't get, truly. Someone *offers* help, but help is refused. He *needs* help, but he doesn't *want* it. He doesn't want to *do* something, to *try* to find a better solution than lying here."

At this, the homeless man awoke from his stupor angrily, shoved himself upward from his lying position, and crossed his legs. His arms became animated as he spoke. "And here's *your* problem. You thinking that somehow I *want* to lay under a tree not knowing where I'm going to eat, going to *sleep*? You think I'm...I'm...*lazy* because I don't *own* a shop to sit around in, so I have to sit around outside. You don't know my life. Man, just head on out of here. I don't need your kind of help."

"Then tell me your life."

"Why should I?"

"Because I'm offering help?"

"Your offering ain't nothing!"

Parrish dropped his head and let it dangle loosely from his neck.

"Come on, Parrish," said Audra. "Let's go."

But the homeless man wasn't finished. "Okay, Jake, answer me one question: Why would I believe you? I don't know you, you don't know me. You yell at me every day up to this one, then one day you want to help? Tell me why I would believe anything about you?" The man's eyes were suddenly, fiercely lucid. He stared steadily at Parrish, exhaling in huffs through his mouth. "I'm waiting for this answer," he said. "You got an answer?"

Parrish shook his head. "No, I don't."

"No, you don't!"

Parrish tipped his weight backward so that he dropped on his rear. The two men sat next to each other in the grass.

"I don't," Parrish said. "You're right. Why would you believe me?"

"Well, I'm glad you finally got that."

"Got it." Parrish sat with his head on his knees.

Audra took a few steps back toward the bench and waited for Parrish to follow.

Parrish, however, pulled backward on the toes of his boots, rocking back and forth. Sitting like that, he brooded. He felt thoroughly wrong. He didn't want to argue anymore. He'd been out-argued by a homeless man, and he was pretty sure arguing with homeless people in general made it on the "wrong" list. He sat with his elbows on his knees, gazing far across the parking lot. Finally, he gave up and stared at the man propped beneath the tree.

Audra called to him softly. "Parrish?"

Parrish leapt up so quickly, she jumped.

"Wait here," he called to her.

He sprang from the patch of grass like a sprinter, then ran across the parking lot, only slowing when he neared the shops. He disappeared inside Mr. Wu's.

When he reappeared, he carried a container and a cup, both Styrofoam, and held a straw in his teeth. As he returned to where Audra stood, she took the straw from his mouth, unwrapped it, then took the soda from his hands. They returned to the spot beneath the tree and sat in the grass on opposite sides of the man.

Parrish opened the Styrofoam container, ripped open some soy sauce packages, and doused the steaming rice. He shoved a fork in the heap of food, then sat the container in the man's lap. The man woke and stared at what was before him, swallowing hard at the thought of eating. He poked at the rice with his fork, picked up a piece of chicken with his hands, and nibbled at it until it all went in his mouth. Audra held his cup, since it wouldn't stand upright in the grass next to the tree's roots. The man chewed and chewed the one bite. It seemed his jaw popped in and out of its hinges as he did so, making chewing a strange effort. He tried to pick up some rice with his fingers, but only made a mess across his coat. Angry with himself, he wiped his fingers in the grass, then tried the fork. His hands shook so tremulously that the rice scattered off the fork before he could reach his mouth.

"Here, let me see that," Parrish said.

Parrish took the plastic fork out of his dirty hand, scooped up a huge bite of rice, held it on the fork with his thumb, then brought it to the man's face. The man blinked rapidly, but accepted this indignity. He let Parrish feed him the entire carton of rice, occasionally picking up a piece of chicken with his fingers and eating that. Audra held out his Coke and matched the straw to his lips as he craned his neck forward. When he'd finished, Parrish smashed all the trash into the Styrofoam container.

The man regained some of his wits once the food began to work on his system. He seemed alive again, human again. Sitting against the tree, fed now, he looked much older than he had when he'd been angry. At the same time, he also seemed too young to look that old, especially his face. It was almost as if there were two versions of him in one body, or like someone else's face peeked out from behind his.

He thanked them and sipped his cola. They sat with him a while longer, until it grew quite dark.

"Can you get back to the shelter?" Parrish asked.

"I take the late bus," he said. "They won't let you in early."

"Do you need money for the bus?" asked Audra.

"Got some."

Parrish smiled at her—a small smile, mostly in the eyes, trying to give an apology in how long his eyes lingered.

Then he turned to the man. "Here's the deal: Starting tomorrow, a free cup of coffee, bathroom rights, you can hang out and get warm. Please, don't trash my bathroom or ask my customers for money. You need something, come talk to me. I'll see what I can do. And when you get ready to put a résumé together, I'll help you type it up and proofread it. If you'll write down your sizes, I'll bring you clothes for an interview, when you get one. You want this deal?"

The man stared at him blankly. "What will I end up owing you?"

"Nothing. Deal?"

"How long?"

"What?"

"You're helping me today, in front of the pretty lady. For how long?"

Parrish released a breath. "Until you can believe me. Fair?"

The man's eyes narrowed slightly. "Can I consider my options?"

"Absolutely." Parrish extended his hand. "I'm sorry I called you Jake. My name's John."

The nameless, homeless man slowly reached out and shook the hand in front of him. "I'm Thomas."

Audra and Parrish walked back to the bus stop. They sat for a while on the same bench, silently. They simply watched traffic, each allowing the other to sort out how exhausted they were by doing the very little they'd done. It was a little thing they'd done, but that little, for that particular moment, had been the right bit.

After a while, Parrish turned to look at Audra. He studied the features of her face, taking his time with each one. Then he stood. "It's too cold to be outside."

Audra stood as well, shouldering her backpack. "Yeah, I need to get home."

Parrish leaned over, picked up her gloves, and handed them to her.

"Thanks," she said, jamming them in her coat pockets.

Parrish cleared his throat. "Would you have dinner with me?"

Audra didn't answer. She just looked at him, surprised — something different, even quieting in his voice.

Parrish smiled. "I know this terrific little Chinese place."

At a small table near the front of Mr. Wu's, Audra pushed her empty plate to one side as Parrish took the last bites of his chicken chow mein. Parrish asked how she'd liked her meal. She'd ordered the sweet and sour shrimp and said it was delicious. He said he hoped it was "sweet" enough, she laughed, then thanked him for suggesting dinner. Left to herself she often forgot to eat.

Parrish understood. "If you drink enough coffee, you can forget to eat for roughly two days before your eyes roll up in your head and you collapse into a twitching heap."

Audra smiled at his helpful advice, then looked at him seriously. "I'm a little nervous."

Finished, Parrish pushed aside his plate. "Nervous about what?"

Audra leaned her face on her hand with a curious expression. "I'm a little nervous about what comes next."

Parrish froze for a moment. He stopped moving completely, even stopped chewing. Then he swallowed what was left in his mouth and slowly cleared room at the table for his elbows. He leaned on the table and spun the twirly-rack of condiments by walking his fingers along its edge.

"What comes next?" he restated, pausing to see if she would offer help.

She didn't.

The rest came out of his mouth in one long tumble. "Okay, yes, I was *going* to ask to walk you home, but that's all. I mean, I barely know you, so I wasn't really thinking about a *next* date, if that's what you mean. Not *actively* thinking, or *trying* not to think actively about that. I'm a very active thinker. On the other hand, my mother raised me to be polite. So sure, I'd *like* to see you again, if that works out and all, but I probably *wouldn't* have asked you out again, not tonight anyway, protocol and all. The plan I was trying *not* to think too actively about was to walk you home so we could keep talking, but definitely *not* ask you out again. Not until tomorrow. When I saw you. That is, if I see you. At the bus stop. Is this making sense? Stop me anytime. I'd really appreciate it if you'd stop me. But since you're not, may I, without any further active expectations of subsequent dates—if in fact, you're counting *this* as one, which by your current silence I'm beginning to conclude is a misperception— Audra, may I walk you home?"

She let him finish and gulped a few times, letting him dig the hole as deeply as he wanted. Then she reached out a hand and stopped the rack from twirling. "Parrish." she spoke very calmly, soothingly. "I'm not nervous about…you. But we're finished with our meal…"

"Yeah?"

"We've finished our *Chinese* meal…" She nodded hopefully, as if this might make him understand. "At Mr. Wu's?"

"Not following."

"When you finish a meal at a Chinese restaurant, what comes next?"

Parrish looked down at his hands, his silverware, his napkin, the empty plates. "Oh! Okay, all right. Very embarrassed now." He leaned heavily back in his chair and pulled at the back of his belt in a manly way.

She laughed at him, but put her hands over her mouth to soften it. "You have to admit, you've built this fortune cookie thing up quite a bit."

"Yep, I do that."

"I'll be frightened to open mine."

"I'm not making any promises for God. The last time there were extenuating circumstances."

They sat and shared a silence—the kind with restrained smiles, jumpy eyes, and unnecessary smoothings of the tablecloth.

Finally, Audra stared directly across at him until she steadied his eyes. "May I tell you something?"

"Oh, I'm not sure. Will it make me talk more?"

"You might like it. It's honest."

He laid his palms flat on the table and bent his neck forward as if on the chopping block. "Ready."

"Earlier today. All that at the bus stop. Thanks for doing that."

Parrish relaxed his shoulders, surprised. "When I argued with the homeless guy?" he asked with a frown.

"Yep."

"We can go find another homeless guy and I can argue with him, if you'd like."

"Be quiet, I'm trying to pay you a compliment. Not the arguing. You didn't like that guy…wait!" She grabbed the back of his hand. "I could see you didn't like him. To be honest, I was pushing you. I did it on purpose, I think."

"Yeah, why'd you do that?"

"I did it before I could stop myself. I mean…" Audra held her hands out and looked around the restaurant. "Here you are, showing up at a bus stop and saying God sent you. I guess that miffed some part of me. So I pushed you, I don't know, to see if you believed your own stuff."

"Audra, that guy's still on the streets."

"True. But you did something, when you clearly didn't want to, when I was goading you, and not very kindly, I might add. When push came to shove, I figured you wouldn't. I wanted to see. Does that make sense?"

"In a spiteful sort of way, sure."

"Stop!" She tilted her head sadly. "That's not what I'm trying to say."

"Audra, I yelled at a homeless guy for being homeless."

"Okay, your good deed, at first, was nearly harassment, but that's not my point."

"So what you're saying is…"

Exasperated, Audra growled, literally. Her hands searched the table quickly, grabbed a spoon, and reached across the table with it, putting it over Parrish's mouth. She held the spoon straight up and down, the bowl of the spoon pressed over his lips and chin. They sat like this for a tense moment, Parrish's eyes darting back and forth, Audra's thumb turning white.

"You lived up," she said quietly.

She waited a moment more, then handed him the spoon.

Parrish crinkled his nose and felt his lips with his hand. He slid the spoon under the edge of his plate, a safe distance away from Audra. "Thank you."

"My pleasure." She folded her napkin, then added, "You changed today. Maybe just an inch, but you did. And I got to see it."

"I forgot that." Parrish watched her take her credit card out of her backpack. "You like to see the stitches."

Audra smiled at him. "I like the good I see after the stitches are gone."

She looked around for their check.

Standing at the register, scratching figures in a ledger, Charles, as always, seemed magically to know when a check was wanted. He immediately stopped his work, dropped the pen on the ledger, and picked up the little plastic tray he had ready. He walked briskly to their table and set it between them. Both Parrish and Audra quickly reached for the check, but froze before the tug of war began.

There were no cookies on the tray.

"Charles?"

"Yes, John?"

"We were kind of looking forward to a fortune cookie."

"We out."

"No cookies?"

"We get some Friday." Charles clapped his hands together once, optimistically.

"Busy week, huh?" Parrish reached for his wallet, but as he took it out, Audra dropped her card in the tray and handed it to Charles, shielding it from Parrish's reach.

Charles took the tray with a sharp nod. Holding the check and credit card tightly in the tray with two fingers, he crossed his arms, striking that wide stance he used for conversation. "No. Medium busy. But your friend come by this afternoon, ask Min San how much for all our fortune cookies."

Parrish gave Audra a concerned frown. "That can't be good."

Charles shrugged.

Parrish tapped the edge of his wallet on the table. "Did he say what he wanted them for?"

"Don't know." Charles gave the back of his head a sudden and thorough scratching. "Your friend bought all the fortune cookies, then he ask my sister out on date. He very strange, right?"

"No comment."

"He one of the same who run out on you and check." Charles shook a finger.

"No comment."

Charles shook his head. "He want to ask out Min San, he shouldn't steal in front of her."

"I'll let him know that."

Charles left the table as briskly as he'd arrived.

Audra sat back in her chair with her legs crossed, bouncing her foot as if she were proud of herself for beating Parrish to the tab.

Parrish snapped his fingers. "Hey, do you want the second one I got Monday?"

"What?"

"The second fortune cookie from that day. It's in my pocket."

Her foot stopped. "Oh...no, I couldn't take that one."

"Why not? It might be a *normal* cookie," he offered.

"Or...," Audra suggested, "it *might* be a normal cookie that's been in your pocket for days."

"Oh, right."

"You keep that. Besides, I'm pretty certain God doesn't have any magic fortune moments for me."

Audra picked her backpack up off the floor and put it in her seat, then zipped it shut. Still seated, she lifted her coat over the back of the chair, slipped her arms inside, then wrapped her scarf around her neck. At the register, Charles rang and swiped, shuffled and tore slips of paper, then he bent down behind the counter and rummaged, popped back up, and arranged the tray just so with the pen. He hustled back over to their table and handed Parrish the tray with the pen. Parrish took his card, put it in his wallet, then figured the tip, signed the receipt, and handed it back to Charles. Only then did Charles give Audra back her credit card.

Audra took her card with confusion. "What just happened?"

"Home court advantage." Parrish grinned. "Thank you, Charles."

Feeling tricky, Parrish laid his right hand palm down on the table, placed a spoon on the back of it, then flipped the spoon in the air and tried to catch it, all with the same hand. It didn't work. Audra and Charles watched as the spoon bounced across the table, off a glass, then onto the carpet.

Charles raised his eyebrows appreciatively, then tore the receipt and gave Parrish his copy. "He give me his card when you two first come in," said Charles. "He win."

Audra flicked the edge of her credit card with her fingernails and eyed them both with a mischievous grin. "Charles, do you have gift certificates for meals?"

"I can make them. You want some?"

"Yes. You've had a medium week. I'm here to change that."

"Whole lot of world-class world-shaking going on here, Luke," Parrish said.

Both Audra and Charles stopped cold and stared at him.

"George Kennedy? In *Cool Hand Luke*?" Parrish explained. "When they bust out of prison?"

"Never saw it," said Audra.

Charles shook his head.

"Forgot where I was," Parrish said. "Never mind."

"Parrish, I don't believe in shaking the world." She buttoned up her coat. "But someone was hungry, and you fed him. So I'm going with you." She followed Charles to the register.

Parrish watched them go, then grabbed his scarf, hung it round his neck, and took a last quick gulp of his soda. He looked around the table to make sure he was ready to leave, to walk her home. He stood up, pushed in his chair, and began to pull on his own coat.

Then, suddenly, he stopped. Or something stopped him, something like the voice inside that sometimes told him to stop talking, to listen.

He stopped getting ready for his next move, sat back down in his chair, and just watched Audra. She stood in her long gray coat at the register, laughing with Charles as he hunched over the counter and carefully filled out certificates. She examined each certificate, blew the ink dry, then put them away in her coat pocket. In between certificates, she withdrew her toboggan and began to fit and push her hair up in it. Parrish looked at her chair. She'd already gathered her things, her backpack zipped and ready to grab. He looked at her again. She'd already buttoned up her coat.

What she *didn't* say, he realized, was most honest. Exceptionally so.

He took off his scarf and dropped it on the table.

Audra returned to their table, folding up her receipt. "That's done. Now we have gift certificates if someone else hungry comes along," she said, then picked up her backpack and adjusted her glasses. "Thank you for dinner, even though you tricked me."

"My pleasure," he said.

As if on cue, she checked her watch, then took a deep breath.

He said it before she could. "You should be going, huh?"

"Yeah, I need to go."

"Thanks for having dinner with me," he said. "Stay warm."

She hesitated for a moment, unsure what had changed, but recovered just as quickly.

"Tell the boys I said hello," she said, grinning, but she didn't wait for a reply. She pushed open the door and stepped through. Outside, after the door shut, she checked her watch again, then glanced back at him through the glass. She mouthed, *See you tomorrow*, then waved good-bye.

Parrish sat for a long while after she'd gone. He played with the spoon she'd mashed over his chin. He slumped back in his chair and buried his hands in his pockets. He sat until Charles turned off the neon Open sign and began to clean up.

Parrish reviewed his day in his mind. He'd only done two things all day worth mentioning, both very small in the grander scheme but both right for their moments. When he realized he was slumped in precisely the same slouch Audra had mimicked earlier, he laughed audibly. Charles gave him a stare, then went back to his sweeping.

Parrish dug in his right coat pocket until he felt the slip of paper. He took out the fortune and reread it, then decided. He grabbed the pen Charles had left on the table, clicked it, flipped the tiny slip over, and placed it on the little plastic tray so he could write on the fortune's blank side:

Is it too early to applaud? Look, she's so beautiful...

Thursday

Thursday was colder. The temperature had dropped drastically overnight, and the sky returned to white and gray, overcast and ominous with snow. The commuter rush proved especially busy—a long, noisy line of winter-clad customers stretched to the front door for two hours while Duncan worked register and Parrish made drinks. Inside the shop, the reliable heaters, the continual opening and closing of the front door, and the constant use of the steam wands kept the windows fogged with condensation, mistily shutting those inside from any sight of the outside world. People held meetings at his bistro tables instead of their offices, as if they anticipated a snow day, treating themselves to the coziness of a warm shop with steaming drinks. Everyone wanted the comfort of a hot coffee when the temperature plummeted.

Parrish and Duncan shared the long day shift together. Though busy, Duncan was unusually quiet, almost reticent. He made beverages without talking to them or the espresso machine. After the rush, he bused the many tables solemnly and ran cups through the dishwasher without having to be told. He wiped things that didn't need wiping, wandered the store looking for things to spray and squirt, polish and wipe, and negotiated the afternoon doldrums with sleepy and compulsory activity. Customers were rung at the register with a minimum of speech, so little that Parrish worried Duncan had caught the flu bug being passed around. He didn't look exactly sad, but his lanky shoulders drooped a bit more loosely, sad-like, and his eyes glanced more slowly about, as if his mind were preoccupied. Even espresso seemed to have lost its spirited effect.

Mason was due to come in at four thirty so Parrish could leave. As four o'clock approached, Duncan watched the clock, agitated and biting his nails. He mumbled to himself as only Duncan could—the half of the argument that was spoken was the dissenting voice, mumbling all that Duncan shouldn't do. He leaned on the espresso bar, nervously patting the top of his head with his hand, as if gentle persistence might nudge his thoughts out of hiding.

Parrish decided to help him along.

"What's up, Dunc?" he asked, giving his friend's back a harmless pop with a damp, twisted rag.

"Huh? Oh, nothing," Duncan said.

Parrish walked away, removed a used filter of coffee grounds from the brewer, threw it in the trash, then put in a fresh one.

Duncan stared across the store.

"What else?" Parrish asked. "Besides nothing."

Duncan shook his head, made two docile fists with his hands on the top of the espresso machine, then leaned his chin on them.

Parrish waited.

Duncan opened his mouth wide, closed it, mumbled to himself. Then he blurted out, "Audra seems nice."

"She is."

"I mean…" Duncan tilted his head, as if he were rolling his thought side to side. "I'm happy for you."

"A tad premature on the congratulations, but thanks."

"And the way that happened—"

Again Parrish waited. He stopped working and crossed his arms, so Duncan could see his undivided attention. "Yeah?"

"The way that happened…" Duncan slid one fist out in front of his nose and regarded it, a personal visual aid. "It was the *cookie*."

"Okay…"

"So I was wondering…" Duncan gave his cookie-fist an inquisitive, confused look. "Could I *borrow* it?"

Parrish processed this, filled in all the gaps and segues that were missing, and rearranged the problem so he could solve for x.

"I don't need the cookie bits. I'm sure you threw those out," Duncan continued, looking at his fist as if it were a very solid thing. "But if you'd let me borrow the *fortune* part, maybe I—"

"Duncan, can I buy you a dog or something?"

"I'm serious."

There was no questioning his sincerity. That was not what Parrish questioned.

"You took a chance, you know?" Once begun, Duncan grew more animated, more convinced. "And it paid off. So—"

The bell above the front door jangled harshly as Mason kicked it open. He used his boot because his hands were filled with plastic shopping bags, six of them, bulging full. Leaving the door wide open to the cold, he traipsed over to the largest table, a four top, and lifted the bags onto it. He started to unload them, then stopped, pointed at the bags as if he were warning them to stay put, and jogged around the counter to get himself coffee. Parrish stepped in his way and gave a mock shiver until Mason went back and closed the front door. Then Mason pushed past Parrish, bumped Duncan aside, and pulled himself an espresso.

"Good to see you too," said Parrish. "You know, Duncan and I were having a conversation."

Mason seemed to notice Duncan for the first time. He raised the small cup of coffee to his lips. "'Bout what?"

"My fortune cookie," said Parrish. "He wants to borrow it."

"Just the fortune," amended Duncan.

Mason downed the espresso in two quick gulps. "Why?"

Duncan looked at his shoes.

Tossing the empty cup in the sink, Mason narrowed his eyes and glanced back and forth between them. "You think there's a busload of beauties waiting for you, Dunc?"

"Leave him alone," Parrish said. "What's in the bags?"

"If you don't want to let me borrow the fortune," Duncan said, struggling as if his topic would be lost forever if he didn't pursue it then, "you have that *other* cookie—"

"Hey!" Mason snapped his fingers. "He's right. I've been meaning to say something. You got two cookies Monday, and one of those is mine." He looked at Duncan. "Or Dunc's." He pointed a finger between them. "Or ours. Collectively."

"I just want to borrow it."

"No way!" Mason grabbed Duncan's elbow. "We have a right to that cookie."

Parrish disagreed. "First, some of you may recall skipping out on the tab."

"Come on, Parrish!" Mason pulled in his chin and threw open his arms. "We were joking."

"Joke still cost me three meals."

"All right, all right, we're sorry! Dunc, pay him."

"Too late." Parrish checked his watch, then pushed himself away from the counter. "I paid the *whole* tab, I get *all* the cookies." He walked toward the back room to fetch his coat.

Mason followed him as far as the hall and yelled to him as he went in the back. "That breaks all the known rules of fortune-getting. One person gets one fortune, not two. Practically rips at the fabric of the whole space-time thingy, people taking multiple fortunes."

Returning, Parrish stopped to button his coat. "Okay, tell me. If a person eats at Wu's one day, then eats at Wu's again the following day, could they have a second cookie?"

Logically, Mason had to agree. "One fortune per meal, perhaps per day, but definitely per meal."

"Well, I ate there last night with Audra and neither of us got a cookie because some maniac had bought them all. Good thing I saved a cookie, so now you only owe me one."

Duncan weighed his vote, then agreed. "He's got a point."

"No," insisted Mason. "Mr. Wu owes him one."

Parrish pushed past. "What's in the bags?" He walked toward them.

"Can I just *see* the fortune?" Duncan pleaded.

"No."

Mason ran around the counter to protect his shopping bags. "Parrish! We ate the meals attached to *that* cookie. We're talking fortunes, not fruit cups. Food you can swap out. Fortunes are connected to the meal-eaters in an entirely different way."

"You're not getting the cookie or the fortune, either of you," Parrish said definitively. "Tell me these bags aren't full of what I think they're full of."

Mason put up a hand like a politician quieting a cheering crowd. "Let me show you. You're going to love this."

He upturned the bags one by one, dumping countless fortune cookies in a heap on the table, so many they spilled over the side and dropped to the floor.

Duncan ran his hand lightly across the wrappers, apparently in awe to be so near a heap of possible dates.

"You have *all* the cookies. Why do you need my one?" asked Parrish.

"This? This is my project." Mason made a grand gesture with his hand. "You got the real deal, we've seen that. And I still want my cookie back. But this, this is phase two."

Parrish sank his hands in his pockets and shook his head. Duncan picked up a cookie, but Mason took it from him and threw it back on the heap.

Mason explained. "Listen, what would the Chinese meal be without a fortune cookie? Ricey. That's all. And why do we expect, why have we come to depend on, why would we not be satisfied without a fortune cookie after a Chinese meal? Marketing, pure and simple. Someone did it long enough until everybody did it. Now it *hurts* to think of a white paper sack with no cookie under all those little square boxes. Right? So…"

He stretched his hands out in the air to demonstrate the marquee.

"'A Cup of Joe and God to Go,'" he said, then watched, waiting for the effect to sink in before he continued. "People want direction in their lives. We can get in on the ground floor. Think of it. When the God cookies catch on, when you can't buy a cup of coffee in America without reaching into the jar and grabbing a God-ordained destiny or directive or theological tidbit, man, it'll be like…like…hash browns. Can you see this?"

Parrish gave Mason the blankest of stares, then walked away.

"I'm totally serious, Parrish!"

"That's why I'm leaving." Parrish opened the front door and shut it slowly as he called out, "Do *not* put those out in my store."

Parrish planned to arrive before the five o'clock bus. Yesterday, he'd missed the bus and ended up waiting forever; a little earlier would ensure he'd meet more people. If that was helping out God, he didn't feel God would mind. Besides, he had arbitrarily decided to go to the bus stop at five every day because that's what he'd done the first day. Why not 4:50? Maybe God, like other professionals, expected him to be ten minutes early so things could get rolling *at* five.

His plan worked.

For a freezing afternoon, the corner was remarkably busy. The bus puffed at the corner with its door open, allowing a line of people to step up, run their bus cards, then continue inside. Audra and Rose sat on their usual benches, knitting and reading, but two other women and a man loitered there as well.

As Parrish walked up to the line waiting to get on the bus, one last passenger shoved his way out the door. He already had a cigarette dangling from his lip, ready to light. When they recognized each other, both he and Parrish turned and walked separate directions. The last thing Parrish wanted on a cold day was to get punched. This put Parrish a short way down from the crowd, nearer the actual corner of street meeting street. Here, he found himself next to a lady listening to messages on her cell phone.

"Excuse me," said Parrish, stepping up to her.

The lady shot up her index finger, signaling she needed a moment more of devoted concentration with her phone, then frowned and used that same finger to plug her free ear in hopes this would deafen the roar of the bus engine as it pulled away. As the cloud of diesel fumes wafted over her, she turned her body away from it, tensing defensively as if a small bomb had exploded behind her, all the while straining to hear the message.

She was no frequenter of buses, Parrish deduced. She wore a stylish brown skirt suit under her expensive trench coat, but both her suit and her coat seemed determined to twist around her body in opposing directions. This peril for the moment proved unfixable, and she wore an afflicted expression, the kind only a person accustomed to the long-held luxury of her own vehicle, who found herself tragically forced into the hustle of public transit could produce. Besides her alligator purse, she also sported a soft leather attaché case, both of which she had deposited on the sidewalk, holding them safely between her feet. She had long, blond-dyed hair, expensively done with wisps of differing shades of blond to accent and give depth. One darker strand persisted in falling into her face. She persisted in swiping it back, a motion between perfunctory and peeved. Had she not been so urgently devouring the messages one after the other, she probably would have become annoyed enough to do something about the wayward hair, but as it was, she punched at the buttons on her phone and listened again. She bent down, exasperated, shoved a hand into her purse, removed a pen, stood upright, then uncapped the pen with her teeth. She jotted a phone number the only place she could, on the thin wrist of the hand that held the phone. Finally, she flapped her phone shut and glared at Parrish.

"What?"

"You okay?' he asked.

"No, I am not okay!" Her neck strained as she yelled. "My fancy rental car is not only currently parked in the middle of some street loaded with honking hillbilly traffic, but also has smoke trailing from under the hood. My insurance agent is suddenly unsure if my puzzling policy covers a replacement rental car for a broken-down fancy rental car. The fancy rental car people are, of course, nowhere to be found. None of which helps *me* to get to the airport, which is where I was told *this* bus let off, and there are *no* cabs in this cabless town! I've called four different cab numbers in your city's phone book, and every time I get the same fried chicken restaurant. How can I help you?"

"Do you need a ride to the airport?" Parrish asked.

The blond woman leaned her entire weight back over one foot. "That's all I need, that and a whiskey sour, but you could be a crazy person, so I'm never getting in a car with you. What did you really want?"

He produced the letter from his coat pocket. "I wanted to know if you dropped this—"

"Oh, my *God*! This stupid purse!" she screamed. She grabbed the letter from his hands, then bent over, more strands of expensive blond hair rebelling and breaking free as she snatched up her purse. Standing again, she rummaged through it dramatically.

"Where did you see me drop it?" She put her purse beneath an arm and held it while she rumpled the paper open and stared at it, then turned it right side up and stared at it again.

"I found it the other day. There's probably no way it's yours, but sincerely, if you need a ride, I work right over there, and my car's—"

"Stop!" She held out a hand to cut off his talking and threw a hip to one side, causing more twisting from the skirt. "If you *didn't* think the letter was mine," she said, holding the disheveled purse accusatively out in front of her, "then why did you ask me to look for it?"

Parrish had no answer, nor time to think of one, because at that moment, two things happened. The woman, dismissing the letter, shoved it back into Parrish's chest. Instinctively, he grabbed it with both hands. As he did so, like a blur, a kid with cropped hair and wearing tattered jeans and a baggy sweatshirt pushed suddenly between them. He grabbed the lady's purse with both hands, hugged it into his stomach like a football, and ran full tilt across the parking lot.

"Thief!" the lady yelled, stamping her shoe and breaking off a heel. She turned on Parrish. "You! You set me up! Where's my mace?"

Parrish watched, too stunned to realize that if she found her mace, it was his eyes she meant to spray. The lady desperately picked up her attaché case, dug through it violently but unsuccessfully. Her mace, of course, was in her purse. She stared in the direction the kid had fled, stomped again, then turned and punched Parrish in the stomach.

Audra leapt up. "Wait, he didn't——"

"Did you see them?" The blond woman screamed to Audra, another woman and a possible witness. "They're in cahoots!"

"No, wait!" Audra said, running up to her. "He asks people about that letter. He does it every day."

The lady seized the collar of Parrish's jacket and yelled, "Police!"

"He didn't have anything to do with your purse!" insisted Audra.

"You should've run when you had the chance, Mack!" the woman said loudly to the back of Parrish's head. He was still doubled over.

"He didn't run," Audra explained, "because he didn't have anything to do with the guy who stole your purse. I know him. He's with me."

The blond woman stared at Audra, sizing her up. With a nasty jerk, she released Parrish's coat and dropped her hands to her side, breathing rapidly.

Audra took Parrish by the shoulders, helped him straighten and stand. "You all right?"

"Good punch, lady," Parrish answered hoarsely.

"Well!" The blond woman glared harshly into Parrish's face. "Even if you weren't in cahoots, you helped!"

"Sorry 'bout that."

The lady huffed. "That's all you have to say?"

"Uh…very sorry?"

Clearly, this was not the answer the woman wanted. She jabbed a long, bright red fingernail into his chest. "Well, don't just stand there!" She stared at Parrish, her mouth clenched tight.

Parrish looked at the blond woman, but he was talking to God. "You've got to be kidding."

It was difficult to run.

His work boots clomped flatly, and his coat, mostly unzipped, twisted and slid off his shoulders as he clumsily picked up speed. After the surprise jab to the gut, he winded easily, but he had the advantage of knowing the surroundings. He knew about the steep dirt incline and the tall chain-link fence that lined the parking lot behind this strip mall. To run behind this strip mall was something of a trap—either come out the way you went in or way at the opposite end. Parrish ran toward the far end. Had the thief known, surely he wouldn't have run back there in the first place, Parrish thought. Unless the thief had a car, or an accomplice, an entire purse-snatching gang waiting silently for their friend's return, sharpening their knives. The pain in his gut tightened with each stride.

Running past the shoe store, the last store, he grabbed the metal post and swung around the corner, then hurried along the brick wall until he came to its back edge and leaned his back against the wall to catch his breath.

Already he'd broken a sweat. His hot breaths huffed out steamily against the cold, and his tongue gave his upper lip a salty lick. Pushing off the wall, he peeked around the corner. He saw no one, just the long row of identical loading docks, raised square structures with cement stairs and yellow lines painted along their edges. He crept out and around the corner, keeping low and close to the wall. Nearing the first loading dock, he crept up the stairs, and from that higher vantage, he spotted the thief.

Several loading docks away, the young man squatted beside a Dumpster with the purse between his knees. He hunched athletically, bouncing on the balls of his feet, ready to bolt away. The thief rifled the purse, threw a few things down, examined others, but finally dumped it entirely onto the pavement. This revealed the wallet more quickly. The thief grabbed the wallet, opened it, thumbing immediately, expertly to the credit cards. He flipped those out, dropped them on the ground between his feet, then turned the wallet sidelong and snatched out a thick stack of bills. He spread the bills quickly through his fingers to take an impatient estimate. Then he dropped the wallet and rocked forward onto his knees to shove the cards and cash into the front pocket of his jeans.

Parrish didn't have much time. He took a deep breath, then jumped down from the dock and ran straight toward the thief.

The young man heard the heavy slap of Parrish's boots instantly. He sprang to his feet, ran straight for the dirt incline, and darted up it with amazing efficiency. As he neared the top he gave a leap, clung to the chain-link fence, and began to crawl upward.

"You've got to be kidding."

This became Parrish's mantra—to himself, to God. He unzipped his coat the rest of the way and wriggled it off his shoulders so that it fell behind as he ran. Moving so fast, he took the first few steps up the incline with a bounding stride, but then stumbled. He caught his fall with both palms, getting a mouthful of dirt, then scrambled on all fours up the hill to the bottom of the fence.

The young thief had made progress upward, but the fence was very tall and the chain links were too small and their metal too slick for proper footholds. The thief propelled himself more by the fast, continuous pumping of his legs, his shoes sliding furiously up and down, and pulling his weight through his fingers' grip. Parrish had no chance of climbing this fence, not in his work boots, not in any case, so he made a last surge to reach out and grab the thief's thrashing foot.

When caught, the thief kicked wildly, both feet pummeling Parrish in the chest and shoulders. Already exhausted, Parrish gripped the ankle with both hands, then heaved himself backward, allowing his own weight as well as gravity to bring the young man down atop him. They tumbled in a heap, Parrish predominately on the bottom, and ended with the thief tossed in a high-flying crash on the asphalt at the bottom of the hill.

Both lay moaning for a moment, then the thief began to roll himself over.

"Can we stop now?" Parrish called out.

"Screw you!" bellowed the young man, not nearly as breathless as his pursuer.

Parrish slid muddily down the rest of the hill, feet first, and landed on top of the thief, who refused to be so easily pinned. The young man twisted his body around, and Parrish's face received the full effect of the thief's feet kicking and thrashing—he'd have a swollen lip, a nasty bump behind his right ear, and he took a dizzying heel to the bridge of his nose.

The thief wriggled loose and crawled a few steps until he could stand. He stooped over a moment to breathe and decide which way to run.

That gave Parrish time to stand. "Give me back her money."

"Who are you?"

"Come on, let's stop."

"Why should I?" The thief laughed. "I'm winning."

"Good point," said Parrish.

They watched each other, waiting to see who'd begin it again. Parrish lunged forward, but the young man darted away, back in the direction from which he'd come. Parrish followed, and the chase continued, but unlike movie characters, neither moved as fast as they had before. In real life, people grow tired of running.

But the thief proved faster and pulled quickly ahead of Parrish by a considerable length. He would have easily escaped had an eighteen-wheeler not pulled around the corner. The young man slowed. Faced with running back toward his pursuer or running forward around the awkwardly angled truck, he slowed. The truck driver blew his horn—one long, deep sound followed by six or seven short bursts, then another sustained blast. The young man halted completely. He turned and saw Parrish close the distance between them.

Penned in, the young man chose the only option left to him and darted between two loading docks. He ran to the only door he saw, grabbed the knob with both hands and shook it violently. It was locked.

"Hey!" Parrish yelled as he ran up, positioning himself between the two docks. "Can we stop, please?"

The young man turned. With a loading dock to either side and a locked door behind him, he was cornered. They both panted, staring at each other.

But just then, the locked door opened from the inside. With a bag of garbage in her hands, Min San backed her way out the delivery door to Mr. Wu's.

Instantly, the thief grabbed her. She shrieked and dropped the bag, her hands instinctively protecting her face. The thief pushed her roughly to one side and grabbed the open door. He tripped once over the bag, tearing it, spilling garbage, until he disappeared inside.

Parrish ran forward and lunged to catch the door.

"Are you okay?" he said, turning to where Min San had fallen.

She pulled herself into a sitting position against the wall, touched her scuffed elbows. She nodded that she was fine.

"Stay here," Parrish said, then hopped the garbage and went inside.

He paused and glanced around, finding only a broom, which he grabbed. Then he ran down the hallway, past the stockroom and washrooms, into the dining room.

"You get outta here!" Charles yelled.

With a baseball bat held high, clutched tightly in his hands, Charles stood blocking the front door and staring at the thief, who had stopped midway through the dining room, between two recently vacated tables. The customers who had been sitting there shoved past Parrish on their way out of the dining room toward the back door. Another customer sat in a corner table by himself, eating happily, as if he were watching a television show. The thief took a step backward, then turned to go back out the way he'd come.

Parrish stood there with the broom.

"Look, it's over," said Parrish, resting the broom on his shoulder. "How about you throw the lady's money on the table, and we're done, okay?"

The young thief reached under his sweatshirt and pulled out a handgun. From across the room, he pointed it at Parrish's face. "How about you throw down your wallet?"

You've got to be kidding. Parrish would have said this, had all the air not left his lungs.

"No, John," yelled Charles. "Don't give it to him!"

The thief spun around and pointed the gun at Charles. "How about you pop open that register?"

"Whoa, whoa, Charles!" said Parrish.

The gun swung back around toward Parrish's face.

"No!" yelled Charles, brandishing the bat higher. "I will *not* give you register!"

The gun turned back toward Charles.

Parrish took several steps toward the thief. "Easy, guy, come on. Take my wallet, here. Look." Dropping the broom, Parrish took out his wallet, then moved another step closer. "But this is his life, his business—"

The gun faced Parrish again. "And this is my business!" yelled the thief.

Charles said. "He can't shoot us both, John, before I knock him."

The thief turned his body so he could better see them both, switched the gun to his other hand, and pointed it at Charles.

"Charles, please, don't talk right now."

The thief kept the gun pointed at Charles but eyed Parrish. "Stay back!"

Parrish held his hands up in the air, stood still. "Easy, okay, easy…"

Then Min San entered the back of the dining room. Seeing Parrish's arms raised, the gun, the baseball bat, she shrieked again.

Now the gun swung toward her.

Parrish had always heard the expression "knees knocking together." He had always thought that an exaggeration, until his did it. He took a big step closer, putting himself between the gun barrel and Min San.

"Don't even think about it!" the thief yelled. He closed one eye and aimed the gun sideways at Parrish. "You want to get shot today?"

"No," said Parrish calmly. "I definitely do not want to be…wait a minute." Parrish took another step forward and stared hard at the gun. Then he lowered his hands.

The young man retreated a step. "Get back! Or I'll shoot!"

"Not with that you won't." Parrish put his wallet in his back pocket. "My nephew's got one of those."

"Get back!"

"Come on, the trucker's probably called the police," Parrish said. "Just give me the lady's money."

"I'm going to shoot you," the thief threatened.

"Seeing as you've already kicked me a hundred times in the face, the little orange dart won't hurt that much."

"This gun is real!"

"It's a toy," said Parrish. "My nephew's is metal too. Looks real, very heavy, but the darts are very plastic."

"I'm going to shoot your face." The thief gripped the gun in both hands and aimed.

"No, you're not." Parrish took another step toward him. "You don't even have a dart loaded."

The thief shifted his feet, then lowered the gun slowly. He took a step closer to Parrish as if he were giving up. Then he pulled his arm back over his shoulder and threw the gun straight at Parrish's head.

It contacted above the right eye, a hard blow. The heavy metal toy bounced off Parrish's face, then landed in a tray of fried rice.

"Ow!" Parrish stumbled backward. "You've got to be—"

The thief turned, ran straight at Charles. He ducked under Charles's swing, knocked him down, then ran out the front door.

Parrish watched through the glass as the young man ran through the parking lot, checking over his shoulder to see if anyone followed. As he looked, he ran straight into the squad car that pulled up. He fell across the hood, slapping it with both hands and sprawling atop it. The officer quickly hopped out and pinned him there.

Parrish leaned against the buffet, holding his head. He felt something warm and wet on his cheek, touched it with his fingers, then checked to see if it was blood. It was. He blinked as a drop of blood caught in his eyelashes. He wiped his eye with the back of his hand, then grabbed a stack of napkins and pressed them over the gash.

He walked out to the squad car, watching as a policeman pressed the young man's chest down onto the hood and cuffed his hands behind his back. The squad car's passenger door opened and Audra got out. Parrish watched as she nodded to the officer, identifying the thief. The officer emptied the young man's pockets of the credit cards and cash.

Audra walked around the car to Parrish. "You're bleeding, John."

"The rest of her purse is out back by the Dumpster." Then he felt his back pocket. "Do I still have my wallet?"

"Come here and sit down." Audra led him to the passenger's seat of the squad car, then examined the cut.

"Ouch!" he yelled.

"I need to clean this off to see if you need stitches."

"No stitches," he barked.

"Do you have a first-aid kit at the shop?"

"Yes," he said. "Audra?"

"Yes, John?"

"Could I have a cup of coffee?"

"This needs stitches…" Audra stood beside him as he sat at a small table in his coffee shop. She wiped at the blood with the only thing she had at the moment, napkins. A pile of blood-messed napkins lay crumpled on the table. Despite her wishes, Parrish adamantly refused to go to the emergency room. After all, he was conscious, he could sit without tipping over, and his eye wasn't hanging out of his head.

"Are you sure we have a first-aid kit?" Duncan asked, coming out of the back room a second time.

Audra tried again. "If this doesn't stop bleeding—"

"It'll stop. And yes, Duncan, we have a first-aid kit. It's against the law not to have one. I bought a brand-new one a couple months ago because you and Mason cut the last one to pieces when you made that newspaper slingshot."

"Yeah, where is that?"

"I threw the slingshot out."

"Why?" asked Duncan. "That was cool."

"'Cause it was supposed to be a first-aid kit!"

"What we cut up...you're saying that was a first-aid kit?" Duncan waited, but received no answer. "It didn't look like a first-aid kit."

"Duncan!" Parrish yelled so loud Audra jumped.

"Parrish, sit still," she said, pressing her hand on his shoulder.

Duncan shook his hands in the air. "I'm sorry, I'm sorry, I'm sorry! Tell me one more time, what does the first-aid kit look like?"

"It's bright orange, Dunc." Parrish blinked harshly and held up a defensive hand as Audra wiped at his face. "Go in the back room and look for the bright orange things."

"Are you kidding?"

"Go!"

Audra closed her eyes for a moment and took a deep breath. "You should have a doctor check this out, even if it does stop bleeding."

"I don't like—"

From the back room, they heard Duncan yell, "Can you come back here and show me? Mason doesn't see it either!"

Parrish took a deep breath to fill his lungs for his next shout. Audra took a step back. "Come out here now!"

With blood on her fingers, Audra used the back of her hand to smooth the sweat off her forehead.

Duncan appeared, both hands empty. Parrish wagged a crooked finger at him. "Look at me!"

Duncan came a tiny step closer.

"You know how, on Saturdays, you like to wear Band-Aids on all your knuckles when you have to work the espresso machine all morning?"

"Sure," Duncan nodded.

"Where do you *get* the Band-Aids?"

"There's like seven boxes of Band-Aids back there in a duffel bag."

"Is the duffel bag orange with a big white plus sign on the side?"

"Oh." Duncan stood blankly. "Got it." He walked away.

"Ouch!" Parrish grimaced as Audra's fingers again explored the cut above his eye.

"Please," she pleaded, "sit still so I can see what I'm doing."

"You're hurting my head. I can see that without an eye."

"Parrish, hold still." She leaned her face closer. "This needs stitches."

"No stitches!" He moaned. "I don't like pain. Ow!"

Duncan returned from the back room, this time with the orange bag. "I think it was the word *kit* that was throwing me."

"Great," bellowed Parrish. "I'll try not to use big words around you anymore."

"Here's ice," announced Mason, also coming out of the back

room. He balanced a mug of coffee in one hand, and the other held a big red bucket heaping with ice. He plopped the bucket heavily atop the crumpled napkins and several cubes tumbled free. Parrish's table shook and wobbled.

"Thanks." Parrish stared at the ice. "Now if I only had something besides this bucket to put it in."

"I know," said Mason, blowing on his coffee. "That's the problem."

"Really?" Parrish twisted around to see him, so that Audra, once again, stopped and waited. "Figured that out yourself?"

"Parrish, hush," whispered Audra.

"Right," said Mason. "If you can stick your head in a *bucket* full of ice, you might as well have just stuck your head in the ice machine."

Parrish's eyes glinted at the bucket, like he might shove it off the table.

Very calmly, Audra turned to Mason. "Could you bring me some towels or rags? Maybe we could twist some ice up in one."

Mason shook his head. "The rags are all dirty. Rag guy usually comes today, but he called blood boy yesterday and said his driver's sick. You don't want a dirty rag for his head, do you?"

"No, you're right." She took a piece of ice to clean some of the blood off her hands. "We shouldn't use a dirty rag."

Parrish torqued around. "I *told* you two to wash out rags last night!"

Audra took some ice in her hand and pressed it to his forehead. "Parrish, hush."

"Ow!" Parrish grabbed the table. "No, I'm sick of this." He turned again and the ice fell from her hand onto the floor. "Why didn't you wash out rags last night like I said?"

Mason scowled. "Well, your royal pain-ness, we were actually *busy* last night, so we didn't have time, so Susan said she'd take a load home and throw them in her washing machine, which I'm sure she did because as we all know she's more reliable than me and Dunc. But Susan's not here yet. That's why we can't *see* her. When she does get here, we can all run out to her car and roll around in the freshly laundered rags, but until then—"

Audra intervened. "Could you maybe take some plastic wrap and make an ice bag?"

Mason looked at her and nodded politely. "Well, Audra, that's a terrific idea. I'll get right on that. Way to problem-solve. Have you ever considered going into management?"

He walked behind the counter. As he did, Parrish threw a handful of ice at him. Audra flinched.

"You shouldn't do that," Mason yelled, ducking. "Susan gets really mad when we throw ice on the floor."

Having brought Audra the kit, Duncan moved out of Parrish's range.

Audra moved the ice bucket off the table and replaced it with the first-aid kit. She unzipped it, then dug through its contents. Parrish watched her pull out gauze and tape, scissors, and a squirt bottle of antiseptic solution. Using some of the gauze, she stopped the bleeding, then opened the squeeze bottle.

"This'll probably sting," she warned Parrish.

"Perfect," he mumbled.

Carefully, she doused the gauze with solution, then held it under the cut so none of the antiseptic would splash into his eye. Then she poured a dab directly on the wound.

"Holy mug of Joseph!" Parrish gripped the table.

"Okay, okay, that's over." Audra cleaned the spot, then looped more gauze around her hand.

Parrish gritted his teeth. "You have *no* idea how fun this is!"

"Oh, I've got my ideas," she said, picking up the scissors and cutting a strip of tape.

"Duncan!" Parrish bellowed.

"Parrish?"

"Make yourself useful and bring a garbage bag for all this mess!"

"Right-o, chief!" Duncan saluted.

"Mason!"

Audra took Parrish's face in her hands and looked him squarely in the eye. "Please! You were quite brave. Now sit still and let me fix this."

For the first time, Parrish actually tried to sit still. But she had to press the gauze firmly while she taped it.

"Ow! Stop it!" he blurted.

Audra shook her head. "Calm down, cranky baby."

"Okay, okay, just hurry up!" he said. "Easy! This hurts, little girl!"

Perhaps it was that phrase, perhaps it was the many other things he'd said, perhaps she'd winced once too often at all their angry replies, but at this, Audra raised her hands in front of her and took a step back. She cocked her jaw as if she tasted something bitter, then bit her lip and rocked her weight back and forth, her eyes filling with tears. She refused them, shaking her head fiercely, and tossed the scissors and the tape on the table in front of Parrish. She wiped her hands furiously with the gauze, dropped it, then walked over to her coat, grabbed it up without putting it on, shouldered her bag, and yanked the front door open.

"Audra…," Parrish tried. "Wait."

"Fix yourself, big man!" And she slammed the door.

That night, Parrish couldn't sleep.

After Audra's exit from the shop, he'd taped the most slipshod and massive of bandages above his eye. It was pitiful—both how it looked and how meagerly it covered the wound. He probably could have used a few stitches above his eye, but instead of going to a doctor, he wrapped his head like a Civil War soldier. He then proceeded to complain and drink innumerable shots of espresso before everyone voted him out of his own store. Back in his apartment, he spent the evening flipping through endless and uninteresting channels until his head began to throb. He chewed aspirin, swallowed ibuprofen, crunched vitamin C cough drops, made sandwiches he did not eat, then put himself to bed.

At midnight, having tossed and mumbled for over an hour, he finally gave up on sleep, put his street clothes back on, grabbed his jacket, and went for a walk. He walked without much of a plan, but eventually meandered to his corner—the cookie corner—and plopped down on the bus stop bench. He stared across to his distant coffee shop, locked up tight, its lights long since snuffed. This late, the dark parking lots, empty of cars, looked completely desolate as the wind tumbled trash across them.

This night was especially chilly, and Parrish took it personally. His head throbbed in the night air. He wished it would go ahead and snow, instead of just threatening. Strangely, snowfall made the air less cold.

"I give up." Parrish said this out loud, looking upward. "You hear me?"

Nothing happened.

He walked over to the route sign at the curb, grabbed it with both hands, and shook it uselessly. The sign, planted deeply in concrete, barely wiggled. So he did the only sensible thing—he kicked it, then limped back to his seat.

"You're going to let me just sit here and give up?"

The streetlight loomed directly above his bench, casting him in a circle of light that only heightened his sense of self-pity. He squinted up at it, wishing it ill, and even glanced around for a rock sizable enough to throw, though the buzzing bulb hovered too high for a likely hit.

"I'm going to keep on giving up until you do something!"

Nothing happened.

Parrish jumped up and gave the sign a second and more thorough throttling.

As he did so, another light suddenly hit him, and a siren blipped twice. Parrish turned and watched the squad car glide to a halt, lurching slightly as the officer put it in park. With the light on the squad car pointing brightly in his eyes, he squinted to see the heavy silhouette of the policeman as he got out.

"You need a sign," the policeman called out, "or are you just tearing that one up?"

Parrish dropped his head, shook it weakly, then raised his face with a gesture of surrender. The officer clicked the spotlight off and turned it downward, the hot bulb glowing orange for the few seconds it took to cool and go completely dark. His squad car still running, the officer closed his door and took a few careful steps toward Parrish, one hand holding a long black flashlight, the other on his holster. He stopped at an official distance, then cocked his head.

"You okay, buddy?"

Parrish blinked, his eyes still adjusting. "Sorry about that."

"How's that head?" asked the policeman.

Parrish raised a hand, only remembering the ridiculous bandage when his fingers touched the gauze. "This? It's nothing, really."

"It bled pretty bad earlier," said the officer, taking his hand off his holster and coming forward. "Did you have someone look at that?"

Parrish recognized him then—the same officer from his purse-snatching afternoon.

The policeman clicked on his flashlight and shone it on Parrish's bandages. "Are you dizzy?"

"No sir. My strangling a bus sign cannot, unfortunately, be blamed on my head wound."

"Whoever wrapped this did an awful job." The policeman lowered the flashlight. "Do you want me to take you to the hospital?"

"I'd be thrilled if this ended with you not taking me anywhere."

"Aw, you can't hurt that sign." The officer tapped the sign with the hefty flashlight, metal on metal. "Hurt you more than you'll hurt it."

Parrish stood shivering. He could feel the tape on the bandages giving way. Soon the entire mess would fall off his head.

The officer glanced about the parking lot. "You on foot?"

"Yeah."

The officer acknowledged this, then rubbed the back of his neck with his hand. "God, I'm tired."

Parrish nodded. "Long shift?"

"Two p.m. to two a.m.," he said, yawning once, then giving Parrish a very official glance up and down. "What are you doing at a bus stop in the middle of the night?"

Parrish sat on the bench to consider his answer. He closed one eye and cocked his head at the officer. "You believe in God?"

The cop gave Parrish a harsh frown.

"You said, 'God, I'm tired.'" Parrish explained. "You sort of mentioned him."

The officer gave Parrish's wounded head a second appraisal, then huffed. "Well, I don't go to church much, if that's what you mean."

Parrish nodded.

After an awkward pause, the policeman relaxed his shoulders and put a boot up on the bench. "Too crowded."

Parrish looked up at him. "What?'

"Church. All those people congratulating each other." He gave a long look across the abandoned parking lot. "I'd prefer a God who hung out in the empty places. That's a God I could use."

Parrish nodded. Then he pointed at the squad car. "Tough work, I bet?"

"It's a job." The policeman spat once. "What about you?"

"Coffee. That's my shop." Parrish pointed across the street.

"Right, your girlfriend mentioned that."

Parrish flinched, but the officer took no notice. He took off his hat and examined the inside band with his hand.

"We give policemen free drip coffee," Parrish said. "Come in anytime."

The officer smiled and arched his back with a stretch. "I'll take you up on that."

The two men remained in the bright pool of light given off by the streetlamp above, scanning the empty parking lot.

"So let me run this past you…," Parrish began.

"Shoot," said the officer.

"Say a person did believe in God, and that person thought God sent him to a bus stop—say, this one. But God didn't say why, just to do it. How does that sound to you?"

The officer shrugged. "Sounds like that gauze might be wrapped too tight."

Parrish reached a hand up and adjusted the bandages so they wouldn't fall off.

The officer took his boot off the bench, planted it firmly on the sidewalk, put his thumbs in his belt, and struck an official stance. "I'd say God could probably do a whole lot more at an empty bus stop than all those church people combined. I bet God thinks church is a bit too crowded most of the time."

The policeman donned his hat again, signaling his break was over.

"I'll let you get back to your...," the officer said, wagging a finger at the sign, then walked back to his squad car and drove away.

Parrish slumped on the bench, exhausted. He had to be at work in a few hours, he should go home and try to sleep. He shoved his hands deep in his coat pockets. As he did so, his left hand felt the crinkle of plastic. He took out the wrapped fortune cookie—the second one—and turned it in his hand.

He didn't open it immediately. He'd opened one cookie and now he had a head wound. Two cookies, he might not live out the week. He looked up at the streetlight above, staring at its glow as if it might be looking at him, then tore the plastic. Taking the cookie out of its wrapper, he crunched it in his hand, put a small piece in his mouth, then pulled the fortune free and closed it up in his hand. He didn't look at it, not until he'd walked the plastic and the rest of the uneaten cookie pieces over to the garbage and thrown them away. He came back and arranged himself squarely on the bench.

Then he read the second fortune: HOPE IS TO REJOICE EARLY.

He nodded with a sense of satisfaction—this, at least, sounded like a fortune cookie. It was vaguely meaningful, the way a cookie should be. More bumper sticker than directive, nothing he had to jump up and do. Good cookie.

He stared at the fortune, turned the phrase over in his mind, tried to recall what he currently had hope about. The shortest bit of reflection revealed he had nothing that qualified as hope. He could come up with a few things he wanted, like an extremely premature Christmas list, but that list was all about things—new chairs for the coffee shop, a flat-screen television, a sports watch with a timer. Things weren't hope.

Then he considered the letter. He could hope to find the owner. That seemed most pertinent—but, honestly, he was sick of the whole letter business. He didn't want to talk about that, not even with God. And if God was nudging him to hope, then probably he *should* hope for peace on earth or something equally auspicious, but that felt a bit too grand for his first run at this.

Then he remembered snow. He liked snow. He could hope for snow, and not to be disrespectful, but that gave God good odds. It would snow again eventually anyway. But technically, he couldn't "hope" for something inevitable. That was cheating. On the other hand, if he shut his eyes tight and demanded snow right then, even if it happened, there wouldn't be any time for the hoping part. Hope needed a time frame, something between the immediacy of a magic wish and a seven-day weather forecast.

Parrish looked upward. Though night, he could still see the impenetrable layer of cloud cover—no moon, no stars.

"God," he began, "I'd like to ask for snow, please. Before the week is out. There. This is a stupid request and there's no reason for you to do so. I'm okay if you don't. But…" He held up the fortune. "Hope is to rejoice early…"

Nothing happened, of course, and it was desperately quiet.

Parrish buried his hands back in his pockets. He didn't *feel* hopeful. He felt absurd, but absurd was better than what he'd felt all day, felt much lighter. Just the thought of rejoicing early for snow he'd requested by the end of the week, this was laughable. But not bad kind of laughing—the mean kind, or at someone's expense. It was a shared laugh, like he and God were up to something.

Moments earlier, he'd almost thrown out the snow idea because snowing was inevitable, but now he was less certain. What if it wasn't? What if *his* snow were the last of the winter? Snow was more beautiful when it was hoped for. Was this what hope did to everything?

On an empty corner at a cold bus bench, Parrish sat looking up at the night sky, expectantly.

Friday

F riday afternoon, Parrish walked slowly across the parking lot to the bus stop. From a distance, he saw Audra on her usual bench, her head bowed over a paperback novel. She was alone. For the first time since the cookie, even Mrs. Miranda was absent.

Sitting at the far end of her bench with her bag gathered close to her, Audra occupied as little space as possible, as if she expected a huge crowd that never materialized. She read diligently. Her hair was pulled up fully, incomprehensibly, inside her toboggan, and she wore her dark gray coat thoroughly buttoned up. She kept her feet tightly together, her knees covered by the length of her coat. It was a cold afternoon. With her thickly gloved hand, she turned a page and started the next with a steamy puff of breath.

As Parrish crossed the street, she refused to look up. He'd timed his arrival late, after the bus had come and gone. Stepping up on the curb, he lumbered down the sidewalk to where she sat. He stood for a moment, shuffling his boots, then leaned his back against the route sign he'd treated so roughly the night before. He said nothing, hoping she might look up. She didn't. He was standing so close, he knew she had to see his boots over the rim of her book, but Audra only leaned her face closer to the pages. Occasionally, she adjusted her glasses with a slow, gloved hand.

Parrish hunched his shoulders, leaned forward, and spoke quietly. "Audra."

She continued to read. With her thumb, she pushed a loop of hair off her forehead and back up into her toboggan.

"I'm sorry," he said. "About yesterday."

Her eyes stopped reading, but she kept them focused on the book. Something fierce played around the edges of her eyes, as if she was ready to give a shove or expected at any moment to receive one.

Parrish squatted by the sign so his eyes would be in line with hers if there were no book. "I was being a huge baby."

"Yes, you were," she said curtly. Without looking at him, she closed her book, laid it in her lap, then took off her gloves and rubbed her hands together. She put her book in her backpack, then folded her hands in her lap. Her eyes focused hard on her own knuckles. She paused for a moment, then said, "When I stormed out, I slammed your door. I'm sorry."

"Audra, it was my fault. You don't have to apologize."

"Yes, I do. I didn't mean to do that. Will you accept my apology?"

"Of course. But I was being a jerk—"

"You did what I expected," she interrupted. Her back stiffened. "I don't know what I expected, but I shouldn't. I shouldn't expect you to be any different than—" She stopped her words and swallowed hard and regained her distant demeanor, both blank and dignified. "I should know that by now, and I shouldn't let it get to me."

"Do you accept my apology?" he asked.

"I already have." There was something brave about the way she held her chin.

Parrish sat on the bench beside her. She showed no response. He noticed how still she sat, so erect and tense, as if waiting for some terrible news to arrive.

He took his hand out of his pocket, hesitated a moment with it in the air, then put it flat on the bench between them. With his finger, he tapped her leg until she felt it and looked down. She tilted her head and stared at his tapping, softening at the silliness and the smallness of the gesture. She reached a finger over and stroked the knuckle of his hand. She almost smiled.

"I'm sorry." He leaned his face lower to see if he could meet her eyes. "Are you okay?"

She took her finger away and immediately nodded.

He wanted to hold her hand. That was something he'd very much like to do for its own sake, but he also wanted to touch whatever she was so afraid of, to grab hold of that hurt so she wouldn't have to hold that weight all by herself. But to take her hand seemed somehow part of what she feared. He put his hands in his pockets, uncertain he could otherwise stop the impulse to take hers.

But that left her alone, and of all the things he wanted in that moment, he most wanted her not to feel alone. She was already working so hard to be alone on that bench. He ended his struggle by leaning and very lightly kissing the shoulder of her coat. Then he settled back into the bench.

Audra turned and looked straight at him. There was no defiance in her face now, no apology or fear—only slight surprise.

She was surprised by his gesture, pleased and surprised, as if she had, say, lost her scarf and he'd found it, returning it by hanging it outside her door, knocking, then leaving before she answered. If, looking for a time down an empty hallway, she then wrapped that scarf around her neck—she wore his kiss to her coat like that. Her breathing relaxed like someone for whom things had finally stopped being too loud.

She hooked a finger in his coat pocket and looked forward again as if nothing out of the ordinary had happened.

A few minutes later, a shabbily dressed man came down the sidewalk toward them. He stopped, stood cautiously for a moment, then asked, "Are you the two who help people at this corner?"

Parrish answered, "Maybe."

"I don't mean nothing, man." The homeless man held his hands out in front of him. "I ain't trying to get something, I just heard you two were—"

"What do you need?" asked Parrish abruptly.

Audra pinched his leg.

The homeless man waited, stomping his feet to shake off the cold. Then he cleared his throat and twitched his head. "I ain't asking for money. He said you don't give out money, but that maybe you'd buy a guy a meal."

"Who said that?" asked Parrish.

"That other guy." He scanned the parking lot. "Homeless guy. What's his name?"

"Thomas?"

"Yeah, Tom. Thomas, yeah."

"You friends with Thomas?" asked Parrish. "I've been looking for him."

The homeless man back-pedaled. "Man, I don't know the guy that well. He said you were crazy. Tom said that, not me. He ain't my friend, but he told me you wanted to feed somebody. Said ask the girl. Said don't argue with the dude, so I don't mean to."

Audra giggled, then she grabbed her backpack, unzipped the side pocket, and fished out one of the certificates she'd bought the other day. "Here you go," she said, leaning forward and holding out the card.

The homeless man never took his eyes off Parrish. He inched forward, keeping his distance, but reached his arm out to take the card. "What is it?"

"It's good for a meal at Mr. Wu's." Audra turned and pointed toward the Chinese restaurant. "It's all you can eat, so knock yourself out."

The homeless man turned the card sideways in his hand and read what little there was to read on both sides.

"The egg rolls are awesome," said Parrish.

"That place right over there, huh?" He flapped the card in his hands, looked down at it again. "Thanks."

"You're welcome," said Audra. "What was your name?"

The homeless man gave them both an uncertain glance. "Me? Uh…Jim."

"Tell Thomas I'm ready to type up his résumé when he gets a chance," said Parrish.

Jim stared at Parrish, nodded and backed away, then quickly headed off to Mr. Wu's.

Audra turned to Parrish, "You're the unfriendliest do-gooder I've ever met."

"Thank you," said Parrish.

"Hey!" a voice called out.

Audra and Parrish looked up. Crossing the street, the man with the St. Bernard tugged and leaned his weight back against the leash.

"Bellamy! Come!"

The short man walked as straight as he could as the huge dog circled and pulled and wandered back and forth. It took a while for them to get to the bench. Panting, the St. Bernard shoved his head between Parrish and Audra. Parrish scratched his ears harshly, shook the dog's head till his jowls dripped and he put a paw up on the bench.

"Bellamy! Sit!"

The man switched the leash from hand to hand, then pushed heavily on the dog's backside, trying to force a sitting position, but the dog and his owner were roughly the same weight. The dog neither sat nor seemed to know his name was Bellamy.

The short man began his speech.

"I don't know what you two are up to, but I wish you'd do it somewhere else. Giving to those bums—I don't mean to sound uncharitable, but you have to stop. It just makes them come back, makes more of them hang out in this neighborhood, *my* neighborhood. I heard there was a purse-snatching in this parking lot yesterday! You encourage these people, and that's all you'll get. More begging, more crime.

"And I've watched you stopping people, asking them this and that. You stopped *me*, so don't try to deny it. I don't know what your angle is, but you don't just pick a corner and start bothering people. What does that prove? You want to help people? Fine, I can get you in touch with plenty of agencies that do just that. I care about *my* neighborhood. I care about the people who live here.

"Mrs. Miranda, for instance. Do you know anything about her life? She has enough problems without having to worry about purse-snatchers. I know that because I know her. I didn't just bump into her one day at a bus stop. But you two, you stir things up—that's all you're doing—and now she's not here today. I'll bet she's afraid to come here because of all that's happening. This is her corner. I knew her way back when she and her husband sat here. She comes here to knit, and God knows she needs to get out of that apartment for a little rest…"

"What's wrong with Rose?" Audra interrupted.

"That's none of *your* business. You two leave her alone. What I'm saying is stop trying to run a homeless shelter on this corner. If you feel the compulsion to do something, go join a club or sign a petition or sell your possessions and fly to Africa, because what you're doing here is a joke. I'm sorry, it is. I wasn't going to say anything, but when I hear of crime on this corner, it breaks my heart. When I see Rose missing, it's just one more good piece of *my* neighborhood disappearing like all the rest."

Parrish had bowed his head to keep from saying something unkind. When he heard this pause, he looked up to see if it was his turn to speak. He patted Bellamy's head, then calmly said, "Has it occurred to you that this might be *our* neighborhood too?"

The short, talkative man grunted. "Has it occurred to you that you're *naive*?" He tugged at Bellamy's leash.

Audra and Parrish watched as man and dog walked away, Bellamy pulling the short man down the sidewalk, occasionally dragging him toward some patch of grass or discarded wrapper.

"He was fun," said Audra.

But Parrish's mind raced in a different direction. "Audra?"

"Yes?"

"Are you thinking what I'm thinking?" he asked.

"Probably not."

"The letter," he said, suddenly enthused. "What if it belongs to Rose?"

Audra sniffled at the cold wind. "I don't think so, Parrish."

"If what he says about her life is true, and she's hiding it—"

"Let's slow down."

"Remember? When I found it, she wouldn't read it for herself." He forced pieces together excitedly. "When I read it to her, she said she didn't like the sound of that."

"John…"

"She said it wasn't hers when I asked, but maybe she felt put on the spot. Do you think she would lie?"

Audra considered his question. "If there's enough sadness, yes, someone might lie."

"Maybe it's hers and she's too afraid to tell us. Maybe *she's* the one we're supposed to help next? Do you know where she lives?"

"No. But, John—"

"That guy with the dog—where'd he go?" Parrish picked up

Audra's gloves so he wouldn't stand on them when he stepped onto the bench. He looked around from that height, but both man and dog were gone.

Carrying a to-go box full of Mr. Wu's, Jim walked up to the bench. "What're you looking at?"

Parrish jumped down. "Hey, do you know the lady who sits here? A bit older, knits…"

"Yeah," Jim said. "I seen her all the time."

"Do you know where she lives?"

Jim hesitated, then glanced at Audra. "I seen her come out of this apartment building once, that's all."

"Can you show us?" asked Parrish.

"Sure."

Audra touched Parrish's sleeve. "I don't think the letter's hers."

But Parrish ignored this. He separated her gloves and shoved one in each of his coat pockets. "You coming?"

The apartment building stood at its own corner only a brief walk away. Jim led them, pointed it out, then disappeared down a side street. The carved granite exterior of the building promised more than the drab interior delivered—a worn staircase, junk mail scattered on the floor beneath the mailboxes, and rows of apartment doors, scuffed and dingy, many with their numbers missing or one digit dangling loosely by a final and persistent screw.

They read the nameplates on the stoop, found her name and apartment number, then slipped through the lobby door as a young lady exited. Inside, old radiators clicked and heated oppressively, and they both shucked their scarves and unbuttoned their coats, Audra releasing her hair from her toboggan.

Climbing the three flights upward, Parrish led with both hands pulling at the handrails, his boots bounding two or three stairs with each jump, Audra plodded along behind. At the end of a long hall, they found themselves standing outside apartment thirty-seven. Beside the door, the bulb in the light fixture weakly hummed and flickered.

"John! What a surprise!" At first, Rose opened the door a crack, then more widely once she recognized his face. "Oh, and Audra! You two must be freezing. Come in."

Parrish waited for Audra to enter first, then stepped to the right, just inside the apartment door, as Rose shut and latched the lock.

"Hope this isn't a bad time," Parrish said.

"Not a bit. Come in." Then Rose noticed the cuts on Parrish's forehead. "Oh my word, John. What happened?" She reached a hand up to his face.

"Commuter rush got a little rowdy this morning," he said.

Rose took him seriously for a moment, till Audra explained the purse chase.

"That was very good of you, John," Rose praised him in motherly tones. "Please sit down and visit."

It was not a large apartment. The room they stood in was cluttered with an eclectic grouping of furniture, too much furniture for so small a room. A television flashed pictures with the volume muted, a worn couch with an outdated floral design held a tight, predomi-

nant spot between two chairs—a rocking chair and a vinyl recliner—
and a low coffee table burdened with a stack of magazines and the
day's newspaper spread open atop all. To the left of the apartment
door stood a small, round, wooden dining table. Beyond it was the
entrance to the kitchen, the table partially blocking the doorway—
this room never meant for use as both sitting room and dining room.

The table had been set with two plates, two glasses, silverware,
and a pitcher of water. Beside one of the glasses, a cluster of brown-
orange prescription bottles stood—five, maybe six, all different
heights. There was a third spot reserved, but without a plate—just
a napkin, a plastic juice cup with a lid, a miniature box of Cheerios,
and a highchair.

Rose wiped her hands on a dishtowel. "John, Audra, this is
Uncle Arthur."

Coming from the back of the apartment, a thin, elderly man
walked spryly through the furniture toward the table. He pulled an
oxygen tank behind him on its two-wheeled dolly, and the tubes ran
up into his nose. He scuffed his feet in a little dance when he heard
his name. "Nice to meet you both."

"Arthur's my late husband's uncle," said Rose. "But I love him
anyway."

"Ha!" He coughed as much as he laughed. "She loves me to
death."

"Arthur's got leukemia, so he likes to play like that. Don't mind
his hair."

They couldn't help looking back at him when she announced
that.

The old man didn't mind the attention. He rubbed the flat of his hand across the top of his skull. "She means the absence of my hair."

"Arthur, we've got company. Put your hat on," she insisted. "You'll scare the children."

"Where's my hat?" The old man looked around. His fingers fumbled and checked to see that his sweater was buttoned evenly.

"You sat on your hat when you were sleeping in the easy chair."

"Why was I sleeping on it?"

"You're a good sleeper. That's all I know." Rose disappeared into the kitchen.

"Found it!" He bent stiffly over, snatched a blue toboggan out of the recliner, then waved it in the air. "We don't often get company."

Arthur stood his oxygen tank upright, then used both hands to shake open the toboggan and pull it on his head. With a finger, he flipped one ear then the other to the outside of the cap.

Rose returned holding a large, square dish with bright red oven mitts. "We were just about to eat. Have a seat."

"Tater Tot casserole tonight, my friends," Arthur said. "It's sloppy and divine."

"Oh no," Audra said. "We didn't mean to intrude."

"You're not intruding." Rose placed the dish in the center of the small table, then slid a wide spoon into it. "I'm glad you stopped by."

"We don't want to intrude on your family."

"You've said that. Now hand me those coats." Rose held her arms out.

They gave up their winter gear, which Rose hustled to the back bedroom.

Arthur took hold of Audra's elbow. "She makes enough casserole for an army, though it's just us three. There's plenty. We usually eat the rest for a week as lunches."

Rose returned. "Sit down. I'll get the extra chairs." She hustled away again.

"I don't know who she thinks I am. I'm not sitting before this pretty young lady takes a seat." Arthur scooted over to the table and placed a hand on the back of the first chair. "Here, sit here." He motioned to Audra, then grabbed Parrish's elbow. "And young man, you sit beside her." Having done the duty given him by his niece-in-law, Arthur went in the kitchen, a wheel on his oxygen dolly squeaking the whole way.

Audra whispered to Parrish. "I think we should go."

"I think we should stay."

"We're intruding," she said.

Returning awkwardly with two chairs, Rose caught Audra mid-whisper. "Stop saying that. Not one more time, you hear? If I didn't want to feed you, I wouldn't."

Parrish leapt up and took one of the chairs from her.

"Thank you, John," she said. "Arthur, here's a chair."

He came out of the kitchen with a bottle of ketchup. "Thank you, Rose." He sat the ketchup on the table, then asked, "You want me to fetch him?"

"No, no. I need to change him. You sit down."

With a series of quick trips to the kitchen, Rose brought out two more settings and placed them neatly in front of her guests, then hurried to the back room. As she did this, Arthur found the chair he wanted, situated his tank behind it, and lowered himself into his seat, tucking his napkin in the collar of his shirt.

"What was it you said you do?" he asked Parrish.

"I run a coffee shop."

"Oh! Rose told me that!" He bobbed a little in his seat, then grabbed Parrish's hand. "I drank some coffee in my time. You used to have that one Costa Rican. What was it?"

"San Juanillo."

"That's it!" He rapped the table with his knuckles. "If there's one thing makes me mad at this cancer, it's that I miss a black cup of coffee in the morning. Rose—this is the fellow who runs that coffee shop around the corner."

"I know," she called happily from the back. "I told you I met him. You two can reminisce about your coffee days."

Arthur turned to his guests. "I'm a teacher. Used to be. High school English. Nothing like being at your desk in an empty classroom early, listening to those sleepy hooligans clattering in their lockers in the hall, the sunrise still pink out the window, and breathing in the steam of a good cup of coffee." He inhaled deeply. "That and a doughnut."

"We sell fritters," said Parrish.

"That's right. Rose! He sells those fritters."

She appeared in the doorway with a wide smile. "Maybe you can have one later this week."

Arthur turned to Audra. "My niece is now my mother *and* nurse. I had a bad morning, so I won't get a decent thing to eat the rest of the week." Then he called to Rose, almost singing. "Except Tater Tot casserole!"

"I shouldn't be feeding you that," she sang back.

"Yes, she should," Arthur said to Parrish.

Seated next to him, Audra touched Arthur's hand. "What happened to your arm?"

Parrish hadn't noticed, but when Audra mentioned it, he looked. On Arthur's outer forearm, a wide purple bruise swelled brightly.

"Oh, that." Instead of being self-conscious, Arthur pulled his sleeve up and held his arm out proudly. "I took a spill this morning. My something-levels were down, so I was dizzier than I thought I was. That floor jumped up and tackled me. Look."

Parrish winced as Audra leaned in close and turned his arm delicately with her fingertips.

"The floor I didn't mind," Arthur said casually. "It was the sink that got me in the ribs on the way down."

"Do you mind if I look? I'm a nurse."

"Well! That's a godsend, isn't it?"

Rose peeked suspiciously around the corner. "Arthur! Keep your shirt down at the table."

"I've got my own private nurse now, thank you."

"Pretty nasty bruise. Does this hurt?" She pressed lightly, but specifically, around the bruised ribs.

"No," he said. "Feels bruised." He lowered his shirt and sweater. "I'm fine."

"To be safe, you might want an x-ray."

Rose came out of the back room with a small, sleepy boy in her arms. He rubbed his eyes with his hands. "Do you think he really needs one, Audra? Arthur, I told you—"

Arthur interrupted her. "My insurance ran out," he confided to Audra. "After I got the cancer, I couldn't work, and when I stopped working, well… We're on a budget these days."

"Does he need to go to the hospital?" Rose asked, very concerned.

Audra shrugged. "It's probably fine. Does it hurt when you lay down?"

"Haven't lain down since it happened," he said. "I'll let you know."

"The arm isn't broken," Audra said to Rose, then turned to Arthur. "But you might want to elevate it to bring that swelling down."

"I'll do that after dinner," he said. "Thank you, ma'am."

"And this," Rose announced, bouncing the boy awake in her arms. "This is Theo."

The boy was maybe two, two and a half. Very cute, barefoot, he wore tiny kid jeans and a little green knitted sweater that looked like Rose's handiwork. Just up from a nap, his hair sprouted in a thick mess and he rubbed at the pillow creases on his cheek.

Audra stood and walked over to the boy. Rose immediately handed him over, and Audra saddled him firmly on her hip, straightened his sweater, and wiped his hair out of his face. Theo took this treatment from a stranger very well, too tired to worry who was holding him, only that someone was. The two women talked quietly for a moment, then Audra put Theo into his highchair. Rose handed him his juice cup, while Audra ripped open the tiny box of Cheerios and spilled some out on the tray for him. They returned to their seats.

Everyone passed their plates to Rose, who served them. "So how are things at our bus stop?" She laughed. "Theo had a runny nose, and with Arthur's spill... He usually watches Theo while I knit. Lets me out of the house for my siesta, as Arthur calls it. Any news on that letter you found?"

Parrish shot Audra a glance. She shook her head so slightly that no one noticed but him.

"We're following up on a lead," Parrish said. "Who's that man with the St. Bernard?"

"Mr. Brooks?" said Rose. "Oh, I've known him forever."

Arthur mumbled. "Bit of a busybody, if you ask me."

"We didn't," Rose said quickly.

"If he can't put a leash on it, he wants nothing to do with it," the old man continued, undeterred.

"Arthur," Rose corrected, "that's not kind."

"Wasn't trying to be kind."

"Well, maybe you should try." Rose held out both hands, palms up. "Would you say grace?"

Arthur put his hand in hers, then laid his other hand upturned on the table next to Audra, who took it. Parrish took Rose's other hand, then Parrish and Audra looked at one another. Parrish opened his hand, held it out to her, and she placed hers in his.

Arthur clamped his eyes shut and began: "God, bless that dog. Send Bellamy an open window, dear Lord, crack that dog a gate. And thank you for casseroles, especially this one I'm smelling, and that I only bruised what I did. Brought me a nurse right here to this table, so I thank you. Send your love down around my Rose and my boy here, provide for them, make them strong. And bless this fine young couple who've joined us. We're glad you sent them. Make their life together smooth and…what do you think, Lord? Make them…delightful. We pray these in your Son's name, amen."

"Amen," followed Rose, who gave Audra's hand a squeeze. Parrish and Audra released hands, and for a while, they couldn't look at one another.

The Tater Tot casserole proved delicious. Everyone thought so, the most praise pouring forth from Arthur. Both he and Parrish had large second helpings, and Arthur insisted everyone try it with ketchup. Theo nibbled a bite, mashed it against the edge of his tray, mostly interested in the ketchup. Audra, the nurse, eyed how much salt Parrish put on his food, occasionally glanced at the bruise on Arthur's arm. Rose tended to everyone's tea, an excellent hostess, and it was fine table conversation, most of it Arthur and Parrish swapping stories about their favorite books, medieval and otherwise, and discussing their top five favorite cups of coffee—where and when they'd had them.

When they had finished their meals, Rose stood and stacked the plates, then whisked them away to the kitchen. She returned with a serving dish half full of lemon squares. Everyone took one, and like Theo, they put them on the table in front of them and ate them with their hands. The ladies set theirs on a napkin, but the men didn't mind at all. Arthur requested a glass of milk, which Rose brought him.

"If I'd known I was coming to dinner, I'd have brought a pound of coffee."

"Your shop's not far, is it?" Arthur suggested.

"Ah! You know you can't have coffee," said Rose. "We've broken every other rule tonight, so let's just stop there."

Arthur settled back in his chair and patted his shirt where a belly might have been if he'd had one. Audra broke a bite of lemon square in smaller pieces for Theo. He stared at her uncertainly, which made Audra mess with his hair.

Finally Parrish had to ask. "Rose, is Theo…yours?

Audra pinched his leg under the table.

Rose gave him a startled look, then burst into laughter. She laughed until Arthur got tickled and laughed. He tried not to look at her, which caused more giggling, and then the old man laughed so hard he had a short coughing fit. That made Rose laugh so hard her eyes filled with tears.

Wiping them, she scolded Arthur, "Why are you laughing?"

"Because you were," Arthur answered.

"I can laugh at my being an old woman. You may not."

"I was laughing at an old woman laughing. And I'm the one who's old, not you." Arthur picked up a fork and poked it playfully into her ribs. "But you *are* too overdone to be having a two-year-old."

This he thought hysterical, especially the fork, and laughed and coughed afresh. Smiling, Rose put her napkin beside her plate and waited for him to finish laughing at his own joke. Then the two shared a quiet look. Though the laughter drained away between them, none of the brightness did.

Then Arthur took off his toboggan, turned to their guests to explain.

"It's all right, I'll tell it." Rose laid a hand over his. "Theo's my grandbaby. My daughter…"

Arthur crossed himself.

Rose continued. "My daughter passed away last summer."

"Oh, I'm so sorry," said Parrish.

Rose accepted his words with a contented dignity. "Thank you."

"May I ask what happened?" asked Parrish.

Rose folded her napkin, smoothing it flat. "She got a headache one day. Next day, it was worse. We took her to the hospital. Two days later she died. The doctors couldn't give a clear answer and wanted to cut her open to find out, but I didn't need to find out that badly. Her name is Evie."

Rose stood and walked over to a table beside the couch. She picked up a picture frame and brought it to Parrish, who then handed it to Audra.

"She was going to be a nurse, too," said Rose. "She applied to two schools. Got in one of them. We got the letter in the mail after she died. I was very proud."

"She'd have been a great nurse." Arthur nodded. "Always help-ing me. Evie was a sweetheart. Do you like it?"

At first Audra didn't understand the question. "Being a nurse? Me? Oh, yes."

"That's good. To like what you do," Arthur said, taking the pic-ture. "That's a handsome thing to see." Even though he'd seen this picture a thousand times, he smiled hugely, immediately, as he would if Evie had walked through the front door.

Audra and Parrish helped Rose with the dishes while Arthur sat with Theo on the couch, entertaining him with a box of toys. Audra washed, Parrish dried, and Rose put things away. Rose found two Tupperware dishes and began to scrape the leftovers into them. Audra took a rag and wiped down the table. Leaving Rose alone in the kitchen, Parrish stepped to where Audra was. He took the letter out of his pocket. Quickly, Audra took it from him and shook her head. Parrish tried to open her hands and take the letter back.

"What's that you have?" asked Rose clicking off the kitchen light. "Oh, is that your letter? Let me get my reading glasses."

She walked over to the coffee table, put on her glasses, then held out her hand.

Reluctantly, Audra handed her the letter. All three sat at the table while Rose peered through her glasses and read it. "Hmm... You said you had a lead?"

"I'm not sure how to ask this," Parrish began.

Audra bowed her head over her hands.

"We had this...conversation with Mr. Brooks. He was walking his dog. And he seemed to think..." Parrish stammered. "Mr. Brooks mentioned that perhaps...."

Audra raised her face. "Tell Parrish that's not your letter, please."

"Me?" asked Rose with genuine surprise. "Why would you suppose—?" She looked at Arthur, then Theo, then Audra. "Oh!"

Her face softened with understanding. She patted Audra's hand, then looked at Parrish with something akin to admiration. She laid down the letter, took off her glasses, pinched the bridge of her nose. After a minute or so, she blinked her eyes and looked at them.

"Thank you. Thank you both for coming here about this. That's the kindest thing I've seen in weeks. I appreciate it."

"What's going on?" Arthur walked over and picked up the letter.

"John and Audra found this letter, and they've been trying to find out who it belongs to. Mr. Brooks led them to think it might be mine."

"Mr. Brooks!" said Arthur. "Don't let him lead you anywhere."

"Now don't—" said Rose.

The old man waved off her correction. "What did he say?"

"Mr. Brooks thought," Parrish tried to explain, "under the circumstances, you might be…unhappy."

"Unhappy!" Arthur dropped the letter on the table. "That dog is unhappy."

"Arthur—" said Rose.

"Circumstances! I'm not under anything!" The old man tapped a bony finger on the table. "That man doesn't mind his own business. And he's not being kind, he's being nosey."

"Arthur, don't get yourself worked up."

"*Mis*-ter *Brooks*." Arthur turned a circle with his oxygen tank. "I'm dying, but I'm happier than he is. Theo, you happy?"

The boy held up a toy figure and made a flying noise.

Arthur finished his circle and put a hand on his niece's shoulder. "Rose? How about you?"

His voice became serious. Suddenly, it was a real question, a gesture completely sincere.

Rose reached her hand up and covered his, then gave it a kiss. "I know an old man who needs to sit down and elevate his arm. That would make me happy."

He stood over her for a moment, squeezing her shoulder. Then he placed his hand on her cheek, leaned down, and kissed the crown of her head. "How did my nephew ever find himself such a beauty?"

"God found us both," she answered.

"I'm glad he did." Arthur cleared his throat. "I haven't thanked you today, have I?"

"You're welcome. Now go sit down."

Arthur walked back toward the couch, whistling as he did, the oxygen tank wheels squeaking in time with his tune.

Rose slid the letter across the table to Parrish. "I'm sorry, but I'm going to be of no use to you two. This is not mine."

"We're sorry to—" Audra began.

Rose turned a stern glance on her but spoke gently. "You haven't, honey. Stop feeling the world's some fault of yours. You two are welcome anytime."

"Can I ask a blunt question?" Parrish said.

Audra sighed, fell back in her chair, and put her hands atop her head.

"You're never blunt, John." Rose gave Audra a wink.

"How on earth do you manage? Financially, I mean," he asked. "How do you survive?"

Rose laughed. "Well, for many years, I worked. I don't have time now, not with Theo, but I used to balance the books at my husband's shop. He owned a dry cleaner's. We met at that bus stop, did I ever tell you that? We did. I guess that's why I like to knit there. Fond memories. Anyway, after he died, we sold his shop and used that money until it ran out. Arthur's savings lasted a while, and now he gets his Social Security. And we have what we've stocked away from life insurance settlements. That'll last us a little longer. I'm hoping long enough for Theo to start school, and then I can go back to work."

"How can we help you?"

Rose gave him a look of genuine but delighted surprise. "That's so sweet of you to ask! Arthur! John and Audra asked if they can help us."

"Help us do what?"

"Just help out, that's all. Isn't that sweet of them?"

"I think they're both sweet."

Rose continued. "God takes care of us, John, so I don't know that we need anything right now. But thank you for asking."

"What if…" Parrish glanced at Audra. "What if I said God sent us here to ask if we could help?"

"Well," Rose thought, "that's different then. Let me pray on it, and I'll let you know, okay?"

"It's getting late," Audra suggested quietly. "Perhaps we should be going."

Rose stood and took two Tupperware bowls she'd prepared out of the refrigerator. She stacked them in a plastic bag, brought them to Parrish, and told him how to warm his up. Audra took the bag and worked it carefully down into her backpack. The two said their good-byes to Arthur and Theo while Rose fetched their coats and scarves from the back room. Once they were bundled up again, Rose opened her front door, then gave them both a hug. As she shut her door, she invited them to come back anytime.

The two turned and walked down the dimly lit hallway toward the stairwell.

"Well, you were right again," Parrish said.

"About what?"

"The letter. You called it. It wasn't hers."

Parrish hummed halfway down the hall before he realized Audra wasn't following. She stood exactly where she had, her hand held tightly to the strap of the backpack over her shoulder, her other hand counting the knuckles of the first—walking up them slowly, spidery—and her eyes glazed but fixed on the tarnished metal numbers on Rose's apartment door.

He took a few steps back her way. "You coming?"

"Yes," she said, looking at him. "John?"

"What's up?" he said.

"Would you walk me home?"

The two sauntered slowly away from Rose's apartment building. Unlike earlier, when Parrish rushed everyone along to find the place, Audra now led their way. She set the tempo, slowly pacing out their walk together—maybe to make it last longer, or so Parrish hoped.

They spoke little, casually, short observations about the sky, the neighborhood, about Arthur and Rose. Audra led by means of an occasional finger delicately extended when they needed to cross a street or turn a corner. It was colder now, but neither of them seemed to notice. Though Audra wore her Burberry buttoned up completely, she wore no gloves, and her hat and scarf remained in her bag.

Parrish took note of each turn, to get his bearings for his walk home. It wasn't so far from his shop. They strolled past the elementary school and a few smaller yards, then cut across the parking lot of a tiny grocery. As they walked, the back of their hands brushed once, and they both bristled with awareness. Audra readjusted the backpack on her shoulder. Very few people were out besides them. Audra let her hand drift into his again, and this time he reached his fingers around and took her hand softly. Neither looked at the other. They just slowed their walking further and allowed their joined hands to swing easily between them.

"Up there, then a left. Almost home." Audra pointed.

Parrish looked around. He hadn't been down this street in a while—he lived in the opposite direction—and he'd forgotten how fine a neighborhood it was. A good mix of houses and apartment buildings—brownstones with three floors and bright, big windows that overlooked courtyards with a tree or two.

"This is nice," he said. "How long have you lived around here?"

Audra glanced up at him. "I grew up here."

"Person could do a lot worse."

Audra pulled herself closer, leaned her shoulder into his as they turned the last corner. A little dog yelped mercilessly as they walked past his stretch of fence.

"He's almost as old as I am. Been barking mad as long as I can remember." Audra smiled. "Here we are."

They stopped in front of the stoop of a four-story brownstone. Audra released his hand, turning to face him.

"Not so far," Parrish said.

"No, not far," Audra agreed. "Oh!"

She set her backpack on the sidewalk and took out one of the containers Rose had given them, then handed it to him.

"Thank you," he said.

"A man needs his Tater Tots." She grinned.

At that, Parrish set the container on the stoop's concrete balustrade so there'd be nothing between them as they stood together. He leaned imperceptibly closer, looking into her face, taking in each feature carefully. Audra kept her face raised, but her eyes glanced at Parrish's coat collar, and she reached her fingers up to flip the coat's zipper so that it lay flat. Then she made herself look back up at him, her eyes blinking behind her glasses. He could smell the washed freshness of her hair and noticed a tiny freckle he'd never seen before, high on her cheek below her eye. She breathed shallowly through her mouth, and her eyes no longer looked away. But when Parrish leaned his face closer to kiss her, at the final moment, she slipped a hand between them, placing it lightly on his chest, and her gaze fell resolutely to the back of her own hand, an unmistakable gesture.

"I need to tell you the truth about something, John."

Parrish laughed nervously. "Are you saying you've been lying up until now?"

Her eyes darted up, pained and hurt, and her fingers on his chest curled slowly, clutching his coat for a moment. She tried to say something, but instead, without a sound, teardrops ran down to her chin and dotted the lenses of her glasses. She stood frozen until one drop fell from her chin onto his coat, then she turned her face away.

"Audra…" Parrish tilted his head to look into her eyes.

She shook her head and pulled her shoulders free from his hands. She wiped the flat of her palms harshly across her face, turning her cheeks away from each hand as it did its work. She pivoted, grabbed the balustrade, and took the first steps of a hurried exit, then returned awkwardly to pick up her bag, letting her expanse of hair fall over her face to hide the unwanted tears.

"I didn't mean—"

"I have to go." Bundling her bag in her arms, she ran up the stoop, dropping her keys once as she fumbled with the front door. She opened it just enough to squeeze through, disappearing entirely before the door had time to puff closed.

Saturday

Saturdays, for Parrish, were a workday like the rest. He shared the shift with Susan, who, not having classes on Saturday, worked as many hours as she could on the weekends. Parrish relished his Saturdays with Susan—the pleasant change of working with someone who worked, the lack of need to beg or threaten, much less progress toward that managerial ulcer. When he turned to ask her to sweep, he found her, broom in hand, sliding tables to one side to clean under them. When she'd finished sweeping inside, she then swept outside—the patio, the walk in front of the store, the curb, and the immediate parking spaces. She swept in front of the two stores adjacent to the coffee shop, picked cups and paper out of the shrubbery, and emptied the outside garbage cans.

By early afternoon they'd cleaned everything possible, and some things twice. The store looked grand-opening immaculate, and, satisfied, both of them leaned against the counter, surveying how well they'd done. Parrish volunteered to make Susan a drink, and she asked for her usual, so he foamed a fine, tall raspberry cappuccino with chocolate sprinkles in a ceramic mug. He didn't approve of pink sprinkled beverages but made a glad exception in Susan's case. He even raspberried the milk before he steamed it, which was breaking basic steam-wand etiquette, but it made the foam pink and berryful, just the way she liked it. When she sipped her drink, she got a tuft of pink foam on her nose. Parrish tapped his own until she took the hint.

"Can I ask you a stupid man question?" said Parrish.

"Uh-oh," she said. "I'm no expert at stupid men."

"No," Parrish corrected, "I'm the stupid man, and it's my question. About women."

"Let's hear it."

"What can you tell me about women and crying?" he asked.

She laughed with a mouthful of pink foam, then wiped her chin with the back of her hand. "Have you been making girls cry?"

Parrish didn't say no.

"A serious cry?"

Parrish weighed this distinction, tilting his head from one side to the other. "Are there categories?"

"Let me go back," Susan said, raising her hand. "Most often, I'd say, a man shouldn't take credit for making a girl cry. In my experience, men are awesome at giving the final push, but there's usually a host of other things going on that day, or for weeks. Men are oblivious, and it's precisely that oblivion that makes them so adept at giving that final shove. But too often, men feel everything is about them. You're not that important—that's the first thing you need to hear. And with men, if they broke it, it's their job to fix it. We don't want you to stop us crying, we want a place to do it, a safe place. So first rule, John: you don't fix crying. Crying happens."

"Hold on. I thought the first rule was 'I'm not that important.'"

Susan smiled hugely. "Very good, John! You've made it to rule three!"

"Where?"

"Listening. Good job. That's really it, I'd say." She set down her mug, which freed her fingers to count off her points. "Not all about you; don't problem-solve; attempt listening."

"Great overview. Now, I need more practical help like...what do I do when it's happening?"

"Oh, okay. Well, stay calm. It's just crying, after all. It'll stop soon enough. Be kind. Don't ask questions, or at least not too many. It's important to stay in the room." She paused, considering. "Unless you feel she *wants* to be alone."

"How on earth would I know that?"

"Well, if she *says* she wants to be alone—"

"No. We both know that's a trick coin—no matter how you flip that, it comes up heads."

"Yes. The key is to figure out if she wants you to call heads or if she wants you to call tails. But be prepared to stay. Her wanting to be alone doesn't mean you *leave* leave. Never go out and have a good time. But we don't want to hear you pacing and tearing your hair out either. It's not all about you, and we don't want to think *your* well-being depends on us. Just don't be gone when we decide to look for you."

"Is this treatable?"

"Forget crying for a minute," she said, her hand giving a wave of erasure in the air. "Tell me, how do you know what to do when the girl's perfectly happy?"

"I don't. They end up crying."

"Come on, you're not that clueless," she said. "Whatever you are at your best, what she most likes about you, be *that* when she's crying."

"What does *that* mean?"

"A person can be hurt by you and still want you. And it's the *want*-able you she needs to be there when she's most upset. Crying in front of you most likely means you're the one she cares about, so much so that *you* get the crying."

"So it's sort of a privilege?" asked Parrish.

"In a way, yes."

"So to clarify, I'm supposed to see that she's crying, but in no way be aware of the fact I made her cry?"

"Be aware, not fundamentally altered."

"If I say I still don't understand, that won't make you cry, will it?"

"Funny, John. But it's not one emotion, okay? It's a bunch all together, too many crowded into the same moment. She's got to pull over, make some get out, and leave 'em on the side of the road."

"So it's like…a circus car with clown midgets?"

Susan closed her eyes with a smile and nodded. "Yes, John. Crying is letting the clowns out to run around the car, then switching drivers."

As soon as Duncan arrived, Parrish grabbed his coat and headed out the door with a cup of coffee. He walked briskly, still wondering what he'd say when he saw Audra, but as he approached the corner, he saw no one there—neither Audra nor Rose, nor anyone else.

It was fine weather—not too cold, sunny enough to leave his coat unzipped. He sipped his coffee, dawdled about, dug a page of that day's paper out of the garbage and perused it. He hobbled along the curb—one foot off, one foot on. Then he checked the times posted on the bus route sign. The buses ran less frequently on the weekends—fewer on Saturdays, none at all on Sundays. And Audra probably didn't have classes on weekends, probably wouldn't show up at all.

Parrish sat on the bench with his cup of coffee, turning it in the palm of his hand while he waited. He wondered if, with God, waiting was typical. Nothing about this cookie experience had been typical, so he sipped his coffee. He'd only been cookie-ing a few days, but in those few, he'd trained himself to look for anything—people strolling down the sidewalk, shoppers fumbling their keys at their cars, angry men sleeping beneath trees, happy St. Bernards—any need at all. The whole world was fair game since the cookie, so he watched with deliberate eyes.

But no one came.

He hummed, he retied his boots. After a while, he turned himself sideways on the bench, leaned his back against the armrest, and put his feet up on the seat. Nearly a full hour passed without a bite, a tug, the slightest nibble. When he finished his coffee, he stood and sauntered the cup over to the garbage can. He leaned against the route sign and buried his hands in his coat pockets. But pocket-wise, something was different. They were too full, too soft. Pulling his hands from his pockets, the fingers of each held a gray wool glove—Audra's gloves.

Maybe she cried because she lost her gloves?

This was a joke, a poor one, and he merely mumbled it to himself.

But God answered quite seriously.

Take the gloves back.

A strange thing and hard to describe. Whenever he tried to explain it (and he did later, when people asked), it always went something like this:

"So...God talks to you?"

Parrish would nod.

"And when God speaks to you, is it an *audible* voice?" they'd inevitably ask.

"If I said yes, would it make me sound *more* crazy?"

"Yes," they'd say.

"If I just nodded, would you still get the message?"

They usually nodded as well.

"So I nod," Parrish would continue, "and the word *yes* appears in your mind?"

"Yes."

"Like that. A speaking in the head. The response to a gesture. One you don't see, but has happened. More than an intimation, less than audible. But words appearing, surprising ones, answers to questions I wasn't asking, hadn't even thought of yet, but they fit perfectly. And there's peace."

God spoke to Parrish, this time without a cookie.

At first, Parrish tried to shake it. He put the gloves away and walked around the benches. He walked across the benches, hopping from one to the other, then took the gloves back out and tried them on. The gloves on his hands, he registered, were too small. Then he realized *this* was talking to himself, but that other thing wasn't. He sat down abruptly, took the gloves off, and twisted them in his hands. *That doesn't happen, God.* But clearly, *that* was his own mind talking. And his own mind was about to answer when he decided to actually address the question to God.

"Can it really be that easy?" Parrish said out loud.

A warm *yes* settled through him again. A strange thing, no doubt.

He'd only learned the way to her apartment the evening before, so it took him a few minutes to find his way back. He took one wrong turn but corrected that, and soon he saw it—her apartment building, the stoop where they'd almost kissed, the stairs she'd run up and disappeared. And to his surprise, he saw Audra. She sat on the stairs, her back to him, her hair pulled back but unmistakable.

But she was not alone.

A young man with wavy, dark hair sat near her, roughly her age and tall—Parrish could tell because his knees were higher than hers where they touched. They were talking, having what seemed like a serious conversation, and Audra had one of his hands clasped in both of hers.

Parrish watched them. The young man talked more than she did. Occasionally he'd laugh, then shake his head. Audra shook her head as well, looking down at his hand, spinning a ring on one of his fingers. Whatever story he was telling, she listened attentively, sympathetically, bringing her face up to smile at him when he paused. She looked up exactly when he wanted her to.

Parrish watched for half a minute, probably much less. He put the gloves back in his pockets, then consciously released his knees so he could turn away. But before he did, he saw Audra push the man's knees gently to one side so she could lean over and kiss his cheek. She wrapped him in her arms, holding him tight. The man returned the embrace, his hand on the back of her head lost under her hair.

"But you *saw* her holding his hand?" Duncan asked.

"No," corrected Mason. "He said she was playing with his fingers. Much worse."

Duncan sat across from Parrish, who played a perfunctory, hostile round of solitaire, while Mason stood over Parrish's shoulder, keeping a keen eye on which card went where. Parrish had filled them in on events, including the part where God spoke to him about the gloves. Having been through the cookie incident together, they weren't interested in that part.

"But you *saw* her," repeated Duncan, leaning on the table so that it tipped slightly. "Her holding his hand, her hugging a guy, her kissing a guy?"

Parrish glanced up. "You can stop now, Dunc." He dealt and flipped cards compulsively, slapping them where he could, missing as many plays as he caught.

"She told you she lived alone?" Mason asked.

"Right," said Parrish, flipping through the deck again.

"Do you think that guy lives there?"

Parrish grimaced harshly at him.

"What? I'm the one who's out of line here?" Mason took a card from Parrish's hand and played it on the far stack.

Parrish dropped the deck on the table, went behind the counter, and poured himself a cup of brewed coffee. Mason asked for one, which made Duncan need one too. Parrish brought the whole pot over to the table with a small stack of cups, allowing them to pour their own. Duncan asked for sugar, so Parrish loudly set the sugar container on the table. Mason fetched an entire carton of half-and-half from the fridge and set it next to the pot of coffee.

Parrish no longer had room to play cards. Duncan watched as he wildly scooted a second table up next to theirs, loaded all the coffee items onto that one, and ordered the other two to move over. Mason held his cup aloft while Parrish rearranged everything, then put his coffee right back where it had been, in Parrish's way. Obediently, Duncan moved his chair to the other table and fixed his coffee by his usual sip-more-sugar-sip-more-sugar-sip method. That done, he suddenly realized he was sitting alone. With his heels, he pulled his chair back their direction in slow scoots.

"Could there be some mistake?" Duncan asked, still scooting.

"There's been numerous mistakes," insisted Mason. "Not the least of which is Audra."

"But I liked Audra," Duncan protested.

"Parrish did too, Dunc. Can you shut up just a little?" Mason tapped a stack, showing Parrish a play he'd missed.

Duncan shook his head and sipped his coffee. He frowned, then dumped in more sugar. "Well, I don't know about everyone else," he said wearily, "but I'm a little shocked."

"Me too, Dunc," said Parrish.

Duncan noticed Parrish had two black sevens and no red sixes and had upturned only one ace, the club. He knew where the two of clubs was—buried under a queen and jack at the top of the deck. Parrish wasn't cheating, but he was thumbing through so quickly that he held the deck faceup, so Duncan had inadvertently seen them.

"Are you sure she kissed him?" he asked.

Mason groaned, picked up the sugar container, unscrewed the lid, and dumped the remaining sugar into Duncan's coffee. Duncan blinked at him, then stirred and sipped, stirred and sipped.

Parrish slapped the deck down again. He paused then blurted, "Should I go back over there or not?"

"Ab-so-lute-ly not!" Mason sang. "No sir! Don't give her *that*."

"He could go back and wait for the guy to leave," suggested Duncan. "He could ask him."

"Ask him what?"

"You know." Duncan stirred, then explained, "What his intentions are and—"

Mason waved this out of bounds. "As men, I don't think we have to hold a big think-tank meeting on what the guy's intentions might be."

"But he should know, too," protested Duncan.

"Let him find out the way Parrish did," Mason said to Duncan, then pointed at Parrish. "No, *you* do not go back. If you want me and Dunc to go wait around for him, just let us know."

Parrish gave Mason a sarcastic grin. "And what would you do?"

"Three guys on a street corner." Mason leaned forward conspiratorially. "Guy stops a guy to ask the time, third guy smashes into first guy with a twenty-ounce cup of scalding coffee."

"You're sick, you know that?" said Parrish.

Duncan pulled up his pants leg and scratched his ankle. "So you think Parrish shouldn't go back over there?"

"Eventually," Parrish interrupted, "I'll run into her again, so how do I—"

"You're done with that bus stop, buddy. You hear me?" Mason went over to the condiment bar, wadding and throwing each empty packet into the trash, one by one. "And when she comes slinkin' in here, wondering where you went, we'll—"

"But the gloves—" Duncan argued.

"Forget the gloves!" Mason yelled. "I'll buy us each a set of darts, and we'll hang the gloves up in the back room." He spun his chair around and sat face to face with Parrish. "You don't need her, Parrish. Not if she's going to be dishonest."

"How was she dishonest?" Duncan asked, matter-of-fact. "Did she say she wasn't seeing someone else?"

"She led him to believe certain things which, apparently, are not the case," said Mason.

"Even if she did," Duncan suggested, "you should still—"

"*If* she did?" Mason glowered at Duncan. "She's dishonest. And if she does that sort of thing right off the bat, you think she's going to honest-up over time? I'll bet twenty bucks the guy lives there, and I'll throw in another twenty that she told him she had dinner last night with her long-lost friend, Melissa."

"Who's Melissa?" Duncan asked.

Parrish fanned through the deck. Now that he was cheating, he went ahead and looked for more cards he needed.

"No," Mason said, "you're better off never seeing her again. She comes in here, you head to the back, and we'll say you've been mauled by a bear."

"Then *we'd* be lying," Duncan insisted.

Mason reached over. "I'm going to shake your head, just for a minute, like this."

"Ow!"

"Don't shake Duncan's head, please," said Parrish.

Mason let go of Duncan's skull, pushed out of his chair, then fled to the back room, slapping his hands along the counter as he went. Soon after he'd disappeared, the other two heard the sound of ice splintering as it was thrown against the back wall.

Duncan watched the cards for a moment, then said, "I'm sorry, Parrish, about what happened. But what I was trying to say…"

Parrish didn't look up, just continued flipping cards.

"I think you should stick with what you think you know, you know? I mean, this whole business—with the cookie, then Audra, then the bus stop—I thought this whole thing was about you *thinking* God told you to do something and then you doing it. And you *think* God told you to take back the gloves. So all I'm saying is…why do you still have them?"

Parrish's hands stopped. He just stared at Duncan.

"Maybe she's not honest," Duncan continued. "But if *God* told you to take the gloves back…you'd better get those gloves out of here."

Parrish looked down, took a card, and flicked it at his friend.

Duncan caught it against his chest. "What?"

Parrish plopped the deck on the table, rose, and headed out of the shop.

As the bells above the door jangled, Duncan flipped the card over on his shirt.

It was the ace of hearts.

At the top of her stoop, Parrish caught the front door before it closed as a man exited. Slightly nervous, he slipped inside then tried to appear normal. Alone in the lobby of her apartment building, he felt an urgency to leave, to get out. This felt wrong in a stalking sort of way. It was only Duncan's simple observation that kept him on track. *Take the gloves back.* It wasn't a phrase you could twist into meaning something other than what it meant. Undoubtedly, Audra would be peeved at his bumbling by uninvited. She would regret letting him walk her home. But he was already in her apartment building, the gloves in his hands.

Climbing the stairs, he realized he had no idea which apartment was hers. It would do no good checking the nameplates outside the front door, because he didn't even know her last name. He'd never asked. He was an excruciating idiot. He considered going back down to the mailboxes—perhaps a piece of junk mail addressed to Audra Somebody in Apartment Such-and-Such would be lying on the floor. He dismissed that as exceedingly creepy.

He went up a flight to the second floor and walked partway down the hall. How would he find her? He felt creepier and creepier.

Then the fear seized him that she would come out of her apartment, a bag of garbage in her hand or a dog on a leash—he didn't even know if she owned a dog. Innocently, she'd open her door and discover him lurking about her hallway.

He turned to leave, grabbing the railing at the top of the stairs, only to hear the quick scuff of shoes below as someone ran up. A young man carrying two plastic grocery bags turned the corner of the landing and stopped abruptly. It was the same young man, the one he'd seen with Audra. They stood like that for a moment, eyeballing each other, then the young man nodded brusquely and continued up the stairs to one side, allowing Parrish to pass.

"I'm looking for Audra." Parrish didn't know why he said it, how he'd made words happen. He wasn't totally sure they *had* happened until the young man stopped and gave him a very suspicious look up and down. At first, the young man frowned, unsure if he approved, then his shoulders relaxed. Apparently he didn't consider Parrish much of a threat.

"Do we know each other?"

"No, but she forgot her gloves."

Parrish extended them. This was the solution: Hand gloves to man, man take them to Audra, everyone would know what everyone knew. But when Audra started knowing, Parrish would be half a block away.

The young man looked at the gloves in Parrish's hand. A stair or two lower than Parrish, they were practically in his face. He nodded, took out his keys, then pushed past Parrish without touching the gloves.

"This way," he said.

Parrish turned, opening his mouth to speak, but dumbly watched the young man saunter carelessly down the hallway, turn to a door on his right, and fit the key in the lock.

"You coming?"

With a conscious effort, Parrish made his mouth close, then walked down the hallway to the open door that awaited him.

It was a large apartment, much larger than he'd expected, but then again, he'd thought Audra lived alone. It had one large room with a sofa, a television, and several comfy chairs. That room split off in three ways—a kitchen off to itself, a breakfast nook with a table surrounded by large, sunny windows, and a hallway that led toward the back of the apartment.

"Take a load off," said the young man, pointing at the sofa. "I'll see if she's home."

Parrish stood precisely where he was, against the wall by the door, as close to the coat stand as he could be without needing to introduce himself. He clutched the pair of gloves in his hands, as if they alone might exonerate him in the forthcoming interrogation.

The young man walked over to the kitchen door, leaned on the frame, and held up the plastic bags to look into them. He took out a jar—spaghetti sauce of some sort—and spun it, reading the label.

"Is this the one you wanted?" he asked. He spoke to someone in the kitchen, holding the jar up for their inspection. Parrish heard no response, but apparently the young man received a nod. He set the jar on the nearest counter, then unloaded both bags as well.

Parrish listened. Besides the sound of jars and cans being piled on a counter, he heard an electric can opener revolving and the splash of water from a spigot turned briefly on, then off. His thoughts formed in vague spy phrases—two targets in the kitchen, possible reinforcements down the hallway. He mentally measured the distance to all the windows and exits.

The young man leaned against the door frame to the kitchen. "You known Audra long?"

Parrish shook his head and slapped the gloves against his palm.

Suddenly the young man turned his head and yelled her name down the hall. He listened toward the back rooms, his head tilted at an angle, but no response came. He turned his face back into the kitchen. "Is Audra here?"

"I believe so."

From the kitchen, Parrish heard a woman's soft voice, and a moment later he saw her—a woman in her fifties wearing a white blouse under a gray long-sleeved cardigan. She was trim, almost un-healthily so, and wore a long, yellow flower-print skirt, which hung loosely on her thin frame. Her hair, which she wore long and tied back, was completely gray. She stepped through the doorway of the kitchen, her hands fretting with a dishtowel, but stopped abruptly, startled by the sight of Parrish. She caught her breath, then touched the finger-tips of one hand to the wall to steady herself.

"I let him in," the young man explained. "He's a friend of Audra's."

"You might have told me we had company," she said, chiding him slightly, but then giving him a weak smile.

The woman drew her sweater more tightly across her blouse,

then pressed her palms to her hips to smooth the skirt. She stepped slowly toward her guest.

Parrish switched the gloves to one hand and held out his other. "Sorry to intrude."

"Mrs. Simms," she introduced herself. She took his hand carefully, not shaking it so much as letting hers rest in his for a moment.

"I'm John," Parrish said. "Audra left these, or I had them—they're hers. I just wanted to bring them by."

It was the young man who responded. "She's always leaving stuff around," he said to Parrish, then to Mrs. Simms, "Where is she?"

"I believe she's in the bath."

"Again?" The young man made a disgruntled face.

Parrish cleared his throat. "I can just leave these. We ate dinner last night at a friend's house, and I found them today in my coat."

Mrs. Simms smiled faintly. "So you're the young man who's been keeping our Audra away these past few evenings?"

The young man walked over to Parrish and stood, face to face. "I'm Neil," he offered. "Don't believe we've met."

"Don't think so." Parrish shook Neil's hand, and each gave the other a firm grip.

"Well, I've already begun supper, so maybe instead of you two going out somewhere, you might like to eat with us, John." Despite her hospitality, there was something distant about Mrs. Simms. Her eyes never lingered anywhere for long, nor did they dart about. They floated—slowly here, then there, meandering. Mrs. Simms turned as if she'd received a reply, then lowered her head and walked primly back into the kitchen, leaving Parrish and Neil alone.

"Have a seat, really." Neil motioned to the sofa. "She'll bathe forever. Want a beer?" Neil asked on his way to the kitchen.

Parrish sat down. He didn't want to. He wanted to leave before Audra came out, but he didn't want to simply walk out the door. He perched on the edge of the sofa, twisting the gloves in his hands and trying to concoct some urgent story as to why he had to leave.

Neil returned with an open can of beer and plopped into the chair, hanging one leg over the armrest. He sipped at the can, then looked at Parrish. "What do you do?"

"I run a coffee shop."

Neil's head nodded lackadaisically.

"You like coffee?" Parrish asked, hoping he might be sent on an errand.

"Nope," Neil said and sipped his beer.

After a moment, Mrs. Simms returned from the kitchen, carrying a plate of cheese and fancy crackers. She brought this to the coffee table and stared down, uncertain where to put it. Parrish glanced at Neil, then leaned forward and quickly rearranged the magazines to make room for the plate. She set it down, corrected a few strands of hair that fell about her forehead, then turned to go.

Parrish stood. "Mrs. Simms…"

He was going to excuse himself, drop the gloves and go, but when the woman turned, she looked at him with a certain forlornness in her eyes—part desperation, part hope, he imagined—as if she so wished to hostess properly and already felt she had failed his approval. She blinked self-consciously, but that too seemed thin. Her self-disapproval only veiled her greater need to have him stay, to make an evening that welcomed a guest well, as if no amount of self-thoughts would feed what starved her.

Parrish didn't know what to say. He felt caught by her, by his wish not to bring any more difficulty to her eyes. Then he noticed something about the strands of hair that kept falling, the way she tilted her head to bring her hand up to them. When she did that she looked just like—

"John?"

Parrish turned. Where the hallway joined the sitting room, Audra stood in a fluffy white bathrobe, her hair in long wet tangles and a towel over her shoulder. She carried her glasses in one hand, and she put them on, then pulled the lapels of her bathrobe closer together. She stared at him, a flush of rosy embarrassment flaring across her cheeks, which then reddened with anger. Her jaw clenched, and she gave everyone in the room a harsh look, one by one, ending with her eyes again on Parrish.

"What are you doing here?" she asked.

Mrs. Simms's face winced, just barely, at the unkind tone in Audra's voice. Neil bristled upward in his chair, as if he might be called upon to intervene. Pitifully, Parrish held up the gloves.

"I thought it would be nice if you two had dinner at home," began Mrs. Simms, "so I invited John—"

"Mother!" Audra whined. She pulled again at her robe, holding it tightly with both hands as she walked over to Parrish and swiped the gloves from his hands.

Neil laughed and stuck his foot out to trip her as she headed back toward the hall.

"Stop it!" Audra slapped his shoulder.

"What's the matter, Sis?" Neil laughed, but stopped short when she turned and gave him a look of betrayal. He reached out, stretching a hand to her apologetically, and tried to grab her hand before she could get away. She slipped free and ran down the hall into a back room, slamming the door behind her.

Neil looked at Parrish, then shrugged. Audra's mother laid a hand on Parrish's sleeve.

"I would like it if you stayed. May I take this coat?"

It took some time for Audra to reemerge. Parrish waited, still perched on the edge of the sofa cushion. He watched Neil finish his beer, take the can to the kitchen to throw it out, then return with a bag of chips. Neil asked if he followed baseball. He said no, commented that it wasn't baseball season, and that ended his conversation with Audra's brother, who picked up a remote and flipped the television to a sports channel, devouring the stats and trades that scrolled across the bottom of the screen.

Parrish ate a slice of cheese and several crackers, only to realize how dry his mouth was. He could barely swallow, so he kept chewing, hoping for moisture. He was working up the nerve to go to the kitchen and ask for a glass of water when the door at the end of the hallway opened loudly and Audra returned.

Her hair was mostly dry now, though still damp at the ends, fluffed and pulled back. She wore a pair of jeans, her tennis shoes, and a heavy, gray pullover sweater with the sleeves rolled up.

Though she'd blushed earlier, hers was now a sensible face, drained of any show of emotion. She addressed Parrish with a very business-like disposition.

"Could I talk you to for a minute?" she asked, more a demand than a request.

Neil glanced between them, whistled once, and sank lower into his chair.

Parrish stood and walked over to her, only to have her spin on her heels and walk down the hallway, escorting him to its farthest corner. There, she spun back in his face. "You're not staying."

"I don't want to," he said, his voice muffled with crackers.

"My mother thinks you are," she whispered, her arms across her chest, her hands tightly grabbing her elbows. She cocked a hip to one side.

"I know she does," he said.

"Why did you come here?" she asked over the rims of her glasses.

He coughed. "To return your gloves."

"You can't stay."

"I'm not."

"Don't be cute. Tell me the truth."

"I've never been cute in my life. And hold on! Speaking of the truth—" He became so animated, he nearly choked, his throat so dry from the crackers. He coughed, swallowed hard, trying to still himself, then hacked and coughed uncontrollably.

"Do you need water?" Audra asked.

"Water," he choked out. "Need it."

She went in the bathroom at the end of the hall and ran him a glass from the tap. She brought it to him, holding it out by her fingertips, her elbow resting on her hip.

Parrish drank half of it, paused, held up a finger to show that this was still a time-out, then drank the rest. "Thank you for the water."

"Thank you for my gloves," she said, taking the glass away. She reached around him and shut the door to her room so he couldn't see in. "I just don't understand how you could invite yourself to dinner—"

"I didn't! Your *mother* invited me," he explained, "when I didn't even know she *was* your mother!"

Audra said nothing but looked at him with the most soulful, sad, damp eyes he'd ever seen.

"Look, you explain it to her," he said. "Tell her I have to get back to the shop. I'll—"

The front door opened. Audra heard it.

"Turn that basketball down," called out a man's voice.

Audra covered her face with her hands and stood helplessly before Parrish like a child, shaking. He had no idea what to do to help. Neil came down the hallway, saw his sister, and put a hand on her shoulder. He gave Parrish a glance, simply to acknowledge he was there, then went into his room.

After a moment, Audra raised her face, then leaned her back against the wall.

From where he stood, Parrish could see Mrs. Simms come out of the kitchen.

"What smells good?" said the loud, deep voice.

"It's been ready. I hope it's fine. I thought you'd be home sooner," Mrs. Simms said.

"I stopped by Reilly's after work. You know that, so don't start."

Parrish saw a man walk over to her and hand her his coat and thermos. He turned and saw the two at the end of the hallway. Audra's shoulders tensed, and she covered one foot with the other.

"Who's this, little girl?"

Audra didn't move, didn't speak.

The man faced them. He stood an average height, slightly shorter than Parrish, but broad shouldered, with a firm, square jaw. He wore a denim work shirt, a dirty pair of jeans, and a scuffed, worn pair of work boots. His hair was black, combed greasily to one side, and he had a thick moustache peppered with gray. "This one of the days we're not speaking?" he asked her.

"I'm John." Parrish walked down the hallway and offered his hand, only to have it crunched by Audra's father.

"Frank. Frank Simms," said her father. He glanced at Audra, who still had not moved. He exhaled heavily, then ignored her.

"John's joining us for dinner," Mrs. Simms said to her husband, "if that's all right?" She waited but received no response. "He and Audra had dinner last night."

"Fine, fine," said Mr. Simms. "You care for a beer?"

Parrish shook his head. Mr. Simms disappeared into the kitchen, as did his wife. Parrish heard the sound of a beer can being popped open.

Audra brushed past Parrish, walked over to the coatrack, and grabbed Parrish's coat.

"Glad to have you," said Mr. Simms, in the doorway to the kitchen. "High time we got a look at the man who's been keeping my daughter out every evening." He leveled a tough look at Parrish, overly tough, then took a huge swig of his beer and gave him a quick wink.

Mrs. Simms came out of the kitchen, carrying a casserole dish. She glanced at Audra, at the coat in her hands. She frowned hopelessly, tried weakly to smile, then her eyes strayed. She set the dish on the table. "Audra, would you set the table, please?" she asked, almost inaudibly.

With a look of despair, Audra gave in and dropped Parrish's coat on a chair by the door. She helped her mother set the table, both of them making numerous trips in and out of the kitchen for silverware, plates, and glasses. She set a pitcher of iced tea near the casserole dish, and her mother brought out rolls in a basket and a dish of mashed potatoes. Mrs. Simms asked for Parrish's help, showed him where to find the extra chair, and instructed him to set it next to Audra's place. Neil returned from his room only when everything was ready and took his place at the table. Audra sat down, as did Parrish. Mrs. Simms stood holding the back of her chair, giving the table a last inventory. Mr. Simms came from the kitchen with a beer can, set it next to his plate, then mumbled to his wife.

"Butter."

Mrs. Simms gripped the chair, a tremor running through her arms as he pointed out what she'd forgotten. She hurried back into the kitchen and returned with a stick of butter on a dish with a small knife.

Once all five were seated, Mr. Simms lifted the dish of mashed potatoes, filled his plate with a fluffy heap, then passed the dish to his wife. Mrs. Simms did not take the dish. Both her hands lay palm up on the table, one to each side of her plate.

"Mom wants to say grace," Neil said to his father.

"Let her say it, then," Mr. Simms said, taking a roll for his plate.

Mrs. Simms's eyes floated up from the table and onto her husband, but not for long. She glanced over at her son, then withdrew her hands and unfolded her napkin.

Neil watched this, then stared at his father. "I think she wants you to say grace."

Mr. Simms popped open the can in front of him, took a sip, and looked around the table, a glance for everyone. Lastly, he gave his wife a heavy stare, one that wilted her shoulders. Then he turned to his son. "Say it, so we can eat."

Neil glanced at Audra, who refused to look up. She held her lips tightly together as if she were trying not to make any sound at all. Parrish offered his hand to her, but she kept her hands in her lap, pretending not to notice. Neil watched his father continue to fill his plate. He reached across the table and took his mother's hand, holding it in between the dishes and the tea pitcher. His other hand he placed on Audra's shoulder.

"Dear God," he began abruptly, his tone defiant. "Thanks for this food and for those hands that prepared it. Bless this food to our nourishment and bless this…family. Amen."

"Amen." Mrs. Simms repeated the word and gave her son a small smile.

"And amen!" said Mr. Simms loudly, with a wild smile at Parrish that invited him into their game. "So what is it you do…uh…what did you say your name was?"

"John." Parrish took a roll from Mrs. Simms. "I run the coffee shop off Belvedeere."

Mr. Simms made a furtive, overinterested face. "I don't remember a coffee shop there."

"It's there. I've seen it," said Neil.

"Well, good, son. Glad to know you get out of the house once in a while. I haven't seen it."

Neil ignored his father.

"Business good?" asked Mr. Simms.

"I do all right," said Parrish.

Mr. Simms nodded with feigned interest.

Their tea glasses had already been filled with ice, and Audra poured tea for everyone, handing the glasses to each person after she'd filled them. Mr. Simms had not been set a tea glass. He drank another gulp out of the beer can, set it down beside his plate, then spooned a huge helping of meatloaf onto his plate and buttered his bread. He scooped a large spoonful of green beans onto his plate in between the mounds of meat and potatoes, then salted and peppered everything with tremendous energy. When he'd finished, he took a last gulp out of the can, tilting the can up high. Before putting the can back next to his plate, he shook it to confirm it was empty.

Mrs. Simms took the cue. She gave a shy glance at Parrish, then excused herself, picked up the empty can and took it with her to the kitchen to get him another. Mr. Simms began eating, seeming not to notice this operation happening so routinely around him. When his wife returned with a new can and set it down for him, he continued eating, his fork in his right hand, but his left reached over and expertly popped the can open.

Though they sat next to each other, Audra wouldn't look at Parrish. She passed the dishes by holding them in her left hand, waiting for him to take their weight, then picked up another. Parrish remained politely silent, answering questions posed him, but not asking any of his own. Neil hunched over his plate, eating quickly. Mrs. Simms eyed everything that happened with a mixture of pride and fear.

"How was school?" Mr. Simms asked Audra, almost mechanically, as if it were his responsibility to fill every silence.

She didn't look up at her father. "Fine."

"Huh?" Mr. Simms said.

"She said 'fine,'" Neil interrupted.

"I didn't ask you." Mr. Simms's voice flared. "I can't hear when she mumbles."

"I don't have class on Saturdays," Audra answered, this time looking him square in the eye.

Mr. Simms opened his eyes mockingly wide and shook his head back and forth. "Was that so hard?"

Audra returned her eyes to her plate and rolled green beans around with her fork.

"My daughter only talks to her father on certain days of the week, John," Mr. Simms explained. He finished yet another beer and shook the can as he placed it beside his plate. This time Mrs. Simms didn't move, but her entire body tensed. Mr. Simms continued unaware. "She wants to be a nurse, but she doesn't work or talk on Saturdays. I just hope I'm never sick on one of her bad days."

Audra listened to all this as she stared at her plate with visible restraint, but at the last words, her restraint drained away and left something much more distant, much more numb, as if she were humming to herself while she poked at her food. For all practical purposes, she'd escaped and was now somewhere else, millions of miles away.

But Neil watched his sister, then put himself in the way again.

"Not everyone's the great conversationalist you are, Dad," he muttered.

Mr. Simms laughed boisterously, cheerfully, too loud for the occasion. He picked up his beer can to sip it, realized it felt too light, glanced at his wife, then set the can down again, this time much closer to her plate.

"This is where the team gangs up on me, John." He leaned toward Parrish as if he were sharing a confidence. "They work their strategies out each afternoon. That's why I come home late from work. Wouldn't want to deprive them of their fun."

He picked up the can, only to realize again it was empty. This time he placed it down hard on the table, looked at his wife, and sighed. He threw his napkin beside his plate and pushed his chair back from the table. "John, you need one?"

"I'll get it," Audra volunteered.

Parrish watched as she stood and went to the kitchen. He couldn't tell if she'd volunteered to save her mother or to make sure her father didn't bring him a beer. She came back from the kitchen holding the can by the top with her thumb and index finger as if it were a dirty thing. She placed it beside his plate, then returned to her seat.

"Thank you, dear daughter," said Mr. Simms, with stressed affection. He glanced at his wife as he popped it open.

Audra gave Parrish a defiant look, her eyes lazily blank but angry. Like she'd given in earlier, holding out Parrish's coat in the hope that he would leave, she now gave in a second time, a more thorough collapse, as if she'd decided to no longer hide this, but to show it all.

Mr. Simms tried a fresh attempt at conversation. "So how's business, John?" he asked, apparently not remembering that he had already done so.

"Good," said Parrish, pretending not to notice.

"Your shop, it's not one of those hoity-toity latte places, huh?"

"We sell those, but mostly black coffee."

"I can't see how a man could make a living off cups of coffee," he said, truly puzzled.

If that was a question, Parrish couldn't answer. He nodded, tried not to look at Audra, and continued to eat his meatloaf.

As the conversation died, Parrish watched Mr. Simms give a long look out the second-story windows that surrounded the table. He sighed, staring down at the street as if he longed to be somewhere else, anywhere but here. His daughter stared out the window in the exact same way.

By this point, Neil had finished his meal. He placed his fork and knife on his plate, chugged the rest of his tea, then wiped his mouth on his napkin. "Food was great, Mom. Nice meeting you, John."

As he pushed his chair back, his father barked, "Where do you think you're going?"

"Down the hall to Kyle's. He bought a huge flat screen and—"

"Sit down," commanded Mr. Simms, pointing at the boy's chair with his fork. "You can wait until everyone's finished just this once."

"I'm pretty sure everybody'll be fine without me," he said, standing and slipping out from his chair.

Mr. Simms stood. By this point, he did so with a slight stagger, resting the fingers of one hand on the table for balance. Parrish couldn't count how many beers he'd had, but he considered the likely possibility that Mr. Simms had drunk before he'd come home. The man's cheeks were flushed, both with displeasure at his son and with alcohol, and his lips began to snarl and slur.

"We have company. You'll stay until we're all done. Like a family does. Please your mother, for once." Mr. Simms said this unsteadily, but when his son made another motion toward leaving, his eyes cleared and narrowed, and his shoulders flexed in a way that was suddenly very steady and imposing.

"I'm going," Neil repeated.

Parrish wondered how Mrs. Simms could eat, but then he realized hers was the smartest choice—finish the meal so the ultimatum would be over. He tried to force himself to eat.

"Neil," said Audra, "tell John about that building you drew."

It was an offer—the whole family understood on some unspoken level—a solution to both men needing to keep face and not back down.

Neil looked at his sister, then took his seat. Briefly, he explained to Parrish that he was studying to be an architect, and that in one class everyone had been given a design project, no big deal really, and he'd drawn up the main draft for a museum, an art museum that would share the plot with the botanical gardens.

"He did it for real," said Audra happily. "He surveyed the place downtown where it could go, and his teacher passed it along to a developer."

Neil leaned back in his chair, crossed his legs, and pulled at the sole of his tennis shoe. "He didn't send it to a developer. It isn't going to happen," he explained to Parrish, grinning. "He just has a friend who's a developer who looked at it and liked what he saw."

"But you did get the highest grade out of, what…a hundred and fifty designs?" Audra prompted.

Neil shook his head, dismissing her. "It's classwork. Nothing really."

"Don't knock it, son," said Mr. Simms. For a moment, Mrs. Simms stared at her husband in disbelief. "That's the most I've heard her speak in weeks," he continued. "Let's keep her talking. God knows how long it's been since she's said something pleasant to anyone."

Audra turned her head with a sad fury, breathed deeply, then excused herself from the table and ran down the hall.

Mrs. Simms stood, picked up her plate, then Audra's, and began clearing dishes to the kitchen.

"What?" Mr. Simms asked his wife.

She continued her motion, her eyes floating again, as if she heard no sound.

"Why do you do that?" Neil said to his father with a tone of pure challenge.

"What?" said Mr. Simms, shaking another empty can.

"Why do you pick on her? You think that will make her *want* to talk to you?"

Mr. Simms squinched his face sourly. "I don't pick on that girl."

"Yeah," Neil said smoothly. "Yeah, you do. Why don't you leave her alone?"

Mrs. Simms appeared at the doorway to the kitchen and stood there with a look of alarm. Her eyes lost their floating quality. Now they gave direct, meaningful glances—toward the table, her husband, her son, Parrish's coat by the door. She looked as if she were planning her escape, or how she could achieve her guest's escape, as if that were her responsibility as hostess.

Audra came back down the hallway. She, too, gave the room a strategic glance—her brother and father, her mother, then hurried over to Parrish's coat and picked it up off the chair.

Mr. Simms stared at his son with a look of contempt, then dropped his fork and knife onto his plate and leaned back. He laughed to himself, stroked his jaw with his hand. "Go on then, leave. Get out of here!"

"Let's all go see Kyle's big-screen television," said Audra.

"No," said Neil very calmly. "He hasn't answered my question."

Mr. Simms frowned deeply, then raised his voice louder than Parrish had yet heard it. "You'd think for a kid who eats *my* food and lets me pay *his* bills, you'd want to watch that *mouth* a little more than you do. I would *never* have spoken to my old man, rest his soul, with a mouth full of *dis*respect—"

"You're right!" Neil leaned excitedly onto the table, pounding it with the tip of his finger. "You never would've said one word to your drunk of a father—"

Mr. Simms stood up so angrily his chair skidded backwards and fell over. Mrs. Simms clutched her arms across her chest, her shoulders tensed as if she were waiting for the crashing sounds to start.

"Neil!" called Audra. "Dad, you want me to get you a beer?"

"Oh, don't you start too, little girl!" Mr. Simms bellowed over his shoulder.

"Frank…," Mrs. Simms whispered.

"Naw, she's got to stop being so touchy. I'm sick to death of it. Need, need, that's all that everybody does around here. How about we show a little gratitude and not make every night the production, huh? Sick to death of it."

Neil leaned back in his chair. He looked carefully at his father, as if appraising—if drunk, how drunk—then called his father's bluff. He smiled cruelly. "I *said*, leave her alone. Talk your crap to me, I'll talk back. I'm not afraid of *my* father."

For a moment, Parrish wondered if Mr. Simms might flip the table out of his way and take his own son by the throat. Instead, the man pounded both fists, short blows but sound ones, into the table-top so that the silverware jumped and rattled. Mr. Simms blinked wildly as he stared at his son, tried to clear his eyes, as if each blink changed who he was seeing. Then he turned slowly, fumbled to pick up his chair, and set it back in place. He collapsed his weight into it, picked up his fork, and looked around at the dishes stacked on the table.

"House full of disrespect, that's what," he mumbled.

Neil stood and looked down at his father. "Yeah," he mumbled, checking his watch. "We're your problem."

Still seated at the table, Parrish kept his hands folded. He tried not to remain invisible, tried for Audra's sake not to feel any of the embarrassment. He glanced at her.

Carrying Parrish's coat, Audra ran to the door, flung it open, and slammed it behind her.

Parrish stood. "Excuse me. I think I should go check on Audra. Thank you for dinner, ma'am."

He went to the door, opened it, and Neil was right behind, following him out. When the door shut, Parrish exhaled deeply.

Neil laughed. "Good times, huh?" he said, swatting Parrish's arm. "Tell her I'm at Kyle's if she needs me. She'll be on the stoop or gone walking. Good to meet you." Neil offered Parrish a handshake as if nothing had happened at all.

Parrish sat on the stoop till it was quite dark. The streetlights flickered awake, and the wind grew colder. The night sky was low, unbroken clouds pressing the cold down, holding it close to the ground.

He shivered. He didn't have his coat—she did, and even his scarf was in his coat pocket. He rocked back and forth, rubbing his hands. For a long while he sat like that, looking up and down the street, but saw no sign of her. Finally, he quit looking. Huddled on the concrete stair, he scooted up against the balustrade to hide from the wind.

Hours later, he heard the little dog bark. When he looked, he saw her walking down the sidewalk, near the fenced yard, which the dog guarded fiercely from the inside. She wore his coat, its sleeves too long for her, but she'd left them long to protect her hands from the wind.

He stood and dusted off the seat of his pants. He didn't walk toward her, nor did he leave.

Audra stopped when she saw him, crossed her arms and stared. Then she shook her head, dropped her gaze to the sidewalk and walked slowly toward the stoop.

"Audra—" he said, but she walked up the stairs right past him, fumbling with her keys.

He stood his ground. "Audra, I—"

She turned to him, staring down harshly, taking full advantage of the height she commanded. "Are you happy now?"

He said nothing.

"Are you, John?" She spoke calmly, not as if her rage had gone, but as if it had turned into something smooth and hard. "Seen all you need to see?" She opened her arms wide, only her fingers showing at the ends of the coat's sleeves. "There's all you wanted to know. That's about everything. Satisfied?"

"I'm sorry, I didn't know."

"No, but *now* you do." She clapped her hands down against her thighs. "So have a good night."

"Audra, wait."

"No, no! You wait! You…you…barge in here, you barge into my life, you and your stupid God games. You've invaded everything and seen precisely everything I didn't *want* you to see. Congratulations!

See me? This is it, here's all my ugliness, all at once, I've nowhere to hide. Satisfied?"

Parrish made no motion, no sound while she gestured and waited.

"Good! That's what I was hoping you'd say. Now…go away."

"Audra—"

"No, John. Turn around and walk away."

When Audra returned upstairs, the dinner scene had been erased—the table cleared entirely, the bowl of fruit back where it belonged, the mail in its stack returned, and the chairs pushed perfectly back in their places. The lights were dimmed now. Audra heard the sink running in the kitchen, the clank of dishes and plates, her mother washing away. She would help her, that was her usual routine, but first she walked down the hallway. She looked in her parents' bedroom and saw her father's clothes strewn on the bed, his shirt sprawled across the floor. The door to their bathroom was closed, and she heard the shower running. Her father preferred his shower at night; he moved so thickly most mornings before work. She tiptoed closer, heard the thud and scuttle of someone dropping a new bar of soap and chasing it across the tile floor of the shower stall. She also heard him curse.

Audra tiptoed out, then down the hall to her brother's door. When she knocked, it drifted open. She whispered his name, but got no response.

She understood.

He would return in his own time, late, or he'd fall asleep on Kyle's couch and come back in the morning after their father had already left for work. She stepped in his room, turned off the lamp beside his bed, fluffed his pillows, and pulled the sheets in such a way that someone might think a body lay there, sleeping. If her father checked, perhaps he might think his son was asleep. It angered him when his boy slept beneath someone else's roof. Audra shut her brother's door and glanced to verify that the crack beneath it showed a darkened room.

That done, she went back to the den. Her father had left the television blaring, and some ridiculous show about cars screamed at the empty room. She turned the volume down and placed the remote on the coffee table by the sofa, where he liked it kept. She picked up her father's boots, aligned them so that they were a pair, then set them at the end of the sofa, where he would be likely to find them. Most often, he fell asleep on the couch, he and his wife spending their nights separately and alone. When he woke in the morning, an early riser, he'd dress in their bedroom closet, then sit with a cup of coffee on the sofa and work with his socks and boots. Audra didn't set a pair of socks on his boots or pick up his clothes from the bedroom floor, not anymore. She'd done that too long. Most often he'd overlook the socks she left out for him and get a pair of his own. She'd found many folded pairs, pairs she had folded, draped over the arm of the sofa when she'd come home from reading at the bus stop.

She went to the kitchen. For a moment, she watched her mother's back, her tense shoulders beneath her housecoat, where she stood at the sink, washing dishes. Audra softly spoke her mother's name.

No matter how softly she tried, her mother always startled. Mrs. Simms jumped, turned to see her daughter, put a hand to her throat, then regained a rhythm to her breathing. She forced a smile at her daughter, then dutifully continued her work.

Audra picked up a dry cloth, wiped down the plates and cups upturned on the drying rack, and put them away in the cupboards.

"Let me do that," her mother chided.

"I'll do it."

"No, make sure they're dry, honey." Her mother stopped her work, dried her hands, then opened the cupboards, took out the dishes Audra had put away, and dried them again. She spun the plates between tight fingers, pressed the dry cloth into them as she turned them, polished away all the streaks until they shined.

Audra never argued with her mother. Instead, she tied her hair back, rolled up her sleeves, and plunged her hands and arms down in the soapy water, washing dishes where her mother had left off.

"I can do that, here…," said her mother.

"Let me help," Audra said softly.

"You run along. I can still do some things," her mother said.

Stubbornly but silently, Audra continued washing the glasses and silverware in the sink. She scrubbed them ferociously, knowing that her mother required more than the removal of stains. She needed to see the effort it took to remove them, so Audra used the sponge and the brush, held the dishes up under the light for inspection before settling them into the drying rack. But this, too, was not enough. Her mother would inspect a knife, a spoon, then sadly, not wanting to upset her daughter, place them on the counter instead of in the drawer, collecting a pile she would later rewash when her daughter would not know.

Audra always knew. She blew a strand of hair out of her face as she washed, trying not to speak.

It took far longer than it should have—Audra finishing a task and moving on, allowing her mother to quietly redo it—but finally they were done. Audra took the teapot down from the top shelf and filled it with water from the tap. She turned on the burner, then set the teapot over it. She took down two mugs, her mother hovering, fingers restlessly pulling the lapel of her housecoat, as if she were uncomfortable with clean dishes being used again so soon.

"You want honey?" Audra asked.

"I don't want any, thank you," her mother replied, tidying her hair and looking away.

"I'll make you a cup, and then you decide."

The water boiled quickly with the high flame. Audra unsheathed tea bags and dropped one in each cup, then poured the steaming water over them. Since her mother wasn't having honey, Audra had none. The two leaned against the kitchen counter and sipped their tea.

Her mother was uneasy when she had nothing to do. She continually pulled at her housecoat and looked back at the counter as if worried it might be wet. Audra reached a hand over to her mother's arm. Mrs. Simms jumped, startled again. She glanced wildly down at her daughter's hand, then looked up at Audra, and forced a smile. She patted her daughter's hand.

"John seems very nice," Mrs. Simms tried.

"He shouldn't have come."

Mrs. Simms began to ask a question, then closed her mouth and patted her daughter's hand again.

From the back rooms, they heard a door banging open, a knob hitting the wall. Then they heard a drawer open and close. After a few moments, the volume on the television increased again. Mrs. Simms jumped at each of these sounds, but at the nearest, the television's volume, she immediately pushed away from the counter, walked to the sink, and dumped her tea down the drain. She took the sponge and washed all of it away, giving the sink another quick wipe down.

Audra turned off the kitchen light. "Come on, Mom, it's time for bed."

Daughter escorted mother from the kitchen, through the den, and down the hall. Neither of them stopped to look at the man heaped on the sofa as they passed.

In her bedroom, Mrs. Simms instinctively began picking up articles of clothing off the floor. Audra took them from her hands and threw them in the closet, much to her mother's dismay. She would have gone in the closet to hang them up if Audra had not stopped her from doing so.

"Leave it!" Audra insisted with a whisper.

Audra sat on the corner of her parents' bed, waiting as her mother applied various face creams, brushed her teeth, picked up towels and rags, and straightened the bathroom. Walking around to the far side of the bed, her side, she slowly took off her housecoat, folded it, and lay it in a rocking chair, then pulled back the covers, sat on the bedside, and slipped her feet beneath the sheet. Audra watched her mother's face as it lay wide-eyed on the pillow. They both wished the other a good night. Then her mother closed her eyes, like a doll whose string had spooled back inside.

Audra never quite knew: Was her mother able simply to choose sleep, or did she close her eyes the way she did to allow her daughter to go? She clicked off her mother's lamp.

His snores could be heard even above the television. She stepped over to where her father lay sprawled, mouth open, and gently took the remote from his hand. She turned down the volume of the television, then placed the remote on the table where she had before and stood over him for a moment.

His hair was damp from his shower; he hadn't dried it. His sides rose with deep breaths, but fell unevenly, with slight jerks and twitches as he exhaled. He was just a human, a man, a big unhappy boy. This was what she most hated about her father—when he was sleeping, she could still love him.

She whispered his name, though she knew he was out and would not wake for a while. She covered his bare, damp feet with the afghan from the back of the sofa, tucking its corner into the cushions.

As she put her hair up in her hat, she glanced down at the chair by the door and saw Parrish's coat atop her own. To return that, she'd be forced to see him again. She considered walking it over to his shop and tossing it at the foot of the door—a cattish thought, to which she gave a sour grin.

Nonetheless, she chose his coat over her own and slipped it on. She rolled the sleeves up a cuff, then buttoned it to the collar.

Outside, the temperature had fallen. She walked in and out of the pools of light from the streetlights, crossed the street, and headed briskly down the sidewalk. Realizing she saw no passing cars, no other people, she checked her watch. It was past eleven, nearing midnight. Most of the windows of the houses and apartments she passed had their blinds drawn, no lights behind them. Somewhere on a Saturday night, people were awake and busy, but not in her neighborhood. Here, all was quiet.

She walked to the bus stop. She had no purpose in going there, other than the walking and that it wasn't home. She sat on her usual bench in the pool of light. The wind picked up, and she wished for her scarf, her gloves. Hunched over in Parrish's coat—it was sizes too big for her—she pushed her hands into the pockets, balling them into fists for warmth. She gave an apprehensive glance across the parking lot, making sure the lights to Parrish's shop were out. It was all dark, no cars at all in the wide parking lot.

Audra certainly never meant to pray. But because she was at this bus stop, where she'd first met Parrish, across from his shop, her memory backtracked through their few days together until she came to the scene, in her mind, of Parrish sitting alone at Mr. Wu's. She pictured him opening the fortune cookie alone at the table, the God cookie. She smirked at the thought of his face—surprised, confused, uncertain—him looking to see if anyone else understood his moment of revelation. How ridiculous a man, she thought. Her mind replayed Parrish's explanation of Duncan's Bible story—the woman who had no child, who wanted a child, and her prayer to God.

Audra understood that sort of prayer—she wanted no father, she wanted a father—the desperate prayer of impossibility.

Her father...

That's where thinking started, where thinking stopped, where all her prayers so long ago had dried up. She no longer prayed, nor even dreamed of changing her father. Her dreams now played variations on the theme of escape. And they were nothing more than that— just dreams, just play. She'd been alone at the end of her dreams so many times before and never had God helped her escape her father, because God couldn't, because she would never escape her need to love him.

Her eyes glanced numbly across the dark parking lot, its pools of light. She blinked without any thought or feeling. This was how it worked—too much feeling until it overwhelmed her, shut her down.

She stretched out her legs despite the cold, crossing them at her ankles. She raised her face and blinked at the sky, her neck exposed without her scarf, but the cold around her no longer as numbing as the flatness inside her. She allowed the cold to creep around Parrish's coat onto her neck, her hands, her forearms, accepting it as her due. She would stay here—a minute more, an hour, who knew—until the cold became unbearable and bore down to the bone, then she would leave.

She bowed her head, sinking her hands limply in the pockets of Parrish's coat. For a moment, she almost borrowed a bit of Parrish's belief, just enough to pray for something, only to realize she didn't want anything to do with a father—heavenly or otherwise.

What God did next for Audra was interesting, mainly because God had been doing it all along. Without disregarding the other purposes—Mr. Crawford and Thomas, Mrs. Miranda, the stolen purse—God's reasons comprised a wider game. Even Parrish's bumbling interruption that evening played its part in bringing Audra to that bus bench that particular night. To redeem her memory, he meant to remake the moment she last held belief, reconnecting her to something sure.

It started with the snowflakes.

After the first fleck brushed her cheek, Audra looked up, only to squint at the streetlight, like a spotlight above her, illuminating her in its pool of light. She squinted so that the light blurred widely, the flutter of snowflakes brushing past her face quickly now, like released confetti. She drew her feet together as if standing on the edge, and a memory collected in the corner of her eyes so that the light became a watery apparition, perhaps an angel or the glow of one, both memory and the present blossoming at once—the bright light, the stage, the bench, the whisper of snow and wind, and the shiver of excitement and cold—all feeling too much inside her, like it might suddenly break free like wings.

Her hands, buried in the pockets of the too-large coat, found and blindly flipped a slip of paper. She took out the fortune and—by sheer accident, like the toss of coin—read the back of the slip instead of the front. Someone else's handwriting, but her memory, and she could hear it, or she was about to hear, if she'd only listen.

Like Mr. Crawford's fondest wish, God, after years of doting preparation, at this corner, suddenly delivered all his correspondence at once, poured out at the feet of his beloved.

Father?

When everything all in a moment comes together, surprisingly perfect, it doesn't prove there's a loving God; but if there is, isn't it perfect when all in a moment, God proves how surprisingly he loves? It was like magic, but so much of magic is about misdirection, whereas so much of redemption is straightforward and ordinary, piercing true and lit with surprise.

She leaned forward, her head swirling because of the speed of her tears, and though the blood pulsing in her ears amplified the silence around her, she heard—as if God now were only a few proud rows away, watching his daughter—*his* whispered voice overheard, so close she could simply fall toward it, despite the dim shadows, from the edge where her toes had too long clutched and curled. A child again with wings, leaping.

Is it too early to applaud? Look…

Sunday

The coffee shop was closed on Sundays.

When Parrish's alarm went off, he rose and brewed a pot of coffee while he shaved, bathed, and dressed. Then he ate a banana, drank the first cup at his kitchen table, and poured the second in a travel mug. Outside, he unlocked his car, put the mug in the holder, and cranked the engine to let the car warm up while he dug his ice scraper out of the backseat. It was an awesome scraper, the kind made for huge trucks. It resembled an oversized dentist's implement, almost three feet long, with a grippy handle at one end and a massive, jagged scraping edge at the other, and when flipped over, there were sturdy plastic bristles on the backside. There was no ice to scrape this morning, so he used the brush side to dust the thin layer of powdery snow off his windshield.

Then he realized, abruptly, that it had *snowed*. He looked up at the sky—partly because that's where snow comes from, but more because that was where he usually imagined God.

"Thanks."

This gratitude slipped from his lips, but too inaudibly, so he said it again, loud enough to be heard—and this time, not upward and away. Parrish discovered he was talking to someone much closer.

So much had happened, in so short a time—it was only a week since he'd opened the cookie, and that week felt to have flown past. But at the same time, it felt so full. They'd spent so much of the week together, he and God. One week of being all-in, and Parrish was talking to God in his driveway like a neighbor who'd stopped by.

"Is *that* how you work?"

Again, he spoke not to some remote God he had to work to get at, like troubling some old radio knob to find the faint and desired frequency. Instead, he posed the question offhandedly across the hood of his snow-dusted car as if to a friend. And at that moment, cleaning off his windshield became incredible with meaning. The cold on his cheeks, no longer a nuisance, became the momentous privilege of feeling. Even the scraper seemed slightly sacred in his hand—not because it was, but because God was near.

He felt a need, almost a pain, to respond, to *do* something— religious or commemorative. Perhaps bury the scraper in the yard and put three large, round stones over the spot. This was, of course, foolish. But that's precisely how he felt—hilariously foolish—and the foolishness of the cookie missions seemed suddenly the only happy way to live.

He wanted to respond appropriately to this God-occasion, so his mind rummaged for something weighty, formal, somber. It was the *Our Father* his mind grasped amid the clutter of his thoughts, and so he began it, only getting as far as the first two words. And again, as abruptly as he'd finally *seen* the snow, he finally *heard* the words, just the two, as if the Christ suddenly appeared and spoke them at the same time.

Our Father. *Ours.*

Whatever that had meant to him previously, it meant something entirely better now. It wasn't a prayer anymore, not really. It became two brothers scraping a windshield to begin their day.

Monday

All three of the boys worked Mondays. They had the Monday before, the fateful day of the God cookie, and they would work the following Monday, whether God was doing things with cookies then or not.

Out of pity for Parrish, Duncan and Mason opened and let him sleep in. Parrish was glad to get the rest. He treated himself to a nice, fat hamburger for lunch and didn't answer his cell when they called to ask him questions. Already, in the back of his mind, he planned to close the store by himself. It'd been a very long time since he'd done so, and he missed the quiet accomplishment of doing everything alone, locking the door and giving that last look through the glass. And nothing was better than opening the store on a morning after he'd closed it. Everything was already done. Push a few buttons, flip the light switches, and drag the patio furniture in place. Then he'd have a cup of his own coffee and wait for the rush. A satisfying plan.

Around four o'clock, Parrish finally made it to work, an unprecedentedly late arrival. When he opened the door, Mason jerked his head spastically and coughed until Duncan ran over to the espresso machine to pull Parrish a couple of shots.

"How's business?" Parrish asked, beating them to the first question.

"Great," said Mason. "We sold a…" He turned desperately to Duncan. "Have we sold anything important?"

"I sold that lady an espresso machine," said Duncan.

"Which one?" Parrish searched the shelves for the empty spot.

"The one with the built-in grinder," Duncan said.

Mason frowned at him. "I thought you sold that last week."

"Yeah," answered Duncan. "Last Tuesday."

Mason blinked vacantly at Duncan, then turned back to Parrish. "See anything different about the mugs?"

Parrish stared hard at the retail wall. "None of them are broken?"

"And?" said Mason with a loud, rising inflection, as if he were a game show host.

"None of them are broken and shoved behind unbroken ones?" Parrish tried.

"The handles! Look at the handles, the way they all point west!"

"Oh," said Parrish. "Nice. Did Susan come in?"

"No! And you're welcome, moron," said Mason.

Duncan cleared his throat gruffly, then wagged a motherly finger back and forth.

Mason sighed. "You're not a moron, Parrish."

"Thanks," said Parrish. "I'd say the same about you, but I'll wait a bit."

The next hour went much the same—Mason trying not to be

insulting and therefore remaining painfully silent, and Duncan trying his best to do the Parrish things, doing them unsuccessfully, then getting out of the way so Parrish could fix them.

Five o'clock came and went with Parrish at the computer in the back room. Duncan walked to the back once, to see that he was still there, and so did Mason. It was nearly six o'clock before Parrish came to the front with a box of new mugs. He set them by the shelves on a small table, then pointed at Mason.

"Since you did so well with the others, could you put these out?"

"Sure," said Mason.

"It's past five," blurted Duncan. At this, Mason gave him a harsh scowl and would have swatted him had Duncan been in swatting range.

"Done with that," said Parrish, to their surprise.

"You're not going to the bus stop?" said Duncan.

"Done with that."

"Good," said Mason forcefully. He poked at the mugs in the box Parrish had brought him, then pulled a chair over to the shelf, stood on the chair, and pushed all the perfectly displayed mugs back into the depths of the shelf to make room for the new ones.

"Do you want me to go over there for you?" Duncan suggested. "Check if she's there?"

"Done with that too," said Parrish, flipping pages on the ordering clipboard.

Duncan and Mason shared a look.

"Did you talk to her?" Duncan asked.

In a quiet but very convincing voice, Parrish answered, "That… is…done."

With great restraint, Mason said, "Could you maybe jot down a list of things we *can* talk about, or are you done with that too?"

Parrish ignored him. He straightened the chairs evenly around the tables, wiped up crumbs, smiled happily at them both, then gave his full attention to the clipboard in his hand. Duncan watched, dabbing a sad finger in the top of his espresso. Mason shoved mugs, one by one, onto the shelf, their handles in no particular order.

Meanwhile, at the bus stop, Audra had arrived well before five o'clock. She'd taken the afternoon off and come home by a much earlier bus to allow herself time to get ready. She wore her gray coat as usual, but she'd chosen a long cotton skirt, charcoal gray and flowing, and tall, stylish brown boots instead of sneakers. She wore no scarf, though the day was chilly; a cream-colored turtleneck sweater kept her warm. She'd pulled back her hair, taken time to pin it up properly with innumerable clips and intentional swoops on the sides, and curled sprigs hung beside each ear, accenting the dangle of her silver earrings. She wore no makeup—she was not a makeup kind of girl—but she'd applied a thin, shiny layer of lip gloss.

When she arrived at the bus stop, Rose was the only one there, sitting, as usual, with several plastic shopping bags around her, busily knitting. They exchanged pleasantries, then Audra paced back and forth, checking her watch and glancing now and again in the direction of the coffee shop. Rose tried not to notice, occasionally glancing across the street as well.

When five o'clock grew near, Audra made herself sit on the bench. She kept her back straight and her hands folded in her lap, sitting professionally as if she awaited an interview, ready but uncertain. She'd left her backpack behind and had no book to pass the time. She took several deep, slow breaths and picked the specks of lint off the sleeves of her coat.

The five o'clock bus came and went, a few passengers disembarking. One or two men she'd seen countless times, for the first time, noticed her. She turned her face down the street, adopting a far and unapproachable look. No one bothered her. After a few minutes, the minor bustle of people dissipated in differing directions, and the corner emptied of all but the two women.

"Audra?" Rose leaned toward her, nearly whispering.

"Yes?"

"You look very nice today."

Audra's eyes fell to her skirt, which she smoothed with her hands. "Think so?"

Rose nodded with certainty.

Audra smiled, but didn't know how to continue their conversation. She checked her watch. It was embarrassing to be caught waiting for someone, especially if that someone never arrived.

Rose sighed. "He came by earlier, before you arrived," she said. "I was hoping he'd come back." She gave a last look across the street, then reached in one of her bags, withdrew a sealed envelope, and leaned across the bench, arm extended. "He asked me to give you this if I saw you."

Audra took the envelope. Her name was written in small cursive on the front, and she immediately remembered the envelopes Mr.

Crawford had shown the two of them that day in his home. She flipped it over, slipped a finger in at the corner, and tore it open carefully. She glanced at Rose, but Rose sank her attention back into her knitting.

Audra lifted the flap and withdrew two separate letters, each folded. One she recognized, one she did not. She opened the new one first and scanned it. It was quite short, too short, and that made her exhale sadly.

> Audra,
>
> Sorry for barging in where you had not invited me. I only meant to return your gloves. I'm also returning the letter—the one whose owner I was sent to the corner to find. I think I've found her. I don't presume to know how to help or even to understand, but if there's anything I can do for you, please, let me know.
>
> Take care,
> Parrish

She read it twice, then folded it along its original creases and placed it in her coat pocket. Then she opened the second letter. As she reread this one, the paper trembled in her hands. She replaced it in the envelope and put this away in her coat as well. She slumped back with her hands deep in her coat pockets, pointing her toes together, no longer waiting for her interview to begin. Her eyes strayed to the glass door of the coffee shop, far across the street.

"And this is from me," said Rose cheerily. She stood, collecting her things. She put away her knitting needles and hung several plastic bags around her wrist, all of the bags but one. This she picked up last and offered to Audra. "A new hat for a new day."

Audra took the bag from Rose's hand and peeked inside. It was identical to her other hat, knitted wool and floppy, plenty of room for her hair. Rose couldn't have made a more perfect copy had she been staring at the original. Except, of course, it was bright green.

"Hope there's no mistake with the color?"

"It's lovely," Audra said softly. "Thank you."

Rose reached out and put a hand on Audra's cheek with a touch of motherly concern, almost as if she were checking her temperature.

"Well," Rose sighed. "Glad there's no mistake."

Audra watched as Rose walked down the sidewalk, her plastic bags bouncing against the side of her leg. Alone, she took the hat out of the plastic bag, put her hands inside it, held it up to see her hands wearing it, then scrunched it up in her lap and leaned forward, keeping her hands inside the hat for warmth.

It was a slow evening at the coffee shop, so Parrish began closing early.

He emptied the containers of half-and-half and whole milk from the condiment bar, dropped them in the back sink, then picked up the broom on his way out the front door. Duncan reached out a hand, his offer to sweep, but Parrish shook his head. Mason busied himself with breaking down the espresso machine, taking off various parts and soaking them in cleanser, then taking a stiff-bristled brush to the filters and steam wand.

No one spoke. Like men, his friends refused to leave him. They settled for silence, busying themselves with the cleaning projects each detested least. It had never been this quiet in the coffee shop when all three of them were present.

When the front door jangled open, Parrish was flipping chairs upside down onto the tables so he could sweep. When he saw Audra, he stopped, a chair in midair. He replaced it on the floor, then leaned on the back of it.

"Hey," he said.

She let the door ring closed behind her. She waved. Her eyes were puffy, and he could tell that she'd been crying.

"I need to sweep the patio," said Duncan as he grabbed the broom.

"I'm going to shampoo the Dumpster," yelled Mason, disappearing out the back.

Duncan apologized as he pushed past Audra on his way out the front door. The door jangled shut, then jangled loudly open as Duncan stuck his head in, reached an arm around the door to flip the sign to Closed, repeated his sorry, then slammed the door shut with a cacophony of bells.

Audra and Parrish stood motionless for a moment, staring at each other.

"Closing early?" she asked, her eyes darting about with self-conscious curiosity.

"It's my shop," Parrish said. "I can do that. How are you?"

She nodded, tucked a strand of hair in her green hat, then forced her eyes to look at him. "I'm not going to cry anymore, so you don't have to worry."

"I'm not worried."

His voice wasn't harsh, but she hesitated, then asked if they might sit down.

Parrish flipped a second chair off the table, set it next to the first, then stepped over to the front door and flipped the lock, jiggling the door to make sure it latched. Audra sat, her hands in her lap. Parrish walked quickly behind the counter, offering her tea as he went. She would have refused, but he'd already ripped open packages of green tea and twirled a ceramic cup under the hot water spigot before she had time to respond. He delivered the steaming cup on a saucer with a spoon and two small packages of honey, then sat next to her.

She straightened her back to begin. "I wanted to apologize," she said. "All those things I said to you…"

"You don't have to."

"I want to. I want to explain why. That day when you read my letter, I didn't know what to say. I didn't think you'd ever meet my father, so I…"

"Audra, you don't have to explain."

"No, I told you I lived alone. I lied to you, and I'm sorry. I *need* you to accept my—"

"I already have."

A confused frown twisted across her face as if she wanted to believe him. But she began her apology again. "I'm sorry that I—"

"Listen," he said, "last time we played simultaneous sorries you took over. It's my turn."

"But—"

"No, *I* need to explain something." He chose his words carefully, not wanting to be glib when she seemed so heavily weighed down with herself. He tried to speak softly. "Audra, this past week, I thought God was telling me things that I was supposed to go *do*. He wasn't."

"Wait!" Audra reached out her hand. "God did. Last night after you left—"

Parrish picked up her spoon, held it up on display, then very gently pressed it over her lips. "Hold that for me."

Despite her heaviness, Audra found her smile. She put her hand over his for a moment, then switched the spoon to her own. She grinned foolishly as she held the spoon over her mouth.

"God," Parrish began again, "is the one doing things, and he very kindly asked if I wanted to join in. So the *listening*, that was the important part. And I don't listen very well, Audra. I apologize. I want to learn, though. To listen." He wagged his fingers at the spoon, then pointed to it. "Now I need that for me."

She didn't hand it to him, instead returning it to her saucer. "No more spoon."

"Not so much fun, that spoon trick?"

"It has its place." Again, she gave him her smile.

Parrish waited to see what she might say. She tried but couldn't continue. Sadly, he watched her smile wither, bit by bit, as her thoughts pulled her inward. He couldn't stand that.

"You want to know what else I want?" he said, clapping his hands on his knees.

Slowly, she nodded.

"I want a do-over."

"Do-over?" she mimicked.

"I want a do-over." Parrish offered his hand across the table. "Hi. I'm John."

Audra rolled her eyes.

He persisted, his hand out until finally she unfolded her hands from her lap and warily shook his.

"And who might you be?" he asked.

She sighed. "Still Audra."

"Well, Audra. I could be wrong"—Parrish paused to remember her exact words to Mr. Crawford—"but I think you might be amazing."

Audra's lips tightened, then the corners of her mouth bent slowly toward a frown and her eyes watered up. She pursed her lips to keep them from trembling. After a moment of effort, she recovered her voice.

"I might be."

She got the words out, but one tear skimmed down her right cheek. She wiped it away with a quick hand, stiffening her neck.

Parrish didn't rush. He waited, then when she said no more, he asked, "Mind if I tag along while you find out?"

Audra nodded enthusiastically, like a little girl. "Yep. I'd like that."

They sat together for a moment, neither speaking, but glancing at each other as often as they glanced away. Then Parrish gave a short laugh, to which Audra furrowed her face. He shook his head as if it were nothing. Her face insisted he tell her.

He looked at her squarely and said, "Nice hat."

She reached a hand up to it, again like a little girl, frantic and afraid she'd lost something dear in the wind. She hadn't, but with her hand on her head, her face tightened, filling with too many thoughts at once, then loosened with emotion. She put a hand over her mouth and burst into tears.

Parrish stood up quickly and opened his arms; she stood as quickly and fell into them, weeping. His hand held the back of her head, and her face burrowed into his neck, his shoulder. She didn't just cry. For minutes she sobbed wildly, heaving occasionally for air, then sobbing again, both her hands clutching the back of his shirt as if she were afraid she might fall off a cliff. Parrish listened—it sounded like years she was weeping out, so many of them, all at once.

Finally, her heart racing, her crying slowed, and she breathed again.

"Sorry I said that about your hat," he said.

She laughed once, coughed, then laughed loud and long.

"No," she said. "I love my hat. It's green-light green."

Parrish handed her a wad of napkins from the dispenser. "Looks more primary to me."

She clutched the napkins in one hand, laid the other on his chest, and looked up at him. "My new favorite."

He sat her down again, convinced her to sip her tea—a most practical cure—and she used all the napkins he'd given her plus a few more, the table as full of crumpled napkins as when she'd nursed the cut above his eye. Parrish gathered up her mess, much to her distress, then took them to the garbage so that their table was clean again.

When he sat back down with her, he asked, "Will you tell me what you want?"

"What I want?"

"Yeah. I wanted a do-over. What do you most want? Please. And I'm going to listen."

Audra giggled and sniffed, continued wiping her nose. "You'll listen, huh?"

"This is me, right now, actively listening."

She waited, her eyes wide with silly patience. When he finished, she opened her mouth to speak, but he timed his interruption perfectly.

"Still listening."

Her entire face smiled, freshly, the way only someone who's stopped a serious cry can. That smile—her eyes suddenly freed, no longer heavy—that was the best part of his whole day.

She said, "Do you remember how that guy walked up to us at the bus stop and asked if we were the two helping people on that corner?"

"Yes."

"I want to be that. Those two." Her eyes questioned his very seriously. "Can we be that?"

"Yep," he said quickly. "I'd like that."

"Good."

Parrish realized he could breathe again. He laid his hands flat on the table and let out a huge sigh.

Audra took her spoon and balanced it on the back of his hand. "So what happens next?"

"Can you eat?" Parrish asked. He stared intently at the spoon as if he were hypnotized, then jerked his hand upward so that the spoon flipped in the air. This time he caught it.

Audra blinked protectively, but then offered a smatter of applause.

Parrish smiled. "I know this terrific little Chinese place."

Extra-Bit:
The Proper Way to Steam and Foam Milk

H ello."

Parrish stands behind the freshly polished espresso machine in his shop, wearing a clean apron and a new blue shirt Audra picked out for the occasion.

"Welcome to the extra-bit," he says. "Glad you could join me. Today, I'm going to give you some pointers on the proper way to steam and foam milk. You'll need a small stainless steel pitcher, a large metal spoon—"

Duncan walks up, eating an apple. "What're you doing?"

"I'm doing an extra-bit for our audience."

Duncan stops chewing. He looks around Parrish, behind him, then looks straight forward, the direction Parrish is facing, squints and stares.

Parrish pours milk into a steaming pitcher. "They're readers, Dunc. You can't see them."

"I was looking for the camera."

"It's a book. There's no camera."

Duncan gives Parrish a puzzled look.

"No camera, Dunc," Parrish says. "We just talk to them."

Duncan chews again, clearly thinking. "So they can't see me doing…this." He does a little dance with his hips, turning in a small circle, then bobbing his head forward and back like a drunk bird.

Duncan stops dancing, laughs heartily, then wipes his nose with the back of his apple-holding hand. "Go on. Don't let me interrupt."

Parrish sighs. "So…I'm explaining some helpful tips to our readers about how to make delicious foamy coffee beverages at home."

Mason emerges from the back room. He's drying his hands with a towel. "What are you two doing?"

"Parrish is explaining to our *readers*"—Duncan waves his apple around in the air, crazily, in every direction. Mason's eyes follow the apple for a moment. He glances up and around the ceiling as if he's supposed to find something there. Seeing nothing, he scowls at Duncan. Duncan continues—"explaining how to make delicious foamy beverages at home."

"Those home machines are crap."

"Yes," agrees Parrish. "But since that's what they're using, maybe simple, helpful, instructive tips…"

Mason frowns. "Can't they use something else?"

"No," says Parrish. His tone is slow, patient. "That's what they're using. Thus, they're reading this extra-bit for help."

Mason shakes his head. "Why don't they just—I don't know—go to a coffee shop? Maybe ours, for instance? Leave this sort of thing to the coffee professionals."

"Okay." Parrish plops the spoon into the pitcher. "First, gasoline's about ten dollars a gallon, so people want to stay home—and fuel costs have cut into their expendable, coffee-shop income. Thus people *read* instead of going shopping or to the movies. They're trying to be cheap, okay? So they sit at home, probably reading this extra-bit to squeeze every last penny out of their purchase."

"I don't care about books," says Mason. "We're talking about *coffee*."

"Right." Parrish resumes his patient tone. "Can I do this, please?"

Mason gestures graciously for Parrish to proceed.

"A stainless steel pitcher, not too large, not too small, and don't fill it full—halfway or less. You're going to aerate the milk and fill the rest of the pitcher with foam. You start with the steam wand submerged, but as soon as you start the steam, bring the tip of the wand to the surface of the milk, barely below the surface. No big schlorking sounds like in TV commercials. Your goal is tiny, staccato schlorking sounds. And it's best to start with very cold milk. Go from extremes: very cold milk steamed to hot makes better foam. Don't know why, just does—"

"Principle of colloidal suspension," Duncan interjects.

"That's redundant," Mason says.

"No, it isn't."

"A colloid is a suspension. Look it up."

"Yes, a colloid, by definition, is a suspension," says Duncan. "But we're talking about the *principle* of colloidal suspension. *Suspension* is more a verb there."

Parrish interrupts. "Shut up, please."

"*Suspend*," corrects Mason. "That's a verb. *Suspension*—never a verb."

"Newton. Einstein!" Parrish yells. "Shut up. Now!" He continues his demonstration. "You want the milk to swirl as it steams, breaking up any large bubbles, making a thicker foam. With the steam wand barely under the surface of the milk tilt the pitcher at an angle so that the milk swirls in a clockwise motion—"

"It doesn't have to be clockwise," Mason mumbles.

Parrish glances sideways at him. "Yes, it does. In the Northern Hemisphere, it's always clockwise."

Mason throws his arms open wide in a gesture of complete shock. "So readers in the Southern Hemisphere should stop what they're doing immediately and go to a coffee shop?"

"Precisely," says Parrish.

Mason drops his arms and shakes his head. "You don't know what you're doing."

"Susan," Parrish asks, "do you foam clockwise or counter-clockwise?"

Susan stops wiping down the table, brushes a strand of hair back, and thinks before answering. "Which hemisphere are we in?"

Parrish and Susan share a smile.

"Fine, fine." Mason rolls his eyes. "You two planned that, you and Susan the expert. If you want foam made by a girl—"

"Mason!" Parrish turns off the steam wand. "Not okay."

Susan shrugs. "This is why I don't make drinks when they're around."

"Technically, Mason," says Audra, looking up from her textbooks and taking a sip of tea, "that last statement… Susan could sue you for harassment."

"He's not harassing me, Audra. But he is an idiot," says Susan. "Can I sue him for that?"

"Can you please apologize?" Parrish demands. "First to Susan, and then to our extra-bit readers."

"Terribly sorry, Sue," says Mason, who then looks up at the ceiling. "Extra-bit readers, my bad."

"An apology"—Parrish is, again, searching for his lost patient tone—"should really involve at least a particle of desire to not be such a jerk."

"No," says Mason. "I can apologize without feeling a thing."

"Exactly. So your 'apology' doesn't really count."

"Parrish is right." Duncan picks apple from his teeth.

"It counts," says Mason. "As a verbal act, it counts."

Parrish shakes his head. "No, the apology must coincide with some inward repentance."

"The apology," says Mason, "is an outward act independent of intent. Intent doesn't matter."

"Of course it matters!" Parrish blusters.

"No," Mason continues, "the apology is for Susan's benefit, not mine. Thus, formally I have apologized. She doesn't know my intent, so intent doesn't matter."

"Even if she doesn't know what you're thinking, it still matters," says Parrish.

"Hey, Mason," Susan calls out. "Can you tell what *I'm* thinking right now?"

Mason blows her a kiss.

"What if Sue *did* know what you were thinking?" asks Duncan, his eyes growing wide.

"She doesn't."

"Apple boy makes a good point," Parrish says, shaking a finger at Duncan. "If she knew your crappy intent, in your weird world, would it still be an apology?"

"She can't. So why worry about it?"

Duncan tries, "But, say, like God, she knew."

Mason raises his eyebrows. "Susan is God?"

Audra looks up from her books again.

"No," says Duncan. "But *like* God, she knows your crappy intent when you apologize."

Mason hops up to sit on the counter. "You can't ever win that. No matter how good you think your repentance is, it is never fully devoid of self-interest. Indeed, the crappier you are, the more tainted your repentance, the more deceived you will be by your own self-interest. So, that's merely shifting the crime to the heart."

"Wasn't that a movie with Sally Field?" asks Susan.

"Yes, *Crimes of the Heart*," says Audra, chewing her pencil. "Sally Field, John Malkovich, and Danny Glover."

Parrish says. "So you're saying it doesn't matter if you're sorry when you say you're sorry?"

"No," says Mason. "I'm saying forgiveness can't be based on our intent."

"Mason?" says Susan.

"Yeah, Sue?"

"I forgive you," she says, smiling.

"See?" says Mason. "God forgives."

Duncan takes a big crunch of apple, chews thoughtfully. "Places," he says. "Not crimes."

Everyone looks at him.

Duncan stops chewing. "Sally Field and Danny Glover. That was *Places of the Heart.*"

"Okay, boys, enough," says Audra. She brings Parrish a sheet of paper. "Here's the recipe you wanted…"

Audra's World-Famous Chocolate Chip Bundt Cake
(sold exclusively at Fritter John's Coffee Shop & Tea Emporium)

Ingredients

1 1/3 cups water

1/2 cup vegetable oil

3 large eggs

1 box Duncan Hines Moist Deluxe Dark Chocolate Fudge Cake

1 large tube Nestlé Toll House Chocolate Chip Cookie Dough

1 bag of Nestlé Chocolate Chips (You can substitute butterscotch chips. Parrish doesn't like butterscotch, but you might.)

1. Okay, preheat your oven to 350 degrees. (There's all kinds of rules about high altitudes and dark coated pans that affect the temperature, but where I live, I've always used 350.)

2. Blend the dry mix, water, oil, and eggs in large bowl at a low speed for, oh, I don't know, about thirty seconds, until moistened. It's a goo with a thick liquid consistency.

3. Then (and this is the best part) after you've greased your Bundt pan, mush the cookie dough in an even layer around the inside of it—almost like a pie crust—but mushed all around.

4. Stir the chocolate chips into the goo batter.

5. Pour your chipped goo into cookie-lined Bundt pan. (See, the cake's inside the cookie crust, so when you flip it out when it's done, the cake's inside a cookie, which is very exciting!)

6. Cook at 350 degrees for 45–50 minutes.

7. When it's done, take it out. Let it cool for 30 minutes or you'll flub it on the flip. After cool, flip it out on a cake stand and voilà!

8. Best served warm with cold, cold French vanilla ice cream. (Whipped cream and chocolate sprinkles optional.)

Serves 8–10 people. (Or 3 people and 1 Duncan.)

LEAPER

I have no pants.

Strange to say, once that moment or two of immediate shock of having instantaneously leapt across space wears off, no pants is still no pants. No matter how fantastically you got there, you're there with no pants.

"Oh, hey, Meg, oh, um, yeah, seems I found the cutting board..."

That wouldn't do. Not pantless.

I pad across the garage to the mail slot in the garage door. It's an old house, an old garage with an old garage door. Meg and I didn't find that mail slot till the second year of our marriage. Along with old bills from some very angry people. We could never figure why anyone would put a mail slot dead smack center in a garage door. Mail gets run over, slips under cars, or is drowned in oily puddles. Sometimes mail takes a fun ride around town on the car bumper. Most of the time we got mail in the mailbox like the rest of the neighborhood, but other times it was shoved recklessly into the least-tidy, least-lit, and least-used room of our home.

But Meg and I found other clever uses for the garage-door mail slot: we watched the neighbors, looked to see which unwanted person was ringing the doorbell, checked for cars parked in the drive.

So I creak open the mail-slot door and crouch to look out. No sign of Meg's Jeep. I had time.

I open the door to the kitchen, stick my head through.

"Hey, Meg!" No answer.

The dogs come bounding around the corner, thrilled to have a guest. Perhaps they still recognized Daddy's voice, but I've often suspected they'd greet uninvited dogcatchers or invading assassins with the same unbridled glee.

"Down! Get down!"

Without clothes, a man shies from large, happy dogs prone to jumping up and flopping a paw on either shoulder.

"Down, buddies!" I hide behind the garage door. They slam into it merrily.

Ponzy is a seventy-five-pound German shepherd known for jumping through the den window at the appearance of the meter man or the sound of thunder. Through, not out. Those windows don't open. Unless a German shepherd shatters the glass. Chunky is a ninety-pound chocolate Labrador who earned his name as a pup by decimating a can of Chunky soup. One morning I found a very thin, shiny, tooth-punctured piece of aluminum on his bed. After looking two hours and finding a couple of stray English peas, I figured out that flat piece of tin was once a full can of Chunky soup left too low in an open pantry. He'd eaten it, label and all, leaving no stew juice anywhere as a clue.

My brutes claw the door and whine affectionately.

"Hold on, boys!"

I sought pants at any cost and pick up a screwdriver to open a few of my boxes. Luckily, I had wrapped a vase in an old pair of jeans so it wouldn't break. Meg had thought this a poor way to pack, but then, she couldn't have foreseen the pants paying off in this particular manner. I pull on the jeans. The vase drops and cracks.

"Hey, buddies! Good boys!" I swat the dogs down with the cutting board as I walk through the kitchen.

"I'm home."

Meg could be home anytime. Fridays were her short day. I still need a shirt, so I go to our bedroom. (Sorry, divorce very recent, my ex-wife's bedroom.) Call it instinct or perhaps desperation, but under the circumstances, looking for a shirt in my old closet wasn't the oddest thing I might have done. I wasn't spying.

And I find one: a white oxford, pressed and starched. I take it off the hanger. I was touched, really, she never did my shirts. Deeply touched and almost willing to forgive a multitude of snips and claws. It was so...

Then I realize: It isn't my size. It isn't mine! It's Doug's. Five white, starched shirts hang in my wife's closet. She'd picked up the man's laundry. She never folded my socks, not once in five years. I ravage the shirt in my hand, wrinkling it mercilessly, cracking the heavy starch until I find the cleaner's tag. "Williams."

She had taken Dougie's shirts to the cleaners, not just picked them up, but dropped them off under her name! Picking up somebody's laundry, you might do that, you know, even for someone you barely knew, if you were going anyway and they've asked, "Hey, can you grab mine?" But dropping off and picking up! Paying to have his shirts cleaned. His shirts under her name.

Her maiden name.

"Down, boys! I'm not in the mood!" I yell.

And my dogs know this other mood. They give up on me and roughhouse each other down the hall.

I pull on Dougie's shirt. Even if it's a bit small, it's better than no shirt. *I'll just roll up the midget's sleeves,* I think. But strangely, the shirt hurts. Yes, it's small under the armpits, but I mean it actually hurts me. Sharp pains up and down my back. Like the financial consultant with the crazy ex-wife cast a spell on his shirts so that only he could wear them. Like how only the Lone Ranger could ride Silver.

When I drop my arms and take a step, pain shoots through my back like a bunch of little pins sticking...

(Of course, I'm an idiot, but this is proof! I didn't black out and wander over to the house after my appointment. On a treatment table, then the garage. No pants. Pins still in my back. I didn't imagine a thing.)

I take the shirt off and hunch toward the bathroom mirror. I rummage the sink drawer for Meg's round face mirror, the one she used to pluck her eyebrows or to check how her hair looked from the back.

I turn like Meg, the mirror in one hand looking for the bathroom mirror behind me. I strain my other arm around to pull out the pins, dropping them one by one into the sink. I get the ones on my neck and the two by each thumb. After a thorough visual check, the best possible without my glasses, I take down a towel. There's no other way. Courageously and suddenly, I dry my back.

No more pain. I had them all.

That's when I hear the front door unlock. Dogs run and skid across the hardwood to greet Mommy's return. Putting on Doug's shirt quickly, I button it up wrong, one button off. I tuck it in anyway.

"Meg?" I call out.

Acknowledgments

My thanks to the good people of Waterbrook Multnomah and, as always, to my editor, Shannon. Thanks and love to Tim and Claudia, Brad and Ashlee, and to the Kallahers—especially the Mongoose. (Wally and Butter say, "Hey.")

About the Author

Geoffrey Wood has been working in both coffee and theater for nearly twenty years—roasting and sipping, acting, writing, and directing. Visit his Web site at www.green-socks.com.